REBEL

The Last American Novel

T.L. Davis

12 Round Productions

Copyright © 2020 T.L. Davis

All rights reserved

The characters and events portrayed in this book are fictitious. Any similarity to real persons, living or dead, is coincidental and not intended by the author.

No part of this book may be reproduced, or stored in a retrieval system, or transmitted in any form or by any means, electronic, mechanical, photocopying, recording, or otherwise, without express written permission of the publisher.

Cover design by: Sammi Lee Davis
Library of Congress Control Number: 1-8932681931
Printed in the United States of America

CONTENTS

Title Page	1
Copyright	2
REBEL	5
CHAPTER ONE	6
CHAPTER TWO	22
CHAPTER THREE	30
CHAPTER FOUR	40
CHAPTER FIVE	51
CHAPTER SIX	62
CHAPTER SEVEN	73
CHAPTER EIGHT	82
CHAPTER NINE	98
CHAPTER TEN	108
CHAPTER ELEVEN	117
CHAPTER TWELVE	128
CHAPTER THIRTEEN	140
CHAPTER FOURTEEN	149
CHAPTER FIFTEEN	161
CHAPTER SIXTEEN	170
CHAPTER SEVENTEEN	181
CHAPTER EIGHTEEN	190

CHAPTER NINETEEN	202
CHAPTER TWENTY	211
CHAPTER TWENTY-ONE	221
CHAPTER TWENTY-TWO	231
CHAPTER TWENTY-THREE	243
CHAPTER TWENTY-FOUR	253
CHAPTER TWENTY-FIVE	262
About The Author	277
Books By This Author	279

REBEL

by
T.L. Davis

CHAPTER ONE

Long's Peak dominates the horizon, a massive, jagged mountain extending high above the tree-line; capped with snow the wind has smoothed to an ice cream finish. The fourteener stands out against the blue, Colorado sky. It was named after Stephen Long, though in Arapaho it was known as Neníisótoyóú'u, but it had been in existence since before humans thought to give mountains names. It was and always had been in my life. It was there for me when shoveling manure out of the stalls, wet with perspiration, I would take a breather outside. I would emerge from the confines of the dust-filled barn with thoughts of nothing but breathable air and would see it: the snowy peak, even on a hot July day, because most years it was snow-capped year-round. It would fill my heart with beauty and I would gaze at it, shovel still clutched in my calloused hand, thinking of how cool the air would be up there, how refreshing to dive into that snow face-first, to wallow in it and be cold.

It was not so appealing when the deep snow of winter surrounded me, clung to my jeans, freezing them solid to the knee as I lifted my leg high to clear the foot or more of snow on the ground. I felt like a mountain man then; rifle in hand in the furthest reaches of our little ranch, tracking a coyote that had gotten brave, lost or desperate; that had smelled our chickens, an unusual odor in the rapidly urbanizing Front Range of Colorado. It was 1977 and everything was changing, except Long's Peak and the hunger of a coyote in a diminishing habitat.

I could commiserate with the coyote; even while I hunted it; as it had hunted the poor chickens huddled fearfully in the coop. It was a cycle I understood as a statement of nature that was eternal, that stretched back to when the Utes and Arapaho hunted these same grounds, when French trappers made their way along the South Platte River and up the Big Thompson all the way to the source. It was a cycle that was understood and celebrated by Mariano Medina when he combined the needs of both natives and trappers at a trading post he called Namaqua at the convergence of several trails like the Cherokee Trail traveled by Utes, Arapaho, French, Mexican and English adventurers, hunters and scouts all participating in the cycle.

Eventually the Overland Stage would take advantage of Medina's efforts and run its line through there along the Cherokee trail. The railroad would follow suit and extend a line to the quarries in the foothills above the town named after the railroad executive W.H. Loveland. It was a town that should have been called, by all rights, Medina, who had recruited one hundred of his fellow residents of Taos, New Mexico to establish a settlement there. Or, the state should have honored Medina's initiative and called the town Namaqua, but it didn't, and I grew up in a town unjustly and irrationally called Loveland.

Perhaps the railroad had a greater impact on the growth of the area than Mariano Medina. Without the railroad, there probably would not have been an effort to build an automobile road through the narrow, towering, rocky sides of the Big Thompson Canyon to Estes Park where wealthy tourists and consumptives sought pleasure or the cure at the Stanley Hotel that offered both. Loveland, until then, was an agricultural community with large tracts of green fields dedicated to growing sugar beets and cherry orchards. Closer to the foothills, where the land was too rocky to farm, ranches appeared and extended all the way into the low mountains of the Front Range. Loveland benefited from an economy built on farming and ranching. Then, the road up the Big Thompson brought those seeking the high, dry climate for their ailments and tourists who would turn into citizens more and more as time went on.

My grandfather, Hugh Daniels, stood on that very ground, smelled cherry blossoms and dug sugar beets. He rode horses and drove mules. He was there when mules were discarded for iron-wheeled tractors and machines tilled the land in immense tracts that would have taken months to cultivate with oxen and a one-bottom plow.

Hugh survived the depression and the dust bowl of the 1930s in Eastern Colorado, but depleted and dispirited he loaded the Model-T with his family and what possessions he could tie on the top or put in the hay trailer pulled behind and drove west until he came to the fertile Big Thompson Valley.

My dad was an infant a decade before they left and there is a picture of him, chubby, white/blonde hair hanging in his eyes, a look of seriousness on his face. The whole family is in that picture, before what can only be described as a shack, dust piled up in the corner of the only window facing the camera, but it was warm and dry.

Luck would be much kinder to them in the Big Thompson Valley, where they would prosper. My dad would grow taller, his muscles thicken and his hair would darken as he aged. Like most farmers who have used mules and oxen to plow the ground, he was fascinated by machinery that would eradicate the drudgery of plowing even twenty acres. Tractors and three-bottom plows turned a mind-numbing, physically-draining weeks of labor into an afternoon with time to spare. Being a farmer stopped being about animals and feed and became about machines and fuel and my dad was right there, breathlessly evaluating the new equipment and imagining the work he could accomplish, the miles he could plow behind the smoke-belching machines.

One day, in the early 1950s when my father was happily tending to a valve job on the tractor, he was informed that the United States of America needed him desperately in Korea to save the world from communism. He was snatched up from the green fields of Northern Colorado, the beautiful towering spires of mountains and dropped rudely on the Korean plain amid thousands of others on the front lines. He sat behind a chattering machine gun he had just learned to operate. All those years of hunting rabbits on the desolate prairies of Eastern and Northern Colorado had paid off in the form of a marksmanship medal and a foxhole.

During my father's conscription, my grandfather was able to run the family farm alone with the help of the modern machines and while that was not always easy, it was possible, at least for the year that his only son would be in a faraway land shooting blindly into surges of humanity dispatched by North Korean and, more often, Chinese commanders.

When my father did come back, it was with an understanding and appreciation of the larger world, a world dominated by machines, a world of gunpowder and horsepower. The farm seemed distant and while he would always love it, the dirt and satisfaction of watching a crop grow, mature and supply the family with all it would require for survival, it would no longer hold his future and he was drawn to the local Ford dealership to work as a mechanic on shiny, miraculous automobiles, helping on the farm in the gaps allowed by regular hours.

My dad was the first in the family to be anything other than a farmer. Eight generations had farmed land in Virginia, Kentucky, Nebraska and Colorado. They were a family of farmers and adventurers, pioneers in every sense of the word, leaving England in the early 1700's to cross a vast and violent sea to a new land, not even a nation of its own, yet. They helped to open the Cumberland Gap and later the great frontier West, all with a plow in the back of a wagon and a mule or oxen up front.

Who knows what impressions the depression and the dust bowl had left on the mind of my father as a small boy? Who knows if it was fear of one thing or fascination with another that led to his ultimate decision to leave the farm? Not even my father would know that for certain. He was drawn away from one thing or toward another and that pull would lead him even further when he heard about an oil drilling rig that had set up north of Fort Collins, near Wellington. His curiosity or pioneering nature led him to the rig, up the steps and into the doghouse where he encountered a driller, a daredevil of sorts, battling the machine and the ground he drilled for control. Chains spinning rapidly, throwing lubricating oil as they spun, giant sprockets rotating at great speed, the pipe in the center of the working floor spinning too fast for the eyes to see, except as a blurred column. Iron, jaw clutches released and pulled back with long handles. It was an iron world, a mechanical maze that wrapped around him, pulled him inside, made him a part of the machine as he watched every move the driller made, understanding how it worked intuitively. He left town as a mechanic and came back a roughneck, spoiled for any other occupation.

The oilfield was a lucrative business, offering him more per hour than the dealership could in half a day, and much more than farming could ever provide, at least on the size of place my grandfather owned. The oil field, for him, was a marriage of interest and income. All it required was hard work and the willingness to risk one's life. Farming had taught him how to work and the Army had taught him how to risk.

With the money dad made in the oil business, he bought a small ranch on the west side of Loveland in 1959, unable to resist the desire for property, cattle and horses. Whatever he sought in a career, there was always the natural desire for the freedom, open spaces and land of his own. Even if it was a hobby of sorts, a supplement of needed ingredients to his life, it made him whole on some level.

It was an old homestead; the house was built in the '20s. It was where he would raise a family, first born was my brother Jon, then me and finally Scott. Dad improved the land with new corrals and an expansion of the barn. It became as much a mechanic's shop as a stable. It was where his battling interests became one.

Mom was born and raised on a farm, too, but a rented place, never one that supplied a sense of permanence or ownership. Their ranch was hers as much as my fathers, but close enough to Loveland that the urban life represented by stores, restaurants and the theatre was available to her. Mom came from a family of musicians, farming being the business, but music the salve for blisters and aching backs. They performed in nearby towns: Fort Collins, Greeley, Brighton and even Denver. It was that urban life that she craved and Loveland supplied, even if it was only in its proximity to vibrant college towns Boulder and Fort Collins.

Education was of interest to my mother, well, our education rather than hers. She was fanatical about our schoolwork and proud of our grades. She did not always understand the drive for hard work that made us want to skip school to finish a job, but she expected that ethic to extend to books and knowledge.

Hugh Daniels farmed his land from 1946 to 1972 when the years of hard work, the hearty meals and physiology combined to produce in his sturdy frame a weakened heart. He died and left behind a farm that by then was worth a thousand times more in land value than any crop he could grow. They sold off the farm to establish a sort of retirement for my grandmother, Pearl, who followed my grandfather in death four years later. The funds not expended in the care of my grandmother were distributed between my father and his four sisters, who had all married and moved away. Somewhere in the United States I had ten cousins, but none were local, none that I knew. I was only able to identify them at the funerals by family pictures sent at Christmas.

1972 was significant. My grandfather died and I missed him, but at the same time, Loveland was experiencing its latest transformation from an agricultural community to a sort of mini Silicon Valley. Industrial areas were rapidly building out, the streets were becoming crowded with station wagons and little, gas-efficient Japanese cars. Hewlett Packard had been around for a long time, having opened a manufacturing site south of downtown in 1960, but it was quickly expanding in 1972 in response to the increased demand for Oscilloscopes nationwide and the perceived coming boom in electronics. Other companies took advantage of the initiative shown by HP and Loveland began to entice a flood of newcomers. 1972 was the last year that Loveland felt rural; after that, it would always be a place of commerce, where I felt more and more a stranger.

As my brothers and I grew up, the city that once was a mile or more away built up and around us, enfolding us in a sea of housing developments. Already our closest neighbors, the Johnsons and the Pulaskis had sold out to the developers; even dad sold forty acres to pay off the other two hundred. The ranch that was my father's attempt to preserve his country roots, to surround himself with the things of his childhood, had become an aberration in an urban setting. It felt as if we had become victims of his nostalgia, stranded on an island of horses and cattle in a burbling urban sea. Our victimhood began at five in the morning when we rose to feed the animals while other children slept undisturbed until seven or even later.

Yet, in a lot of ways we were city kids, too. My mom had combined her skills as a seamstress, learned in the cold winters of her childhood, with her desire for a business of her own. In 1972 she purchased a fabric store. We rode our bikes into town to help her out when needed and to visit friends who lived in the surrounding housing developments and similarly surrounded farms and ranches.

In the day to day chores and obligations it was easy to feel lost in the dismal routine, but I stood on the cusp of some incredible changes. I could feel it welling up from within, a change in my outlook. There was a transformation taking place in my surroundings, in the children I encountered in school, who were no longer from a rural background, but from Palo Alto, Rochester and Austin. They looked on us as outsiders, because we were not like them with no recognition of our culture or traditions that were formed over hundreds of years.

Agriculture built the university in Fort Collins, which started as a land-grant college founded by local farmers seeking technology and a competitive advantage. Agriculture drove industry, the sugar beet farms enticed Great Western Sugar Company to build factories all through the area to process the beets into the valuable commodity. Still, the newcomers dismissed us as backward relics of a distant past.

I first noticed the new attitude at the end of eighth grade when a group of us were called into a special meeting. I didn't know it was a special meeting; I didn't know anything about it, except that I was told to attend. I thought all the students were similarly engaged somewhere else in the school. I found out later that they were not.

I was oblivious, because I hardly ever looked at my report card and never read any of the bulletins posted outside of the office. I knew I was passing my classes and was not curious about the degrees by which I passed them. An "A" meant no more to me than a "B." The only thing that mattered was that I was trying my best; I left it at that.

The meeting that I didn't understand was a gathering of students who had been on the honor roll. The others in attendance were the really smart kids, the ones who were called on to explain to the rest of us dolts the principles covered by the teacher. I didn't know how I had gotten lumped in with them. I didn't belong there. I thought it was bad luck that had gotten me listed alongside them. What I didn't know, understand or even care about is that I had been on the honor roll all of that year.

I sat at a desk, trapped behind brick walls interrupted only occasionally by narrow slits for windows, offering only a glimpse of the outside world where freedom could be found. It was stuffy and exemplified everything I hated about school: the fluorescent lighting, the brick walls and the other kids. It was an atmosphere designed to stifle and smother freedom. It was prison: dehumanizing, degrading and every minute controlled by a strict schedule. Was it my ancestry of pioneers and individualists or the history of the area populated by the same demand for freedom that made me jealous of my time and how it was spent? There was something internal and deep down that caused my antagonism toward anything that would limit me or confine me without cause and school was just one. One did not have to like something to be good at it.

There I was, among the bespectacled, self-consciously meticulous intellectuals, in my "cowboy" clothes: the boots, belt buckle and Western shirt. I had an International Harvester cap setting in front of me on the desk. Alan Nelson, the smartest kid I ever knew, stared at me and joked with his friends about my presence and my attire. I knew he would humiliate me. He couldn't help himself and why not? I was easy prey for those who held people born and raised on the disappearing farms and ranches in contempt.

As the brochures for several universities were being passed around and the others were talking about their plans and strategies for higher education, I rose from my seat and prepared to leave. I wanted none of it. I wanted to work and be outside, no matter the weather.

"Lane, don't you want to see some of these brochures?" Alan asked, calling over the short distance, training the focus of the room on me as I rose.

I stopped and turned to look at him. When I did, I saw Millie Anderson. I had gone to elementary school with Millie and had always liked her, even wanted to date her as I grew older, but she seemed out of my league. Millie was pretty, blonde hair in curls down the side of her smooth cheeks. Red lips distracted only slightly from her deep blue, almost purple eyes and she was brilliant. I had heard her discussing Hemingway's *The Sun Also Rises* in English class and I was stunned by her command and knowledge of literature. I didn't even bother to read it. She made me feel like an idiot and maybe I was. Now, thanks to Alan's taunt, the things I would say about Alan would insult her as much as him and any chance I would have with her would vanish.

I took a few steps toward Alan; my cap held tight in my fist.

"I don't know, Alan, maybe I should."

Alan walked toward me, a smug look on his face, knowing somehow that while I could beat him senseless, that I wouldn't do it in that setting, no matter how perfectly he justified it.

"What are you even doing here?" he asked, crinkling up his nose.

"I don't have the slightest idea, Alan. If I'd known this was all about college, something that won't happen for at least three years, I wouldn't have bothered at all."

"You don't think you should plan your future?" he asked, shaking his head in fake disappointment. "Maybe, you don't have one."

"I'll tell you what I think, Alan," I said, taking an intimidating step toward him; pushing a desk out of the way to get closer, causing him to take a step back. "I think the future is dictated by forces none of us understand, could never understand and you want to plan it, like a school project. All you're going to do, any of you, is drive yourself down a narrow path to your death and experience nothing; feel nothing that isn't provided for you, sheltered so you can partake in it without danger. You will see what every other college graduate working in an office or a lab will see and you'll tell yourselves that you're fortunate, better than me, but I'll know the smell of dirt, tired muscles and honest love, not for the social position, or the trust fund or prestige, but because neither of us gain anything by it, except each other."

I finished and walked out, not knowing what they thought of what I had to say, but I immediately felt stupid and clumsy, like some big oaf trying to sound clever and deep. I imagined them laughing at me, thinking that I was trying to be like them. What I said had a much bigger effect on me than it did them. It was the first time that I verbalized my deep desire to be free and in voicing it, I realized how much it meant to me. It quickly became a goal I needed to attain.

As I walked down the hall, the sunshine beckoned to me from around the corner. When I emerged from the depressing halls, I burst through the door of the building and out into the spring air, gulping it as if I had been smothered. I did feel imprisoned and the clean mountain air invigorated my need to be liberated.

My understanding of the unreliability of the future probably stemmed from my father's work. The oil industry was a dangerous, unpredictable place, where people got hurt, sometimes killed, trying to make a living. I had known people who would, due to injury, be missing when I went out to the rig. I would never see them again.

"Where's Bill?" I might ask innocently, but instead of receiving kind, sorrowful looks and commiserating tones, I would be met with: "That stupid sonofabitch got his damned hand cut off. Stupid bastard."

Then, there was the time my father came home in a somber mood and gathered Jon and me to his side.

"I don't think I want you boys working on the rig," he said and looked down.

"Why?" we asked in unison as both of our future plans began with the oil field and a job on the rig. Everyone that worked for dad had lots of money, new cars and expensive toys: motorcycles and boats. Even if it wasn't a lifelong career, it was a great place to start.

"Someone got killed today. I got there just as his brains spilled out onto the ground. I don't know if I should keep working there, much less risk the two of you."

Despite what dad told us, he did continue to work there and our plans, temporarily shaken by his fear, were restored, but things like that happened to people. The oil industry demanded physical risk, hard work, in sometimes bad weather, with no days off for long stretches at a time, but they compensated their workers well and advancement was often rapid. Those conditions were acceptable to us, Jon and me, even though we were years away from being able to take advantage of it.

Jon was closer to realizing that future than I was. He had just turned seventeen and had only one year of school to endure before he would be venturing out into that world, the world of freedom and commerce. I had three years before me and the changes that were taking place, even at that time, were pushing me further from that path, not toward it. I didn't think I could wait until I was eighteen to start my life.

All of that was in the past, and while it remained in my mind, it did not alter my thoughts. I walked over to the corral looking every bit the cowboy, the whole history of the area somehow imbued in my nature. I scattered a bale of hay into the feed trough. The horses walked toward me, the big gray horse and the smaller, reddish, brown one, smelling the hay, a moment that might have existed two hundred years ago as easily as then.

I had been working odd jobs, putting money aside for a car in anticipation of getting my driver's license in a few months. My friend Ronnie asked his parents if I could work with him to earn some extra money. He needed the help and I needed the cash. They relented and I had been going there to work for a couple of days. When I got done with the horses I had to wait to be picked up and taken to work.

While I waited for Mrs. Flanders, I fed the chickens and filled the water trough. She arrived in the brown Chevrolet van she always drove. In the seat next to her was Beth, Ronnie's little sister. I knew it. Beth was always there. She was a cute kid with big brown eyes, a bright smile and shoulder-length, brown hair that had lighter streaks in it, but she was thirteen and an annoyance.

I opened the side door and climbed into the back seat of the van. It smelled of cigarettes. Beth turned sideways and looked over the back of the seat.

"Hi," she said, her broad smile beaming.

"Howdy."

Mrs. Flanders pulled out of the driveway and onto the street. She looked up into the rear-view mirror.

"They're working on the fence around the north half-section. You boys have about a week."

I nodded.

"Pretty soon, you won't have to pick me up."

"It's no problem," Beth interjected, still looking over the back of the seat.

Mrs. Flanders glanced at Beth.

"Turn around and sit down."

The Flanders ranch was a big, grand place, much bigger than ours. Thousands of acres instead of hundreds. They had a large steel building that housed most of the equipment and provided a place to make repairs. It smelled of oil and dust. They had several stacks of hay, most of which had been grown on property they owned further away, along the foothills. The value of their property was in the multi millions, but they showed little of their landed wealth, driving older vehicles and well-maintained, but older tractors and other equipment.

Ronnie was waiting when we pulled into the yard. He was about my height, muscular as we all were due to the type of work we did. Brown hair protruded out from under a baseball cap. A slight grin edged at his lips. He had the sort of looks that made even his friends feel inferior, especially me.

I stepped out of the van and walked up to Ronnie.

"We're taking the motorcycle," he said, as we walked toward the steel building.

I could tell he wanted to say something but was waiting for the right time to bring it up.

"Just say it," I said.

"Say what?"

"Whatever it is that put that stupid grin on your face."

Ronnie laughed, but changed the subject as we entered the building.

"Grab that bag over there with the pliers and shit in it," he said as he fiddled with the motorcycle, checking it for gas and oil.

I looked along the wall where tools and such were piled onto a work bench. Among the dust and tools was a canvas bag containing some fencing pliers and a bunch of wire stays. Next to the bag was a wire stretcher, I grabbed it and the bag as the high-pitched engine of the motorcycle cranked up. Blue smoke belched out of the exhaust pipe and hung in the air, the shaft of light from the open doors illuminating the blue cloud. Ronnie threw his leg over the seat and sat down. I climbed on the back and dangled my feet only inches from the ground. We sped out of the open doors and into the yard.

Beth stood on the porch of the house and watched us leave. She was framed there, like an oil painting, but without the flowing print dress and the wide-brimmed hat so many paintings seemed to feature. Instead, she was the image of a country girl, boots, tight jeans and a loose-fitting shirt that hid the swelling breasts of a rapidly-developing thirteen-year-old.

We bounced out onto the dirt road running by their place and headed north. I reached up and pulled the bill of my cap down to keep it from getting caught by the wind. The mountain range sped by on our left, reminding me of what I loved about Colorado: when all other things sucked, there were mountains. It was probably the same way people felt about the sea, a permanence, a reliability that when all other things were transient, the sea could be relied on for inspiration and beauty in a dark and dismal world.

We rode the motorcycle north a couple of miles along a dirt road hemmed in by grasses and pulled up to a gate made of four strands of barbed wire stapled to a wooden post. The post fit into two loops of wire hanging from an anchor post, one at the top and one at the bottom. I stepped off the motorcycle and set the bag and fence stretcher down to open the gate. Minutes later we were idling along the fence line looking for damaged strands of barbed wire.

"There's one," he said and stopped the motorcycle next to a strand of wire that had broken; the loose ends hung down to the ground.

We worked all morning pulling broken strands together with the fence stretchers, which took up the slack that naturally occurred over the years. We would splice them together, a practice taught differently by his father and mine, so we did it different and argued about it. The splice held, either way.

The sun rose higher into the sky and the July heat began to build on the deep green of the pasture.

"Should have brought some beer," I said, joking.

"Good idea, should have put some in the bag."

"Maybe your mom could bring some out."

We laughed at the silliness of the idea. Ronnie's mom didn't like it when she found out we had been drinking beer, but Ronnie's dad, Ron Sr., would occasionally let us get a can or two out of the cooler if we had worked hard. We hadn't worked hard enough to earn a beer, though.

"So, what happened?" Ronnie asked, a wicked smile on his face. He usually had some sort of sexual aside or crude comment to make.

"What happened with what?"

"Annie Brewster," he said, then looked at me with a concerned look on his face. "Annie, man."

"What about her?"

"Are you shitting me?"

"What?" I shrugged. "She was at the party," I said, which was as much as I knew.

"After. What happened after?"

"Nothing. Jon came by and got me. Oh shit, then we went to the burger joint and there were all these…"

"Shut up, wait," he said, holding his hand up. "You just left?"

"Yeah."

Ronnie looked at me trying to figure out if I was teasing him or just stupid.

"You're kidding, right? Did Jon give her a ride, or what?"

"Who?"

"Annie."

"No, he just pulled up and said, 'get in' and I got in and we left, but then we were at the burger joint. You know the one on Eisenhower? There were all these hoods hanging out and they started some shit with us, calling us 'goat ropers' and…"

"So, you left Annie just, what? Standing there?"

"Huh? Yeah, I guess, I didn't think about it."

"You're an idiot," he said, looking at me with skepticism.

"Why?"

"Annie was all over you, man. She laughed at every stupid thing you said. She didn't even see me. I was standing right next to her."

"Yeah, I thought that was weird. She was laughing at stuff that wasn't funny."

"She was coming onto you." Ronnie shook his head and looked down.

"That ain't it."

"Yes, it is."

"Look, I don't believe in all that shit about body language and signals. What are you supposed to do with it anyway? So, they laugh at some joke you tell and that means they like you? Too vague, too unreliable."

"Well, you don't leave them standing in the middle of a party, alone, I can tell you that much."

We looked at each other and broke out laughing.

CHAPTER TWO

  I got home from Ronnie's at six that evening. Mom was cooking chili; I could smell it from outside, which is where I preferred to stay until supper. There was usually something to do out there. The chores were endless on a ranch, even a small one. Getting caught up was the most anyone could expect. Instead of going inside and hanging around the kitchen, annoying my mom while she cooked, I stayed outside and greased the tractor we used for moving hay from the stacks to the corrals. It was a Farmall M with a bucket on the front and leaking hydraulics. It was painted red, but years had faded it to nearly orange. I had seen such tractors restored and the red was always bright, but every Farmall I had ever seen in the field featured a badly faded red paint.

  The conversation I had with Ronnie kept playing over and over in my mind. I didn't know anything about girls and what little I did know, I didn't trust. Ronnie was different; he had sisters. Ronnie knew how to talk to girls, how to take a "no" and turn it into a "yes." I had seen him do it any number of times, but it didn't rub off on me, because I didn't have the looks to go along with the patter.

  The difference in us that Ronnie didn't see, or wouldn't acknowledge, was that he was more attractive than I was. I could see it whenever we got near a group of girls, they would all drift toward him, instead of me. That was the part that vexed him at the party when it came to Annie Brewster. It was also the reason I didn't understand her behavior. I thought she was sticking it to Ronnie for one reason or another, purposely ignoring him. Even having thought it out, I was no closer to understanding anything about the other night. Just because Ronnie said

Annie was coming onto me didn't make it true.

Jon pulled his pickup into the yard while I was putting the grease gun back in the barn. I came out of the barn when he was closing the door to the pickup. We caught each other's eye. There was a lot in that look. We were brothers and we had scaled the heights and plumbed the depths of that relationship. I would die to save his life or be willing to take it myself and that's how it was. I would look at him in his nearly adult form, but all I would ever see is the child. The younger version I knew when we had faced hostile neighbors, got into serious trouble for driving the pickup into town when we he was fourteen and I was twelve, or when we brought the rattlesnake into the house and it got away overnight.

When we were small, we had gotten hold of a tape recorder and we would spend hours playing the interview game. The interview game was played like this: one person would be the interviewer and he would imagine an insane occupation for the interviewee and the interviewee would have to improvise answers to the off-the-wall questions asked by the interviewer. One lost the game when he could not answer a question or the interviewer ran out of questions to ask. Holding onto the role of the interviewer was the goal, because it was fun to put someone under that sort of pressure and sometimes the funniest responses would come out, but also some of the lamest.

Some of my fondest memories of my brother involved the snowy, winter days playing the interview game and it was hard to see him as any older than he was then. The game called on intellectual qualities of wit and humor that somehow burrowed deep into aspects of personality that no other game could touch. Those winter days were spent playing a lot of board games and the like, but the interview game was hilarious.

"What's for supper?"

"Chili."

Jon nodded, adjusting the cowboy hat on his head, his lean muscles flexing as he pulled up on his belt buckle.

"Vince is still in jail," he said, referring to the event at the burger joint, the night I left Annie at the party to go with him. Vince Ciroli, whose parents owned a big dairy in the next town, had gotten into a fight with a hood and put the boy in the hospital. Jon had almost been arrested trying to keep Vince from being arrested. If Jon would have gotten arrested, I would have, too; trying to defend him. That was how we had to be, us cowboys in the middle of a thriving city. We had to stick together, because we were perpetually outnumbered.

"What about bail?"

"Ten grand."

"Shit."

"Yeah, they think they'll get it reduced, but they have to hire a lawyer. It's turning into a huge deal. I have to work for both of us while he's gone."

"The guy's going to be all right, though, right?"

Jon shrugged.

"Don't know," he said. "I guess that's part of it, see how he comes out. Better not die."

Everyone is born into a world that they come to understand and their actions are in reaction to what they experience and how they are treated. The people we knew were all longtime residents of the area and most of the people with whom we interacted had moved into town a few years before. The town had doubled in population from 1960 to 1970 and was on its way to doubling again before 1980 came around.

To some degree, we were all lost, our home taken over by outsiders. No one cared that we had been there for generations. They didn't care that the town had once been an agricultural community and we used to fit in. They saw it as a growing metropolis, a bedroom community for Denver or Fort Collins. To them, we were hicks and shit kickers.

To be honest, we had treated the newcomers with some contempt when they came into our community and began to control the city council, the school board and spread their wealth to redesign our world. So, no one was innocent and the hostilities were let loose in school, where the attitudes of parents played out among their offspring. Those hostilities extended to social interactions at football games and school dances. Late at night, they played out at the burger joint; the only thing open at one in the morning when parties all around town broke up and the varied cliques congregated there at different levels of intoxication. It was a volatile situation that sometimes got out of hand.

We went into the house together, like old times, in a way, as friends, a feeling that often got lost in our competitiveness. Brothers, especially those so closely matched in age and size as Jon and I were, rarely got along, there was too much friction, too much competition.

As we stood before the pot with our bowls and spoons at the ready, we nudged each other, using our weight to try and push the other away from the pot, like two dogs fighting over scraps.

"Knock it off, you two," mom said, knowing her admonition was a formality at best. "Don't make a mess," she said, louder, with more authority as we shoved each other and tried to maneuver our bowl under the pouring stream of chili. The ladle was pushed around, wavering dangerously over the stovetop and floor as we struggled to win.

Scott stood back, with his bowl and spoon, waiting for us to move along and allow him to get some food. Scott benefited from our left-over minibikes, our forgotten toys and especially our punishments. He was allowed to do things we begged to do at his age and were denied. We broke all the ground for him to exploit and he took advantage of it with an infuriating smile.

Gathered around the table, with hats and caps hung on the high-backed chairs, we ate. Bread was passed around and milk brought home by Jon from the dairy was poured into glasses. That sort of meal was becoming an oddity as we all grew and found distractions away from the home.

"So, you're gonna ride?" Jon asked, glancing at me as he took a drink of milk.

"Yeah, I suppose, just steers, though."

"That was bs," Jon said, referring to the junior rodeo. He would ride in the senior rodeo, where full-sized bulls were ridden by contestants sixteen and older.

"I've been riding bulls all summer getting ready," I said, disappointed.

"You should go to a school."

It was an old argument between Jon and I. Rodeo schools were great, a guy could ride up to ten bulls with pros giving classes and hands-on instruction. But, they were expensive and I was saving for a car. Besides, I didn't take rodeo as seriously as he did. I didn't take anything as seriously as he did. I wanted to ride when I got a chance, for something to do, that's all. Jon was dedicated. He wanted to excel at everything he tried and I just wanted to have fun.

"Yeah," I said, without commitment.

"Half-assed," he remarked, smirking and rising to refill his bowl.

How could I tell him that I knew it wasn't for me, that I had other things in my future. In order to be good at rodeo, one had to ride, which meant joining an association, which meant making a commitment to something and I couldn't; I had to keep my options open, I just felt it.

"I've been to the buckouts, riding bulls when I can, how the hell is that 'half-assed?'"

"You need to be trained."

"For steers?"

Jon stood at the stove and looked over his shoulder at me.

"The point is, you don't take anything serious, you don't dedicate yourself. How are you ever going to get anywhere, just floating along like you do; getting jobs to make money; riding bulls when everyone else does; taking tests, but not caring about the outcome? You never buckle down to do the hard work or care deeply about anything."

"I'm fifteen, I don't even have a car. How am I going to make a commitment to anything when I can't even get my ass from one place to another?"

"Hey!" mom yelled from the other room when she heard the curse word.

"Sorry, ma'am," I replied, then continued. "What am I going to do, pay three-hundred dollars for a school and not be able to go, 'cause I don't have a car?"

Jon walked back to the table and sat down. He pointed his spoon at me, chili dripped off.

"That ain't it and you know it. We could go together, you could ride with me; if you really wanted to do it, but you don't."

I shrugged, because he was right. I was just making a good argument, just to argue. I finished my meal and walked the bowl to the sink, rinsed it and set it in the basin.

Scott sat, watching the exchange, knew more about us than we knew about ourselves. He stayed out of the fray, but he learned from everything we did.

I took my cap off the back of the chair and went back outside. The sun was drifting toward the sharp peak of the mountain that was framed by the orange light of the dying sun; it was beautiful, but the cars passing by on the street kept it from being peaceful.

I walked out to the corral and climbed up to sit on the top rail where I liked to think.

Jon was just part of it; everyone thought I should be someone else. My dad wanted me to like mechanics, but I didn't. I was a good mechanic; I could troubleshoot a problem as quickly as anyone I knew, but I didn't like being on my back looking up at the dirty underside of a car or pickup; greasy dirt dropping into my eyes; my neck aching from being strained at odd angles and never having enough leverage to break rusty bolts out of their holes without using every tool in the garage.

My mom wanted me to be a student, to take pride in my grades. Like everyone else, she mistook the A's for effort when they were really indictments of the school system. She read my report cards and thought I had huge promise. She was sure that it would pave the path to my future if I would just knuckle down and try harder. But, no one talked about college, least of all me and I had already gotten the lowdown. High school was to prepare students for college, that's all. For guys like me, it was a fraud.

All I wanted to do was to buy a car and see the world. I was willing to work odd jobs to earn gas money and a meal here and there, but I wanted to be free. A few more weeks and I would have the money to buy a car. It was all arranged; I would buy one of dad's old crew cars that he used to transport the guys in his crew back and forth to the rig when he was still a driller, before the promotion. It was a Ford, a two-door LTD, kind of rare, actually. Most two-door LTDs were fastbacks. This one was a sedan. A few months after I bought the car, I would have a license to drive it on the streets.

I might have been only fifteen, but I knew how to run a life. I knew it took hard work and saving to pay for things like rent and food. The only thing holding me back from pursuing my life was age. I was not old enough to drive, though I had been driving for a long time. I wasn't old enough to work on the drilling rigs with my dad, though I had been out to fill in once or twice.

I felt stuck, trapped, held hostage by time.

"What the hell are you doing up there?" Jon asked from behind me. I hadn't heard him come out of the house or walk up behind me. Knowing him, it must have taken some willpower not to push me off.

"Just thinkin'."

"Thinkin' or dreamin'?"

The light was fading and the shadows were growing long across the yard. A golden hue was cast on the barn, the tractor and across the grassy prairie beyond the corral.

"Thinkin'."

"About the ride?"

"About life, when I'll be able to run it myself without so many helping hands like teachers, parents and older brothers."

"That's dreamin,' not thinkin. You'll never be there, that world don't exist, not like you think, anyway. Once you get rid of all that, you'll have a wife to help out and kids and bosses and finances."

"That's what I'm thinkin' about, planning to make sure that don't happen, not for a while."

"Okay, smartass, but I've seen it happen to friends of mine already. You know Cary, right? Big football player, maybe college, even? He got Elizabeth pregnant late last year, now he's workin' for her dad, his dreams shot to hell in a second. Vince is in jail over something stupid, just defending himself from that creep and his bunch."

Jon reached up and pulled on my shirt to make me look at him.

"You're fifteen, be a kid for a while. Stop trying to be an adult so quick, it ain't no fun anyway. If Vince had been sixteen or seventeen, he wouldn't have gone to jail, but he just turned eighteen and they booked him. Now, I have to go back out there to do his work for him."

"I just want to live," I said.

"All right. Fine. Fuck it, I tried to talk some sense, but no one gets through that thick head. I tried to be a big brother, to give good advice, but you just spit it back in my face. So, don't, go screw it up, it ain't my problem."

Jon walked off and got into his pickup. He pulled out of the yard, tires spinning, pissed off at me again.

CHAPTER THREE

As it grew dark in the yard, the yard light was turned on, probably by mom, it illuminated the area between the house, the barn and the corrals. The yard was a wide graveled area where vehicles, including semis could be turned around and backed up to the corrals to load cattle. Beyond the trees, a tall, illuminated oil company sign could be seen marking the location of a convenience store a mile away.

The heat of the day had long-since passed and the cooler air encouraged me to consider a trip to the convenience store. I had to walk or ride the minibike along a path next to the street. Sidewalks didn't begin until the housing development west of our place. From our place east to the convenience store was a footpath through the weeds between the street and our land. Our property ended where the barbed-wire fence ended about a quarter of a mile away, after that it was the Pulaskis' old place that was now being prepared for construction. Their house had been moved out already. I watched them do it, it was interesting how they put steel beams under the frame of the house, through the old foundation, then loaded it on a truck and drove it away. The story was that the construction company sold it for a couple of hundred dollars. I could have bought it with the money I had saved for the car, but I couldn't drive a house. A house would not enhance my freedom.

I got down off the corral and looked over at the minibike Scott had been working on. It had its ignition cover off and the points exposed. It only had one cylinder and I thought I could probably get it going, if I wanted to, but it was Scott's project and I decided to let him learn how to fix it himself. I turned and walked out the drive and along the path.

Cars zipped by on the street. Tin cans, plastic bags, fast food bags and wrappers occasionally littered the roadside. Dad would make one of us pick it up when it got bad enough to annoy him. It was one of the reasons he was hostile to the newcomers. We rarely had trash in front of our house before the housing developments started cropping up. A tin can would appear overnight now and then, but nothing like what had occurred the past couple of years. Whether we had anything to do with the trash or not, it looked like we didn't care about our property. Nothing could be further from the truth, so we would wind up having to pick up after everyone else. I felt like picking up the trash as I walked along, without his demand, but I didn't have anything to put it in. I walked along the path and kicked the cans away from the street, where it would be safer to pick them up later.

A semi roared past and almost blew me over when I was off balance, kicking a can. I was across from the Pulaskis' home site and nearing the convenience store. I heard a loud car nearing from behind. I glanced over my shoulder and saw a red '70 Chevelle with black stripes running lengthwise over the center of the car. It was sharp, jacked up a little in the back, with a hood scoop. It roared past and pulled into the convenience store and up to the gas pump. Three high-school-aged guys got out, hoods.

I thought for a moment that I should wait them out, let them get gas and leave before I went up to the store, but shrugged off the idea. I couldn't be afraid to go to the store. That was ridiculous. Despite what had happened to Vince, I had to assume that they wouldn't bother with a kid.

Bright lights flooded the parking area of the store. Advertising for everything from pop to cigarettes were splashed across the windows making it hard to see inside. The hood filling the car with gas had long, dirty-blond hair, skinny arms protruded from a tank top and spindly legs extended down from a pair of cut-off jeans.

I walked in front of the other cars there, a Datsun and a Volkswagen. Approaching the doors, I hesitated, thinking that the others might come out before I went in. My caution was warranted. I grew up with tension between us cowboys and the hoods that we derisively called hippies.

No one came out of the doors by the time I got there, so I went inside. The girl behind the counter, Sally, looked up when I came in. She was twenty or so and nice-looking. She worked most nights, but sometimes an older lady with black hair worked that shift.

"Welcome to Maxi-Mart," she said, by obligation.

"Howdy," I said, walking back toward the coolers.

The other two hoods were hanging around the beer section, screwing up courage or pooling their money together, I couldn't figure out which, but they were huddled, whispering back and forth. One of them was a heavy-set guy about my height with brown, curly hair. The other was tall, six one or two and muscular, with a tight T-shirt and tie-dyed shorts.

I was stalling, I wanted them to do their business before I did mine. At the time, the late seventies, it was legal to sell 3.2% alcohol beer to eighteen-year-olds, so they could very well be old enough to buy it, but they seemed suspicious to me. I kept glancing at them, waiting to see what they were going to do. Giving up and seeing the driver approaching to pay for the gas, I went up to the rack and grabbed a can of chewing tobacco. I looked at the date on the bottom of the can and placed it on the counter with a dollar bill to pay for it.

"Will that be all?" Sally asked.

"Yes, ma'am," I replied, feeling the presence of the hoods right behind me as if they had been waiting for me, while I waited for them.

"Yes, ma'am," the fat one mocked me, but I ignored him as best as I could with his hot breath on my neck. The other one came through the door with a ten-dollar bill in his hand.

Sally handed me a quarter and I put the can of tobacco in my shirt pocket. The driver brushed by me on my way out as he handed the ten to Sally. He smelled of beer and weed. I couldn't wait to get outside. I pulled the door inward and threw it wide so the hood could make it through before it closed; it was the best I could do to be civil.

I stepped in front of the cars parked in the lot feeling like it was going to end peacefully and that I had escaped some danger. I got to the corner of the building when the hood called out to me.

"Hey, kid."

I paid no attention to him, thinking I stood a better chance of avoiding conflict if I didn't respond.

"Hey, you, goat roper!"

That was it, there was no getting out of it. I stopped and turned slowly to see the driver walking toward me as the other two approached the car with a twelve-pack.

"Yeah?"

The driver had a big nose, I hadn't noticed before. He kept walking toward me. He didn't speak again until he was very close.

"You want a beer?" he asked, his watery blue eyes darting around, then settling on me.

"For doin' what?"

The driver glanced around to see if anyone was close enough to hear what he was going to say.

"Where can I score some weed?"

I was taken aback by that. What made him think I had any idea where to buy dope? I knew some guys who smoked it, but not in my circles. We spent our time trying to get beer or whiskey, not dope.

"No clue, man," I said.

"Aw, you're shittin' me. I won't tell no one, if that's what you're worried about."

"I drink," I said, thinking that should suffice.

The tall muscular guy leaned out the passenger side window and yelled: "Come on, man. Let's go.

The driver looked over his shoulder.

"No weed, no beer."

"Guess I'll have to do without," I said and walked around

the corner, toward the path. It could have been worse. I felt fortunate to get off without some altercation. I heard the car start up behind me. The engine revved and the exhaust popped as the tires squealed, spinning on the concrete. It was a pretty car and I glanced at it as they pulled up to the stop light at the intersection. The turn signal was on, so they were going to drive right past me. I would get another look after it passed.

The engine revved again as the car came around the corner. I kept walking, but I was low, down in the embankment and I didn't think they would see me. I kept expecting the car to go by, but it didn't. A can of beer went sailing by my nose and bounced off the ground, skidding to a stop and spraying foam in an arc. A great roar of laughter came from the direction of the road before the sound of the engine and squealing tires erupted. The driver's arm was extended from the open window. He was giving me the finger as he sped off.

"Yeah, fuck you, too," I said and kept walking, knowing that if I returned the gesture things would go bad, fast. The thing that really irked me, was that I would have to pick up the beer can somewhere along the line.

When I got home, Jon had already made it back from Ciroli's dairy. He probably knew the guys in the car. They would have gone to school together. All the kids his age went to the same high school, but they were building a new one and it would open in the fall. I would go to it, as would Jon. But, those guys had most likely graduated in the spring.

Our house was built in the 1920s and my dad upgraded the wiring and plumbing in the '60s. We remodeled it one summer, too, upgrading the appliances and such, but it still felt old every time I entered it, like taking a step back in time. The outside looked just as it did when it was first built and was a decided contrast from the new houses popping up everywhere with complicated rooflines and split basements. It made me feel poor.

I walked into the kitchen with its linoleum counters and real wood cabinets. The hardwood floors gleamed and area rugs spread out through the rooms and under furniture. Mom was sitting in the living room watching some program on television.

"Dad still working?"

"Huh? Yeah, they're finishing a well. Won't be back until morning."

I turned toward the doorway that led to an enclosed staircase leading up to my room. At the top, to the right was Jon's room. Mine was directly in front of me. I paused at Jon's room and listened, thinking about talking to him about the guys in the Chevelle, to see who they were, but decided against it. We all went through that sort of thing. It was another reason I couldn't wait to get a car.

I went into my room, kicked off my boots and hung my cap on the bedpost. My cowboy hat was upside down on the dresser. The rigging bag with rodeo gear in it was in the corner. There was a light on the nightstand beside the bed along with a copy of *On the Road* by Jack Kerouac. I was only reading it because the idea of it appealed to me given my dedication to the idea of getting my driver's license and pursuing freedom with a religious devotion. *On the Road*, right? I was not prepared to read so much about towns and cities with which I was so intimately familiar. Nor did I expect to find commonality in many respects with Sal Paradise, in thought more than deed, but nonetheless.

I had to read something. *On the Road* was not something I sought out and actually went against a lot of what I had decided would be in my life, but in killing time in a downtown bookstore, a smelly, dusty, crowded hardwood-floored maze of books, I ran across the title. As I had recognized on other trips, the books often found me, all I had to do was walk around until they reached out to snare my attention. This was my discovery of *On the Road*. It was a title that appealed to my every thought, which was to eventually escape from my limited scope and burst out into the world. Besides, there was nothing else to do in the room, no television, not even a radio and the nights were long without one. It was hard enough getting to sleep as it was, my mind kept running through events of the day and imagining confrontations like the one with the hood at the convenience store.

Mom liked the idea of reading over television for her children. She did not ban us from television, but did not encourage it in our rooms and certainly wouldn't buy one to put in there. She believed reading books would enhance our minds and imagination, which she thought would somehow solve all of our problems. The only thing school ever did for me was cause problems. Getting good grades made my friends think I was weird or something and it didn't change the fact that I was a goat roper to the rest of the kids like Alan Nelson and Millie Anderson. The smart kids all thought I had somehow rigged the system to get the kind of grades I did.

I turned off the ceiling light and turned on the lamp beside the bed. It was nearly ten at night and I wasn't tired. I looked forward to the next day and working at Ronnie's again, but I wouldn't be able to go to sleep without reading the book. Every day I worked at Ronnie's I got closer to owning the car. Once I owned it, I had to get a license to drive it on the street, but first things first.

I stripped out of my clothes and got under the thin cover. It was hot on the upper floor of the un-airconditioned farmhouse that we lived in, even with the window open. Only rarely did a cool breeze come through the opening. I reached over and opened the book to the bookmark.

The characters were undefined in age and it was easy to place myself in the role of Sal Paradise and Ronnie in the role of Dean Moriarty. Ronnie was a conman in his own right, slippery and unreliable in many ways, especially when it came to women. His good looks produced opportunities that he could rarely resist and I had a suspicion that when questioned about some of his dalliances, he made me the fall guy, whether I was present or not.

I had my own issues with girls and was suspicious of the boyfriend/girlfriend dynamic that seemed too serious in people my age or even a little older. Jon had never brought a girl home, though I know he had been with a few at parties, dances and rodeos. Girls my age liked Jon and asked me about him, whether he was seeing anyone or not, a question I honestly couldn't answer. They thought I was vindictively refusing to offer information about him, but they didn't understand us. We didn't huddle together every day and discuss our lives, loves and ambitions. A week might go by before we talked at all.

I did not view the novel with anything like a lust for a similar situation, instead, I thought that several of their difficulties could be avoided with a little more common sense. In fact, it was hard to see in it what the nation had latched onto that created the "beat generation," but I excused that as a reaction from a person who had lived through the further development of the philosophy and so did not see it for the novelty that it must have been at the time. From my view they would have benefited from being a little less naïve. I was more circumspect with my commitments; some would call it "cagey." People wanted to know if I would come to work for them and I wanted to know what the "work" entailed and who was the "them" that I would be reporting to and taking direction from? Working at Ronnie's was easy, I knew I would be working with Ronnie most of the time and at worst under the direction of his father, who was strict and demanded hard work, but who recognized a good job and paid promptly upon completion. That was not true of everyone.

The Taylors, Jim and Adele, had hired me to help build a corral for their horses. I started off with Jim, he had a tractor with an auger run by the PTO shaft that we were using to dig the post holes, but the tractor broke down halfway through and instead of fixing the tractor, he handed me a pair of manual post-hole diggers, essentially opposing shovels hinged so the dirt could be squeezed between them and pulled out of the hole, and left. I spent three days digging the rest of the post holes by hand in the hard clay. Jim came back long enough to help me set the posts in the holes and make sure they were lined up and straight, but when it came time to mix cement to put in the holes, he was gone again. That took another week. Jim did show up to bring more cement and gravel as needed, but he did that after I had gone home for the day.

After spending nearly two weeks doing what should have taken a couple of days with a tractor and two people, I decided we were far enough along that I could let Jim handle the rest. I asked for my pay and told him I had been shirking my chores on our place to help him. That's when it got ugly.

"Well, I ain't paying you until the job is done," Jim said, growing angry.

"As far as I'm concerned, it's finished. Just pay me what I have coming."

"I'm not paying you for a week's work that should have taken a few days."

I knew what he was trying to do; I had been through it before with other people. Jim wasn't planning to pay me at all. When the job was done, he would come up with some excuse and try to put me off until I gave up trying to collect. That's why I stopped when I did, when I had some leverage.

"Just pay me what I have coming and I'll go back and work at our place for a couple of days and if you still need me, I'll come back and finish up."

"The job's half done. I'll pay you half of what you have coming and the rest when you come back," Jim offered.

He was clever and had done this sort of thing before. He was a cheat, simple as that and I saw him for the lowlife that he was. It was not just a matter of not wanting to pay or not having the money or feeling like I hadn't worked hard enough, cheating me was figured into the budget. Jim Taylor calculated that he could cheat a kid a lot easier than an adult and with fewer consequences. He probably only wanted to pay for three or four days, but that was up to him. He could have fixed the tractor, or helped, but he did neither.

"I wasn't being paid by the job; I was being paid by the hour. I want paid for the hours I've already worked," I said, standing my ground.

"I'm not sure you worked all them hours. You might have been loafing around half the time for all I know."

"I worked all of the hours I wrote down, sixty of 'em. If I didn't work, I didn't write it down. If I was waiting for you to bring supplies, I quit working and wrote down when I quit and went home. That's better than most people. No sir, I want paid for those sixty hours, one-hundred and twenty-six dollars."

I stood there and watched his face grow red with anger. He was bigger than me and an adult. I was just a kid, but the hard work I had always done reflected in my biceps and chest. If it came to a physical thing, I was pretty sure I'd lose, but it would cost him some bruises, cuts and maybe a handful of hair to get his way and that registered on his face when he saw me stiffen.

"I don't have the money right this minute," he said and probably never had it.

"You got a horse," I said nodding toward the makeshift and dilapidated corrals on the other side of the barn, the ones we were replacing. If I had reached out and punched him in the face it wouldn't have affected him more.

"That horse is worth a hell of a lot more than a hunnerd and twenty-six bucks," he sputtered, spit forming at the corner of his mouth.

"Then, you'll be sure to pay me to get it back, right?" I watched him think about it. "You know our place; I'll take good care of him over there. He'll fit right in with ours."

"You wait right here," he said and went into the house.

I didn't wait right there; I walked over to the barn and started looking for a bridle among the hay bales and tools. Hanging on a nail near the door was a bridle and I took it down and walked out.

Jim Taylor met me at the corral with one-hundred dollars in twenties.

"Here, that's all I got," he said, taking the bridle from my hand and putting the twenties in my palm. "Now get outta here. I don't want to see you around here no more."

CHAPTER FOUR

It was early August and fair time in Loveland. A carnival had been set up in the parking lot of the fairgrounds, flashing lights and barkers enticing young men to impress their girlfriends by throwing balls at dolls and swinging oversized hammers trying to drive a piston up to ring a bell. There was a parade in town earlier that day with dignitaries riding on convertibles and American flags being waved up and down the procession. It was the only time that the community cared a whit about its agricultural roots. It was the only time anything was dedicated to the people who spent generations building the accommodations the newcomers enjoyed.

The fairgrounds in Loveland featured a huge arena where the rodeo and some concerts were held. There were stock pens for cows, horses, goats and sheep that would be shown by 4-H kids. I was one when I was younger, but I was growing up, getting too old for such things. I was a cowboy, but a different sort, kind of a roughneck, like my dad. To me there was a difference between a cowboy and a farmer. A cowboy was a little more of a reckless sort, a daredevil, as attested to by the concept of rodeo.

There was the McMillen Building on the midway, a large metal building with a concrete floor. It was where country dances were held all year round. The only time I ever felt at home was at the dances. But, dancing wasn't the attraction. It was the country music favorites played by local bands; it was the opportunity to meet girls; it was the beer and whiskey in the parking lot. Conflicts were often settled there and though the police and parents might not like the idea of us fighting; we did settle a lot of disagreements in the dirt parking lot before someone came along to break it up.

I was working my way back to the area behind the chutes. It smelled of manure, straw, hay and dust. It was where the contestants got ready to ride; rosining their bull ropes and bareback riggings. Some of them were from Fort Collins, but most were from Loveland, guys I knew. I went to school with some of them, others went to the other junior high. Our few allies in town, the other farmers and ranchers, would get split up again when they opened the new high school, the one they called Thompson Valley. Stupid name.

I dropped my rigging bag at an open spot on the fence, where I could hang up my bull rope and grind the rosin into the handle with my glove. Looking around, a lot of the other bull ropes were hung from the top rail of the fence with gloves secured to the handle. I took the goatskin glove out of the bag; it had a piece of rawhide strip laced through a couple of holes. The rawhide was used to tie around my wrist to hold the glove on, otherwise, with a big lunge, the bull could pull the glove off my hand and I would be whipped to the ground.

"Lane, hey man, how ya doin?" Will Pulaski asked, stepping up to me. He was the grandson of our neighbors. His dad had gotten into real estate years before, recognizing the opportunities to sell off property to the developers. His bona fides as a rancher helped him in negotiations with his neighbors. Will's family had grown wealthy but living in the big house on the lake had not changed him as much as I thought it would. He clung to his country roots with an iron grip.

"Good, you?"

"Fine. Fuckin' steers, huh?"

"Yeah, first year they pulled this shit. Last year the cutoff for junior boys was fourteen, not fifteen. Hell, I practiced all summer on bulls. I didn't find out it would be steers until I had to sign up for an event and saw thirteen to fifteen had to ride steers and sixteen to eighteen would ride bulls."

"Yeah, I saw that, too. Bullshit."

Will was a tall kid, blonde hair, blue eyes. He was too tall to ride bulls anyway; he would have done better with bareback horses where height was an advantage. He had the same problem I did, though. It was a lot tougher to find practice horses than bulls. Everyone had bulls and only a few of the contractors ran buckouts for horses for the same reason, there were fewer contestants looking for horses.

"You done here?" he asked.

"Yeah, I guess," I said, shoving the glove in my back pocket.

"Let's go check out the grounds."

We left our rigging bags behind the chutes, like everyone. No one worried about their gear getting stolen, it just wasn't like that. Someone might get into your gear if they needed some rosin or a rawhide strip, but that was acceptable.

Will was not a friend of mine, exactly. He lived on the other side of town, always had. His grandparents lived next to us and we would hang out if he came to see them, but it didn't go as far as friendship. We didn't visit each other. We didn't go to the same school, even.

We walked out of the arena and into the stock pen area where kids were washing their steers and horses or grooming their sheep. We were looking for girls, really. So, we walked, chatted and looked around. I thought I might run into Ronnie somewhere along the line. He would be riding, too. I didn't want to run into Beth, because she would want to come along with us and that was uncomfortable; a little girl hanging around with boys looking for dates.

There were girls, all right, but they were with their parents mostly. We were only fifteen and so were most of them; it was an awkward situation. We walked all through the area without any prospects and wound up at the carnival. I stopped, but Will kept walking until he realized I wasn't next to him and he turned around.

"Come on."

"Naw, I don't like the carnival, I'm going back."

Will was confused and a little perturbed.

"Come on, let's check it out."

"What are we going to see? I've seen rides and shit before."

"What are you afraid of?"

"Nothin' man, I just don't like the people. I don't like being yelled at to try some stupid game that's rigged anyway. They just want our money and I don't have enough to throw away on that shit."

"Don't have the money?" he laughed.

"I don't."

"Everyone knows your old man's raking it in. That ain't no secret. He made a lot of money on that forty acres he sold; my old man told me."

"That ain't me, though."

"No, but if you spent a few bucks having fun, he'd make it up."

"Oh, would he? You know him better than me, now?"

"Don't get all pissed off."

"Then don't say shit that pisses me off."

Will shook his head. This is why we weren't friends; we didn't see the world the same way. It's why Ronnie and I were friends.

"Just come with me. I don't want to go in there alone."

There it was, that was the real reason he brought me along. It had nothing to do with friendship. It was protection, something I could understand. None of us could wander around town without some backup and the carnival attracted the hoods. It attracted people like those who had thrown the beer can at me; it attracted the kind that jumped Vince at the burger joint.

"For a bit," I said, relenting because I finally understood his motives and because I was somewhat honor-bound to do it; we all were. If we didn't back each other up, there would be places we would not be able to go without taking an ass-beating.

We walked into the carnival. The hackles on the back of my neck stood up. I glanced at the booths with stuffed animals lined up on shelves waiting to be knocked down by some sucker throwing a ball. There was a place with pop bottles where one was supposed to try and pitch a plastic ring around one of the bottles. The men running the booths looked like they had been shooting heroin or something, scraggly looking with long, dirty hair.

The attendants started calling to us, trying to get us to throw a ball or pitch a ring. I knew they would and I didn't like it, but I pretended that they were calling to Will, not me. We walked the gauntlet and arrived at the Ferris wheel.

The girls looked different at the carnival, too. They had shorts with long, tanned legs, tank tops, tube tops and too much makeup. A lot of them were holding hands with hoods, big muscular guys and skinny little ones. I just wanted out. Nothing good could come from being there. Eventually, we would attract attention and it would all go sour.

They say that when confronted with a perceived threat, everyone is predisposed to fight or flight. It's a natural reaction to do one or the other. I had been through it enough to know that my predisposition was to fight and the odds were bad at the carnival. The thing that made me uneasy, is I was not sure what Will's predisposition might be. Ronnie and I were friends because I knew his predisposition was to fight and he wouldn't leave me to get my ass pummeled alone. Will might.

"We done, or what?"

Will looked at me, a big smile on his face. "Huh?"

"We done here?"

"No shit, you don't like this? Look at some of these chicks, man. That one," he said nodding and I looked to where he had indicated.

She was pretty, I had seen her earlier. She had long, dark hair and was built like a model, short-shorts and a Denver Broncos T-shirt stretched out of shape.

"Nice," I said.

"I'm gonna go to talk to her," Will said, walking away from me.

I didn't want to follow along, but felt I had to. I was a few steps behind, dreading the likely outcome, which was some conflict with her boyfriend. Girls like that didn't wander around carnivals all by themselves, as if dropped out of the clouds; they were smarter than that. Will was almost to her when some big biker came up to her and threw a tattooed arm around her neck. Will froze, looked left, then right and turned around to face me.

"Oops."

"Yeah," I said. "We're leavin'."

We walked back through the gauntlet of carnival barkers and onto the midway of the fairgrounds. There was a concession stand in the arts building across from the McMillen Building.

"Let's get a coke," I said, which was a euphemism for pop. It didn't mean an actual Coke, except that was all the concessions stands sold. They had big banners advertising the fact.

"Screw that, let's get a beer," Will said.

"Beer?"

"Yeah, Kevin has some in a cooler in the back of his truck."

"Where?"

"Across the river."

We walked through the midway, past the stock pens to an old iron bridge that spanned the Big Thompson River as the river curved along the fairgrounds and eventually out of town. The river would continue east until it met up with the South Platte coming out of Denver somewhere around Evans, Colorado.

Across the bridge was a corral where horse events were held that were not part of the rodeo competition. Next to the corral was a large open field where those who came to the rodeo in big recreational vehicles could park them, but it worked as overflow parking as well, since the actual parking lot had been turned into a carnival. It was also an area where underaged kids could sneak a beer now and then and was not generally patrolled by the sheriff's deputies. But, even when the deputies did come around, they were easy to spot, riding horses and visible above everything else.

Kevin Pulaski was eighteen and could buy and consume 3.2 beer, though his true intention was to come into possession of the stronger stuff and the weak beer was a concession to legality. Will led me to Kevin's pickup, a new Chevrolet with two-tone paint kind of a brownish-brass color on the top and bottom with a cream color in the middle and cream top. It was not much different from the 1976 model with the squared front end and the rounded rear corners with turn signal lenses that wrapped around the corner. All in all, not a bad design, but I liked the Fords better simply because one was either a Ford or a Chevy guy and my dad had worked for the Ford dealer as a young man. The Fords just looked classier to my sensibilities.

Will climbed into the back of Kevin's pickup, opened a cooler and tossed me a Budweiser. I liked Coors. Nothing Will did or liked was consistent with my preference. Even his taste in girls drifted to the carny-type while mine remained among the more homespun, less flashy type. To me, the carnival girls seemed like cotton candy, while the girls I liked seemed like steak and potatoes. I didn't know how else to think of it.

The beer was cold and refreshing in the heat of the day and dust of the parking area. That first one went down fast and I was light-headed by the end of it. We squashed the cans with our boot heels and pitched them under the pickup.

"Another?"

"Naw, if I have another, I'll want another after that."

Will nodded and we went back to the arena. The sun was starting to drift toward the horizon, casting longer shadows. The steer riding was in the middle of the rodeo, so we still had some time, but getting ready seemed reasonable.

By the time we got back to the area behind the chutes, it was crowded with contestants. We nodded and otherwise acknowledged those who acknowledged us. Ronnie was there already talking to one of the Gonsalez boys and Brad Romero. I knew Brad better than Gonsalez. But they were deep in conversation and I walked on by to my rope hanging from the fence.

I reached into the bag and brought out the small, cloth bag of rosin. I pulled the glove out of my back pocket and pulled it on, tying the leather strip around my wrist. I dug out a nugget of the amber-colored chunks. There was powder rosin, but we all liked the rocks; they fit better in the hand. We used friction to melt the rosin into the crevices of the plaits in the bull rope. Starting at the top of the handle, with the rock between my fingers and the rope, I squeezed the handle and pulled down quickly, heating the rosin, melting it into the plaits. I was busy doing this when Ronnie walked up behind me.

"Brad says you were in some big hassle down at the burger joint."

"Yeah," I said, laughing. "I tried to tell you that a number of times, but all you could talk about was Annie Brewster."

"She's here, you know."

"No shit, where else would she be?"

"She's looking for you."

"She ain't lookin' for me. Stop buggin' me with that shit."

Ronnie laughed and I knew he was lying.

It was dark by the time I got the call to ride. I had helped Ronnie get down on his steer and pulled his rope for him. I was expecting the same from him.

"Daniels, get ready," I heard the chute boss call out.

I straddled the steer; the toes of my boots stuck between the boards on the back of the chute and the gate while I dangled my rope down one side. Ronnie held the wire hook and fished under the steer for the rope. He caught it and brought it up to me. I ran the tail end through the loop and worked the rope around to where the handle was on top of the steer. I pulled the rope tight until the handle set just to the left of the steer's backbone. I handed the tail end of the rope to Ronnie and put my gloved hand, the left hand, into the handle. Ronnie pulled up on it with all his might. When the rope felt tight enough to crush my hand, I knew it was tight enough. I had him loosen it just a bit so I could adjust the handle a little further to the left and he pulled it tight again, this time it was right.

"That's good," I said, taking the tail end of the rope and wrapping it loosely around my wrist.

"Daniels, come on," the chute boss prodded an old contractor trick whose reputation was improved by unprepared cowboys coming out and bucking down. It made his stock look tougher when he approached other rodeos for the contract.

I knew better than to let him rattle me. First rule in rodeo: take the time to make sure things are right.

"Just a second," I said, laying the tail end of the rope in my clutched hand, beating on my fingers to tighten my grip. I lowered myself down on the back of the steer and let my legs fall onto each side, my spurs digging into the thick skin in front of the rope, wedging the spurs into that crease. I pulled my cowboy hat down onto my head and raised my right arm into the air.

I nodded and the chute gate flew open. The steer jumped out of the chute left and then to the right and I threw my right arm across my chest to center myself in the middle of the steer's back. My left hand was held tight in the handle, stuck together by the thick rosin. The steer began to run. That was not what I wanted. I wanted it to buck. I watched the steer's head to see which way he was going to go. The ground flashed by underneath, but no bucking.

The score was the product of two judges, each rating the steer from zero to twenty-five points and the rider from zero to twenty-five points. So, the best score for a perfect performance from the steer (massive bucking) was fifty points and the best score for a perfect performance from the rider was fifty points. Perfection on both counts was a total of one hundred points.

I kicked the steer to try and make it buck, but it just ran across the arena. The buzzer sounded and I rolled off the steer's back. I was angry. It was a waste. I deserved a re-ride. No matter how well I scored, half of the total would be the score of the steer, that did nothing.

I picked up the bull rope that lay in the middle of the arena and gathered it in my hand. I took off my hat and set it at a different angle as I walked back to the shelter of the chutes. I was the first one to ride a steer.

"Daniels scores a sixty-nine, placing him in first," the announcer said over the speakers to a big round of applause, though sixty-nine was a dismal score. The steer just did not buck. By the time I got to the chutes, I was pissed.

"First place," Ronnie said cheerfully, but even he couldn't make me feel better.

"It sucks. The damn thing just ran," I said, throwing my gear down, toward the rigging bag.

"Least you stuck yours; I fell off," Ronnie said.

"Yours bucked," I retorted as I arranged the gear in the bag and zipped it shut.

Ronnie shrugged.

"Let's go see if we can find some beer," Ronnie said.

While I was curious how everyone else would do, I was too disappointed in my score to care. By the end of the night I would probably be second or third and by the end of tomorrow, I would be lucky to be fifth or sixth. The problem is, the rodeo only paid to fourth place and that seemed out of the question.

"All right, let's go," I said, picking up my rigging bag and taking it with me.

Together, we walked through the darkness to the bridge and over to Kevin Pulaski's pickup, where several other pickups were parked in a semi-circle. Jon's was not among them, but then, I didn't expect him to be there. Jon ran in his own circles, especially since he began work at the dairy and they hardly ever overlapped mine. Kevin and Jon, being the same age, had some hostility toward each other over something or other. In truth, I didn't get along all that well with Will, but he had beer and that covered a lot of ground.

As we got closer, we could hear the music being played; Waylon Jennings' Outlaw album. Ever since that album came out, the year before, it got played everywhere. The best bands would play "Good-Hearted Woman" and the worse bands stuck with Porter Wagoner.

"Five bucks," someone said out of the darkness, holding

his hand out to us.

"A piece?" Ronnie asked.

The dark figure nodded.

Ronnie and I dug in our pockets until we came up with ten dollars. I think Ronnie covered for me by a buck or two, but we were allowed to drink our fill having paid the price. Getting our money's worth was our goal.

While we were drinking our beer, a bottle was passed around to us. I couldn't see exactly what it was; I thought it was whiskey, but it had no smell. I took a deep drink of it and it must have been Everclear, because it was flat out alcohol and as soon as I took a breath, my lungs ignited into instant heartburn.

CHAPTER FIVE

I woke up under a massive cottonwood on the bank of the Big Thompson River. I blinked and looked around. My head was pounding and the more I tried to remember what had happened, the more my head throbbed. My breath smelled like feces. I couldn't shake it. My hat was laying a few feet away, thankfully not destroyed, as I feared.

I rose up to a sitting position. I could feel my hair poking out away from my skull. I shoved the hat on my head. I needed water. My mouth was dry as a bone and I thought about getting a drink from the river, but I figured I was as likely to drown myself as to get a drink. To make it even less enticing, the big flood of '76 had only happened a year before, so there might be all manner of decomposing things in that river. I thought about the coolers that had been in the backs of the pickups and used as seats for those who had been partying there. There would be water in the coolers. I looked for Kevin's pickup, but it was gone; so was everyone else who had been with our group. My rigging bag was in the back of Kevin's pickup, I remembered that.

There was a cooler outside, next to a camper. I eased over to it; afraid my actions would be mistaken for sneaking about. I opened the lid and started scooping the melted ice, the slightly dirty water into my mouth with one hand. There was a bottle of beer floating around in the cooler, but I paid it no mind. It was in the way, an obstruction.

I had a vague recollection of stumbling through the darkness. Ronnie was there, but out of the fog, I remembered an argument or a conflict of some kind between Ronnie and I. I didn't remember seeing Will at all. I continued alone past that. Some sort of dance was taking place, at least a band played in my obscured memory, but tripping over someone's feet, falling, then being shoved out the door was a vivid recollection. I recalled hitting a bench and lying there staring up at the sky, a silver web of spinning stars.

When I had gotten my bearings enough to rise from the bench, I staggered around until the bridge appeared out of the darkness and I crossed it. I didn't remember much more of the evening than that, but there was a sense of embarrassment for the way I had acted; the degree of intoxication I had achieved. An apology was due to Ronnie, I was sure of that.

I ventured back across the bridge to the fairgrounds to see if I could spark a recollection or find someone who had more information about what had taken place the night before. I didn't have to look long before I encountered someone, but it was not the "someone" I wanted to find.

Jon came walking toward me in the stiff-legged manner of someone who's angry. I stood my ground as he neared.

"You been here all night?" he asked, calling across the remaining distance. "Drunk, I heard, stumbling around the fairgrounds."

When he reached me, he grabbed me by the collar and started dragging me toward his pickup, which was parked along the road that ran by the fairgrounds. He pulled me along for several feet until I jerked out of his grasp and stood there, my chest heaving, ready for a fight.

Jon hit me so quickly, I didn't see it coming. My head snapped back and to the right. I brought it around and stared at him through bloodshot eyes. He took another swing at me, but I pulled back out of range, except he clipped me very slightly on the chin. His right hand clutched the back of my neck and he started pushing me toward his pickup. I bent over at the waist and turned out of his grasp.

"I'm going," I said and walked with him, about five feet distant.

We got into his pickup and he started it, revving the engine, the pipes roaring, echoing off the building and the train cars on the railroad tracks just to the west of the road.

Jon didn't say anything the rest of the way home, he just shook his head occasionally as if he couldn't believe what he knew to be true. It seemed inconceivable to him, outrageous. I didn't mean to do it, so I understood where he was coming from, but I couldn't change anything. I got a lot drunker than I had intended and nothing went as planned.

We pulled into the yard. I was hungover, tired and thirsty. I dreaded facing mom under those conditions, but I knew I would have to. I got out of the pickup and walked to the door. I entered, taking off my hat.

"Where have you been?" mom asked, her eyes flashing, brows arched.

"At the fairgrounds."

"You couldn't call?" she asked, getting closer. I tried to stay away from her, but she kept getting closer. "You've been drinking, too?"

I nodded, ashamed. There was nothing wrong with having a beer now and then and my parents didn't give me a lot of trouble when I was responsible but getting drunk and not coming home was irresponsible and inexcusable.

"Go out and do your chores," she said, unable to look at me, turning away.

I went outside and dawdled around with different things, mostly just staying out of her way. There were a few minor chores to do, fill water tanks, bring some bales of hay over to the corrals, though the horses and cows had already been fed.

Jon leaned out from the open door.

"She wants to talk to you."

I went back to the house feeling like mom and Jon had talked it over. Without dad around, Jon did a lot of the parenting, especially when it came to me. I walked back into the vintage kitchen, taking my hat off. I stood just inside the door to hear the verdict.

"I was supposed to go down and help you get your permit to drive next week, but having pulled the sort of crap you did, I won't sign for thirty days."

"Thirty days? That means I won't be able to get my license until December," I said. It was more than the official license; it was freedom that I was being denied. It was being able to get to jobs on my own, going to school on my own, without the bus, or having someone drop me off or pick me up.

"I just can't help you get a driver's license until you can prove that getting drunk is not going to be a habit. You can't do that if you have to drive. If I hear a peep about this sort of thing again, I'll put it off another thirty days until you get the picture."

"I think you're getting off easy," Jon said, staring me down, ready to smack me around if I objected too strenuously or disrespected my mother in any way.

I nodded and went back outside.

It was easy to get the wrong impression of my relationship with Jon. I respected him as a substitute father figure, in a way. My dad had spent most of my childhood working odd shifts on the drilling rigs, instead of meting out punishments to us kids. When he did have time off, he wanted to teach us how to do tasks on the ranch: how to fix fence, fix a tractor, drive a tractor, stack hay properly so the stack wouldn't fall over in a stiff wind. That left Jon to deal with me on a physical level.

Jon did the best he could; he was still just a kid, too and I was far from the easiest person to deal with. I didn't care about getting smacked around, I was tough enough to handle it. In fact, a swat or a punch only liberated me from further shame. It put a cap on the punishment.

Grounding me from my driver's license was a brilliant move on their part. That would have an impact like no physical punishment could. I would get over a spanking or any other form of punishment but being unable to obtain my driver's license would force me to acknowledge my misbehavior every time I had to explain to friends why I didn't have it. It was all I had talked about for the past year.

I went back outside and began to consider my life in relation to the restriction. I walked over to the minibike. Scott had gotten it back together and it looked like it would run. Maybe I would have to negotiate a deal with him to ride it to high school. I laughed at the thought. Me riding a minibike to school every day. No, I would have to endure riding the bus for a few months, yet.

I hung around outside doing odd jobs until Jon came out. He was going to ride that afternoon and would be going back down to the fairgrounds. I caught him as he opened the door to his pickup.

"Give me a ride back down to the fairgrounds, will ya?"

Jon looked at me.

"If you get drunk, you'll lose your license for another month, you know that, right?"

"Yeah, I know. I don't feel much like drinkin' anyway; I left my rigging bag in the back of Kevin's pickup. I need to catch him down there, if I can. I'll watch you ride later on."

"Get in," he said.

For a while, we were just brothers again, punishment meted out and accepted. Jon plugged in the eight-track tape of the Outlaws album. The windows were down and fresh mountain air pulsed in as Waylon Jennings poured out. We sang along with *Honky Tonk Heroes* and between Vince's incarceration and my juvenile delinquency, it seemed as if we were riding the edge of the outlaw-country movement.

That was the part that no one really understood about Jon and me. One minute we were worst enemies, the next minute we were best friends. When people talked about brothers, about family, I knew they didn't mean it on the same level that I understood those things.

The exhaust pipes crackled and popped when Jon let off the accelerator and roared when he got back in it and swooped around a slower car. I suppose the adrenaline was rushing through his veins as he thought about the bull that he would ride later on.

Jon trolled along the car-lined road outside the rodeo

arena, looking for a parking spot closer to the chutes. It was a solid line of cars.

"Aw hell," Jon said, then turned the pickup toward the arena, stomped on the accelerator and the tires spun as the rear end of the pickup came slowly around.

I started laughing.

When the pickup was pointed directly at the railroad tracks, he got off the accelerator and the pickup jumped forward aiming right for a narrow gap between two cars. The pickup fit nicely at a perpendicular angle between the rear bumper of one and the front bumper of the other. The pickup climbed up the embankment and we got out. I fell, unable to keep the door open and climb out at the same time. The door slammed closed behind me. I was picking myself up off the ground when Jon came around from the other side with his rigging bag hanging off his shoulder.

"You okay?"

"Yeah, fine. Hell of a first step."

Jon grinned and walked away. That was it, that was the extent to which we would be together. The rest of the time was reserved for his rodeo pals. I watched him walk away, knowing I would remember that moment, remember those feelings.

"Honky Tonk Heroes," I whispered to myself.

I walked past the area behind the chutes, busy with older riders getting ready. Those were the serious riders, like Jon. They were the ones who had joined Little Britches that held weekly rodeos all over the state; they attended the rodeo schools Jon talked about and I had no business back there, so I continued on under the bleachers on my way to the midway. I dug in my pockets for some money, but I only had seventy-five cents. It was enough to get a pop, though.

When I came out from under the bleachers at the ticket booth, it was crowded with those paying to watch the rodeo. I hadn't paid to watch a rodeo in years. I was glad they did, though, because if I did win some money it would be their money I would win.

To my left was a bunch of picnic tables set out and Ronnie was talking to Lisa over there, standing next to a table. I didn't know if I should bother. An apology was due, if he would listen to it, or hear it even if he did let me make it. Besides, Lisa was often angry with me for some trouble Ronnie had gotten into that he blamed on me. I walked on by.

"Lane," I heard Ronnie call, but pretended I didn't. I kept walking.

I wanted to check out the standings, to see if I had already been knocked out of the money.

"Lane!" I heard, louder this time, as if he were getting closer, so I turned around.

"What?" I asked, letting myself sound annoyed.

"Where you goin'?"

"To look at the standings," I replied, noticing Lisa was standing beside him, her fingers entwined with his.

"Man, you were fucked up!" Ronnie said.

I blushed; I could feel it creep over my face.

"That's what I hear," I said, looking at Lisa. She was a very pretty girl, a good match for Ronnie.

"You don't remember it?"

"Not much," I admitted. "Someone gave me some hard stuff and the rest of the night is sort of sketchy. I remember being thrown out of some place."

Lisa started tugging on Ronnie's fingers, trying to pull him away from me or trying to get free, I couldn't tell which. Ronnie glanced at her, but looked back at me with eyes expecting something, an explanation or the overdue apology.

"Look, I don't know what all went on, but I think I owe you an apology for something. I'm sorry I don't remember what."

"Sssshhhhh," Ronnie hissed, wagging his head as if it wasn't worth the recollection. "Don't worry man, we were both a little buzzed. No big deal."

I shrugged. If he was going to let me off that easy, I wasn't going to push it.

"You gonna stick around for the dance?"

Lisa looked at me, waiting for my answer with expectations beyond my understanding.

"I don't know. I'm gonna watch Jon ride, maybe pull his rope, if he needs it. Depends on, after that."

"Lisa can take you home, if you can stay."

Lisa was sixteen, older than both of us. That's how attractive Ronnie was, he even got the girls older than him. None of the rest of us could do that. A lot of the girls our age were going out with older guys. Somehow, Ronnie got Lisa, or Lisa got Ronnie, however one deciphered it.

I looked at Lisa, who was slightly shaking her head, a signal I took to mean that I should refuse the offer. So, I did.

"Naw, if Jon ain't staying, I'll just go home with him."

"Suit yourself," Ronnie said, letting himself be pulled away by the hand. "Oh, you're second right now with one more go-round."

"You saw it," I said over the growing distance, "the damned thing just ran, not one buck. I should have gotten a re-ride."

Walking away from those two, I went through the alleyway past the stock pens and toward the bridge. At the other end of the bridge was the corral where some horse events were taking place. A lot of parents sat in the cheap bleachers. Girls in expensive English riding attire were atop beautiful horses, slicked down and gleaming for the event. That was not my scene; I didn't understand what went on over there and I didn't want to. I averted my eyes and started looking up and down the row of vehicles for Kevin's pickup. Where the hell was Will? I couldn't shake him the day before.

I saw the sheriff's deputies riding along on their horses looking things over. I was surprised I was not introduced to them the night before. That was lucky. I dodged in between a car and an RV to avoid them and ran right into Annie Brewster. I stopped short, blinking, resisting the urge to flight.

Annie looked up at me with a twisted grin.

"Hi."

"Howdy," I said, easing forward, as if to slip by her and continue on my way. She didn't budge.

"Heard about you yesterday," she said, her green eyes wide, dark eyebrows lifted in evaluation.

That was as much punishment as I thought I deserved, explaining it to everyone I met for months to come. She waited while I looked down at my boots, the brim of my hat hiding my face.

"That was bad," I said, preferring to look at my dusty boots rather than the amused ridicule her expression had to offer.

"You took first, at least for a while," she offered.

What was she talking about? The ride? I lifted my gaze to gauge her intent.

"The ride?"

"Of course, the ride."

"That was bad, too," I said, laughing.

"Bad? You took first," she said, confused by my reaction.

"Annie, they were steers and mine didn't even buck, it just ran around the arena. I could've done that blindfolded."

"Is that why you got drunk?"

I felt like I got hit by a board, stumped, dumfounded, unable to speak.

She stood there, expectantly in her tight jeans, peasant-girl shirt, blonde hair and flashing green eyes.

"Is that why?"

"No."

"Then why?"

"Why? Because they had beer and someone gave me something hard, Everclear, I think. It was dark, I didn't see what it was. I didn't know it was going to affect me like that." I didn't know why I was explaining it to her, what right did she have to ask me about it?

"Your mom and dad know?"

"Yeah."

"What'd they say?"

I didn't know why I stood there answering her. It had to do with not wanting to appear afraid of it. If I did it, I could stand up to the consequences of it, but Annie was nobody to me, except that I felt a little ashamed of leaving her alone in the parking lot of a party.

"My mom grounded me from my permit. I won't get my driver's license until December."

"Huh," she said.

"Well, I gotta find my rigging bag. I left it in Kevin Pulaski's pickup last night. Have you seen him around?"

"I'll show you," she said, shooing me back the way I had come.

I walked backward until we were out into the trail through the field of cars. I didn't want her to show me, I wanted her to tell me, but she had other ideas. We walked together through the double line of vehicles parked reasonably in rows with the odd vehicle at the wrong angle or parked too far out into the road so that the rows looked jagged and unruly. Her blonde hair seemed to glow in the sun.

"Are you going to the dance tonight?"

"I don't know."

"You don't know?"

"Jon's my ride and if he goes home, I gotta go home. If he stays, I gotta stay. Unless, I find another way home. I hate not having a license."

We walked in welcomed silence until we got to Kevin's pickup. I jumped in the back. There was my rigging bag pushed up against the front corner of the bed. I grabbed it and jumped over the side of the bed, landing in the fine dust, causing a cloud.

"Phew, thanks, that saved some time," I said, looking her bravely in the eyes.

Despite what Ronnie told me, I was not sold on the idea that Annie liked me and even if she did, what would she expect from me? I was not interested in having a girlfriend, at least nothing long-term. I was fifteen and those relationships, like

Ronnie's with Lisa, seemed silly and a complication to an otherwise already difficult school day. I had seen him with other girls, trying to catch them at their locker, notes left on his locker, jealousy, anger and arguments over nothing, miscommunication. It just seemed like too much. There was plenty of time for all of that. My focus was on a car and a driver's license and a chance to see something new.

With all of those thoughts passing through my mind, I didn't know what to say to her.

"I better go," I said, easing past her, squeezing between her and the pickup.

"Where to?"

"See if Jon needs help getting down on his bull, maybe watch him ride," I said, walking away from her, feeling a sense of freedom, out from under the inquisitor's glare. She was pretty though, but I didn't know what she wanted from me, if anything. Did she want to come with me? Behind the chutes? If so, what for? What would it mean?

CHAPTER SIX

That was it. Jon rode his bull and eventually took second, winning two-hundred dollars. I barely hung on to take fourth and won seventy. I bought the car I could not drive and spent some time making sure it would be in good mechanical condition. But, the rodeo was the last bit of comfort I would feel for a long time. All the stock was loaded into big-rig trailers and shipped back to the contractor's ranch to wait on the next rodeo. Everything good about being a cowboy or a farmer slipped away as the crowds emptied out of the arena. Me and people like me were left surrounded by a thriving city of people who did not understand us, care about us or find any use for us at all except as objects of ridicule. We stopped being cowboys and became "hicks," "goat ropers" and "shitkickers." That fact was made clear to me the first day I walked into the cafeteria of the new high school and heard calls of "yeeeeha!" lift up into the huge space filled with laughing hoods and jocks. They had to do it, I supposed. It made them feel superior in a way, but I had dealt with it all through junior high, so it didn't matter. What mattered, is if they got close to me and attempted to ridicule me and subject me to physical humiliation. That was a different story. That was when I would fight, when I would expect some of the other cowboys to come and lend a hand, to even the odds just enough that whatever I felt I had to do to defend myself would not necessarily result in a serious beating by hostile classmates. That was the code, unwritten, unspoken, but there nonetheless. I had done it any number of times and most of the time, just showing up, demonstrating that whoever they had targeted would not be alone was enough.

Crowds are inherently cowards; I learned that early. But,

there were so few of us that any real conflict, usually arranged for after school, would mean that we would be outnumbered by three to one. The thing that saved us then, was that we were all ready to fight and most of them were just tagging along to feel tough. We were fighting to keep from getting pummeled and they were just there, because it was the cool place to be. Those dynamics saved us, unless it was at a football game or a school dance, then it was different and we didn't come out so well.

The newcomers saw the football games and the school dances as their territory and us backward hicks as invading their space. They were right in a lot of ways. We knew they considered that their turf and if we did show up, we usually showed up en masse with the explicit intent to stake out our rights to attend as much as anyone else who went to school. They treated us with as much hostility as we would if they showed up at the McMillen Building. While there was no declaration of these facts, they had been established years ago, when the first city kids from Palo Alto or Rochester showed up, demanding attention and a modern city rather than the agrarian burg they had landed in. By 1977, it was all routine and the same situation that existed at Loveland High transferred to the new high school.

I stood at a table in my boots, belt buckle and Western shirt, my International Harvester cap in my hand and heard the catcalls and annoying epithets, but paid them no mind, because I knew, in a one-on-one situation, they wouldn't be so brave. They never were. If they could stand in the crowd and make their friends laugh with their ridiculous insults, they were fine, but none of them were so brave with even odds. None of them came to our table to do it.

Jon came in just after me and stood at my table. Ronnie showed up next and the catcalls ended all together, especially when Brad Romero came in with the brothers Gonsalez, Juan and Francisco, who liked to be called Frank. Juan was Jon's age and Frank was a Junior. A few more of our group showed up with the arrival of several buses. In all, there were ten of us, the rest were at the other high school, the Pulaskis for sure, Robertsons, a boy and a girl and several others, some I didn't know or care to know.

The girls in our group of cowboys and farmers did not have the same problem with fitting in that the boys did. There was not the physical element to their relationships with other girls that there was among the boys. They had conflicts, too, but it did not result in their absolute segregation as it did us.

When all of us had gathered we counted our numbers and it was pathetic. We looked at each other and shrugged.

"Here we go again," Frank said, who was not given any slack by the others because he was of Mexican heritage. He was a cowboy and that was enough. Both the Romero and Gonsalez ranches were big and had been in existence almost since the first Mariano Median's time. Their fathers had arrived at the turn of the century to work in the quarries where they made enough money to purchase some property outside of town, between Loveland and Berthoud. They were solid cowboys and were hated as much or more than we were. They had the added burden of taking criticism from some of the other Mexicans for being cowboys instead of hoods or "Chicanos" as they called themselves. It came with the territory and they understood it. We stood beside them and they stood beside us, no matter who was on the other side of the line.

The bell rang and we all went to our homeroom classes to get our schedules. "ten" was all I could think as I walked down the hall amid the mass of students going in the same direction. It was going to be a rough year. I walked into the classroom and took a seat in the back, next to the door.

The teacher, a tall man with glasses, a thin tie and a green jacket stood up front. He didn't know anyone's names, so he called out to us as he read our names off of the schedule in his hand. We came up front, one by one, to retrieve the slip of white paper that would dictate the routes we would take through the school for the next semester.

I stood, blinking, halfway back to my seat, staring at the

piece of paper. I looked around at the other kids, did they have the same nonsense on their schedules that I did? Was it some joke?

"When you have your schedule, please sit down until the bell rings," the teacher said, as if to no one, but he was talking to me, standing in the middle of the aisle.

I sat down, angry, trying to think of what I should do. My first class was swimming! Swimming of all things! It meant that I would get up, take a shower or get dressed if I had taken a shower the night before. I would go out, do my chores, wait for the bus, ride to school, take my clothes off, put on swimming trunks, jump into a pool full of water, swim around for a while, get out of the pool, take a shower, put on my clothes and then go to school. To learn what? How to swim? I knew how to swim. I was infuriated at the massive waste of time.

The bell rang and I was the first one out the door. We would see if I was going to swim or not. I walked toward the pool, where my next "class" was to take place looking for Ronnie, Jon or anyone I could complain to, but I didn't see any of them as I made my way down the long, sloping hall to the pool. I didn't even know swimming was a graded class, I thought it was an extracurricular activity.

I went through the double doors and saw where others had already taken up seats on the fold-out bleachers along the east wall. All boys. I looked at their faces, none of them seemed as irritated as I was. There were no cowboys there with whom to commiserate, so I took a seat away from the others. I knew some of the kids from junior high, but I preferred the company of the cowboys and farmers with whom I shared some commonality of outlook, who would be doing chores after school as I would, instead of riding skateboards, playing basketball or fucking swimming.

The instructor came out from somewhere, but seemingly just appeared in blue shorts and a white T-shirt stretched over a protruding, but solid looking belly. He had a tanned bald head with receding blonde/white hair. A whistle hung around his neck and a clipboard was clutched in his left hand. He blew the whistle to get our attention.

"Welcome to Swimming Class. You will be getting a grade for this class and it is a required class. If you don't pass this class, you will not be able to graduate high school. We will be teaching you…"

I stood up; my hand raised.

"Sit down, I'm not done talking," the instructor said, then continued, "…we will be teaching you skills that will make you a better swimmer…."

I had not bothered to sit down or lower my hand.

"Is there something important? Are you going to die?"

"I know how to swim; do I still have to take this class?" I asked. "Can't I just test out of it, or something?"

"Sit down!" he bellowed.

With all the others staring at me open-mouthed, sneering at me or shaking their heads, I sat down.

"Class, what did I say at the beginning? Did I not say that this is a 'required class?' Did I not say that you cannot graduate high school without passing this class? Okay, how many brought their swimming trunks today?"

The great majority of kids raised their hands. I was stunned by it. I didn't even know there was such a class, but these guys were prepared for it.

"All right, change out," the instructor said and blew his whistle.

The other boys scrambled off the bleachers and to the locker room. The instructor walked back to wherever he had come from and disappeared. I sat with three others on the bleachers and felt no kinship with them. They had not brought their swimming trunks, but they would. They would happily don their suits and gleefully jump into the water if given the chance and the attire. Not me. It was a waste of time, taking the place of something I might want to learn, something that I needed to know.

I put it off for a week.

"Daniels, where's your suit?"

"I don't have one."

"Daniels, where's your suit?"

"We couldn't get one, maybe tomorrow."

"Daniels, where's your suit? I talked to your mom and she bought one for you. She told me you hadn't said anything about it. So, where is it?"

"I forgot it."

"Bring it, tomorrow," he instructed.

"Daniels, where's your suit?"

"I forgot it."

"Get to the office, I've had enough of this!" he yelled.

"Finally!" I yelled back, getting up and tromping down the bleachers. I burst through the double doors on my way to the office. It would be my first introduction to our principal, each grade had its own. Anything was better than participating in a class for which I had such contempt, such hostility.

I walked up the sloping corridor that emptied out into the cafeteria. The whole building seemed deserted during class time. Big shining hallways, brick walls. It was a nice school, shiny and clean unlike that of our junior high which was old and no matter how hard they tried to keep it up, it seemed dirty and uncared for.

I crossed the cafeteria and walked into the bustling office. The staff was busy keeping track of a thousand kids or more. I stood in front of the counter and waited.

"Can I help you?" a blonde woman with long, dangling earrings asked, her face heavy with makeup.

"I doubt it, I just got kicked out of Swimming."

"Already?"

"Yep."

"What grade are you in?"

"Tenth."

She looked at me and her eyes narrowed in suspicion or recognition of a problem.

"Take a seat, Mr. Schmidt will be with you in a minute."

I looked around and there was a chair with a fabric seat and back with shiny, metallic legs. It looked like it cost about five dollars. I sat down and waited and waited.

Two girls came in and leaned on the counter in a familiar sort of way that made me wary of them. They were probably seniors. One wore a cheerleader's outfit with short skirt. The other one was dressed in jeans and a white top with narrow straps over her tanned shoulders. I figured they had spent their summer lying about the pool or down at the lake, not bucking hay or fixing fence.

They seemed to recognize my presence all of a sudden and looked over their shoulders at me and giggled. I looked darkly up at them from under my brow. I had been ridiculed by girls like that since junior high. It was easier to take from someone like Millie Anderson, who was clearly smarter than me. What did the girls in front of me have that allowed them their ridicule? Was it a rich father? Is that all it took for one person to be better than another; shiny cars, big houses, lots of money and vacations? Was that the sum of a person's value? Or was it that I did not have movie-star looks, or the right clothes…the "in" clothes? Was it that I didn't care about their fashions, their music or their perspectives on life that relegated me to the trash heap of humanity?

I was brooding about all of that when Mr. Schmidt came in, heavy, sweating, bustling to get to his office and take a seat. He plopped down into his chair and sorted out the papers on his desk.

"You can go in now," the woman said to me, causing the girls to turn and look, sneering smiles on their faces, big eyes taking in the failure, the defeated, the subjected, before them.

I walked past and into the office.

"Close the door if you would," Mr. Schmidt said, breathlessly.

I did as he asked and took a seat in a chair just like the one outside.

"I just talked to Mr. Worthington. He says that you did

not bring your swimming suit for five consecutive days, that he spoke to your mother about it and she assured him that you would bring it to class. Now, are you going to bring your swimming suit to class and participate with all the other children, or are we going to have to take additional steps?"

"I guess we're going to have to take additional steps," I said, resigning myself to the punishment if it got me out of that class.

"It is a required class, did Mr. Worthington explain that to you?"

"Yes."

"That you cannot graduate high school without passing that class?"

"Yes."

"Then, you know you're going to have to pass it sometime, why not just get it out of the way?"

"Because, it's stupid. I don't understand why there is such a class, how the school can hold my diploma hostage to something that pointless. Unless, you have to justify that big, expensive pool..."

That was it; it finally donned on me that having had the taxpayers pay for the pool, requiring a class ensured its use, so it wouldn't look like all that money was spent just to satisfy the needs of ten or fifteen kids on the swim team. The football stadium made some sense. At least it could be used for other things, graduation ceremonies, track and field, gym and theoretically, the football and baseball stadiums brought in concessions and paying crowds.

"Now, you just wait," Mr. Schmidt said, getting nervous. "Don't go off spreading rumors like that. It is required that we offer swimming as an extracurricular activity, part of being in the school district comes with certain obligations."

"I don't care about none of that," I said. "All I care about is that I don't want to have to go to that stupid class, the class I don't need, don't want and won't attend."

My heart was racing with the exhilaration of the debate. I

felt like I had him on shaky ground and it felt good, like I had accomplished something.

"All I can do," he said, shuffling some papers in front of him, "is put it off. I can arrange it that you don't have to attend until your senior year, if that's what you want, but you will have to go."

It was a small victory, but it felt like a victory of some sort and I walked out of the office feeling like something had changed. At least, I didn't have to go to swimming the next day and sit on the hard, wooden bleachers watching other kids do as they were told, without question, without an understanding that they were being manipulated, coerced into doing something ridiculous and irrelevant on the mere say so of a school board. I looked out over the empty cafeteria and took a seat at a table. I looked up at the big clock across from me. I still had twenty minutes until my next class.

That was on a Friday. On Monday, I got my new class schedule from Mr. Schmidt and looking down at it, I saw that it said "Art." Art Class? That wasn't much of an improvement, but I walked the down the hall until I came to the open door. I went in and saw, in the back of the room, Jon sitting in a chair. It was the only class we had ever had together. I showed my schedule to the teacher and took a seat next to Jon in the back.

"Wait," the teachers said, her addled, '60s, free-love brain confused by the fact that now she had two Daniels' in her class instead of one. She pointed at Jon. "Are you supposed to be in this class?"

Jon got up and walked to the front of the class. When he did, a big, muscular kid stood up, a Junior from what I could tell, a jock. He walked to the back of the class and took Jon's seat. It could be considered nothing if not an act of intimidation, suggesting that Jon wouldn't contest the issue. The jock was wrong. He didn't know my brother, who was not as muscular, but I knew from experience, he could strike like a rattlesnake.

"I wouldn't sit there, if I were you," I said, trying to help the guy out.

He just looked at me with a moronic grin and kicked back in the chair, getting comfortable.

"All right," I said, grinning and putting my head down on my forearms, looking up from under my brow to see Jon's reaction.

Jon seemed to have gotten things sorted out with the teacher and started back to his chair. He stopped short when he saw the jock in his chair. Resolve came over his face and he continued to walk back and stood next to the jock.

"Get outta my chair," Jon said, standing casually by, waiting.

"My chair, now," the jock said, grinning, bluffing his way through as seemed to be his custom. He was used to getting his way by being intimidating and nothing else.

Without another word, Jon reached down, wrapped his arm around the guy's neck and yanked him by the head out of the chair and threw the guy over his hip into the peg board stand with art taped to it, knocking the peg board over, breaking it into pieces as the jock landed on top of it.

The teacher was screaming invectives at Jon, words I had not heard come from a teacher before, but Jon stood over the jock.

"Get up and try again," Jon said, grinning down at him, then stomped the guy's testicles.

The jock had lost interest in demeaning Jon, playing him for a fearful pussy.

"Get out of my class!" the teacher screamed, but Jon just walked back to his seat and sat down.

"I told him," I said, shrugging.

"He knows now."

"You get out of my class, right now!"

Jon stood up.

"Fuck this class!" Jon said, flipping the whole table over. "Fuck this school."

That was the last day Jon went to that school. From that day on, he went to the school in the nearby town where Ciroli's

Dairy was. They played it off that he lived with the Cirolis, which he nearly did anyway. It was often late at night before Jon got home from the dairy and that was during summer; working after school he had been even later, rarely eating at home anymore.

Jon would join the football team at the other school and letter in every sport he went out for, nearly winning the state championship in wrestling, a reason the jock did not see the hip move coming that Jon laid on him so effectively. All the Ciroli boys wrestled and spending so much time with them, Jon had learned a lot.

I had been looking forward to having my older brother in high school with me; it had been since junior high that I had seen much of him and he was a good fighter, it was a big loss. But, his life was better in the other town, where cowboys and farmers made up the majority of the school kids. It was a much smaller school, so they needed everyone to participate or there would be no school plays, football teams or bands.

CHAPTER SEVEN

The next class I had trouble understanding was oral communications. It was, after swimming, the stupidest class imaginable, to the point of literal distraction. We would go into the classroom, sit about and talk to each other about the topic of the day, whatever that was. It was, in some way, designed to teach us to communicate with each other beginning from a given baseline of understanding. I tried to let it prove itself, to show me some instance of value, but after weeks of great tolerance, I gave up.

"Today, class, we are going to discuss the effects of socioeconomic strata of a given audience and the means of effectively communicating with different strata."

I kicked back in my chair, folded my arms over my chest and stared past the jock sitting across from me.

"Look at you," he said. "What does that mean, that you're too good for this class, or just too stupid?"

I pulled my gaze from the wall behind him to his face. He was a jock, had been in junior high, too. He played football and ran track, a big chested kid with short dark hair and green eyes. His name was Bret Lloyd, but I didn't call him by his name, because that would have intimated some degree of respect and I had none. He was one of those who called us names in the cafeteria surrounded by others of the same conceit, comfortable in his physical presence and superior attitude. Accustomed to exploiting his vast numerical advantage as a bludgeon against us.

"You think I'm stupid? You sit here in this class day after day talking about all this retarded shit and think that makes you smart? Holy shit."

Bret leaned forward, a sort of physical threat, but I

blinked lazily, discounting him, showing him that I did not consider him a threat.

"You don't give it a chance," the girl I knew as Chloe said, as if cajoling me into acceptance or compliance.

"I've given it two weeks, waiting for something, anything that would make it worth it and all I get is more talk, just everyone discussing this nonsense as if you're actually saying something, but you're not. These are just words repeated over and over."

"What's going on over here?" the teacher asked, stepping up to our table.

"Daniels thinks this is a stupid class," Bret said, smirking.

"Is that right?"

"Don't you?" I asked the teacher. "Don't any of you?" I asked the class, looking from face to face. "Really?"

"Maybe you'd like to take this up with Mr. Schmidt."

"Why not?" I asked and stood up, preparing to leave. It was the second class I had been kicked out of in the first month.

"I haven't dismissed you."

I stopped, annoyed and turned back to face him.

"This class is designed to help you become a better public speaker, it is for those who will go on to become leaders, perhaps politicians or CEO's. Am I right in assuming that you don't see yourself in those roles?"

There it was. He just couldn't restrain himself from making some sort of criticism, as if not being interested in his stupid class consigned me to perpetual servitude. I laughed at the thinly-veiled, clumsy insult.

"That's funny?" he asked.

"It's funny that you think listening to you drone on about socioeconomic strata when what you mean is stupid, poor people versus brilliant rich people is going to somehow turn me into the President of the United States."

Some of the other students chuckled.

"That's it, get to the office."

"Yeah, I seem to have trouble with that public speaking

shit, huh?" I said as I gladly turned and walked out.

I walked along the wide, newly buffed floor of the hall on the way to the cafeteria where the principal's office sat just off to the right of the main entrance. I was free of the insipid class, but I was not free of school. They would just find another class for me to attend, something just as useless in the end, because none of it was designed to educate those who would not go further. High school had already been revealed to me as a giant waiting room where college students gathered their needed credits and grade point averages and the rest of the students were warehoused for three years until they would be allowed to pursue their careers in mechanics, farming, industry of one sort or another, the building trades and the like. It was a fraud in that sense, an illusion of obtaining something we already possessed. I could already read, write, speak, calculate wages, make change, multiply, divide and subtract. I could recognize the nuances of speech required to make a point effectively to others. I attended high school to obtain the knowledge that I did not have. I had no problem with science, for instance, but they had stopped teaching me all the things I wanted to learn, like government and history. I could use more English, but that had been replaced with oral communications.

I entered the office and stood before the counter. Mrs. Vincent – I had come to learn was her name - looked up from her filing and recognized me.

"Yes?"

"I got kicked out of oral communications."

"Already?"

"Hey, I gave it a chance."

"Two weeks, you call that a chance?"

"For that class, it's an eternity."

"Have a seat."

I waited for Mr. Schmidt, who, when he entered the office, walked past me with an air of weariness and waved his arm for me to follow.

I went in and took a seat in front of his desk, my

cap clutched in my hand. He sat heavily behind his desk and straightened his tie.

"What am I going to do with you?" he asked and I understood that to be a rhetorical question - something I had not learned in oral communications - so I kept my mouth shut.

"You can't just go to the classes you want. There is a curriculum that must be followed. You can't graduate without having passed certain classes."

"It's oral communications: if I talk to you and you understand me and you talk to me and I understand you, that's oral communications, what else is there to know? Why does it take a whole semester to learn that?"

"You have to take the class."

"Because, being unable to speak in public is going to affect my ability to stack hay, or feed cows? I'm going to work for my dad on the oil rig when I turn eighteen. What does public speaking have to do with that, and, by the way, who says I can't speak in public? No one has asked me; no one has given me a chance to prove it one way or the other."

"You still have to pass the class, but if you don't need it, as you claim, then you should get an A."

"What am I going to do with an A?" I laughed. "Can I build a fence with it? Can I buy a candy bar? A gallon of gas? Does it have any value to someone who is not interested in college?"

Mr. Schmidt seemed confused by that question and fumbled with some articles on his desk.

"I'll get you into health, that's the best I can do, but you have to pass that class, too."

I left the office wondering what world these academics lived in and why their world was so much different from mine. How is it that people who do not understand the world I live in insist on teaching me? If I didn't know high school to be a fraud, it would be easier for me to accept these dictates, but I did.

I sat at a table in the cafeteria and waited for lunch to start. Oral communications was my last class before lunch, so I waited it out there, listening to the clanging of metal pots and the rattling of silverware in the kitchen.

The cheap plastic chairs in the cafeteria were uncomfortable, but I didn't spend much time in them. Lunch was horrible and expensive at school, so I didn't eat there. During lunch, I would go out and hang out with the other cowboys, who didn't bother to eat lunch, either.

When the children started to empty out into the halls, I went out front of the school in the fall sunshine and felt momentarily free. Ronnie came out with Brad Romero and Zach Pritchard. Zach had a football and threw an arcing spiral in my direction. I broke to where the football was going to be and caught it.

We spent the lunch period playing a game of football. A few more of the guys came out to play with us and we played our brand of football, which was brutal without pads. The unspoken intent was to injure someone along the line. Our tackles were at full speed, with shoulders driven deep into the ribcage of the runner or receiver. It was the sort of football that bull riders would play.

When we were done, we were sweaty and blood smeared down our arms from minute cuts or rashes where we slid along the grass. Zach had ripped the knee out of his jeans. Brad looked like he was going to have a black eye. It was exhilarating, because it was done on our terms, by our rules, not dictated by some old, fat guy with a whistle. We jostled each other and recounted our greatest catches or runs. For a moment, we were just boys, not hated for our clothes or where or how we lived. It lasted long enough to enter through the glass doors of the main entrance, then all of the social derision crashed down on us with the first "Yeeeeha," that burst forth to remind us that playing one of their games did not make us them.

We split up, each going his own way in grass-stained jeans. I went down one of the two west halls toward the library and took a right where I was met by Mandy Bankhouse, a short blonde with large breasts. She was condescendingly friendly as if being friendly with me proved her goodness to and invisible witness.

"Hi," she said, falling into step.

"Howdy."

"That was some show you all put on."

"What was?"

"Playing football."

"That wasn't a show," I laughed. "Zach had a football. We do things beside rodeo, you know."

We reached the classroom and went in. Mandy sat by the wall with a friend. I sat in my usual seat and leaned back in the chair. I had no homework. The other kids opened their books and started studying.

I watched minutes click away with nothing to do. I should have brought a book to read, but that would have put me to sleep. I looked forward to science in the next period. It was the only class in which I was getting an A. There was a significant difference to me between something like oral communications and science; there was new-age mumbo jumbo and an opportunity to learn something. But, while I sat there, a girl approached the open doorway and stepped in. She handed the teacher a slip of paper.

"Lane Daniels?"

"Yeah?"

"You're wanted in the office."

I looked over my shoulder at Mandy, the closest thing I had to a friend. I got up from the desk and went to the teacher. I took the slip of paper and studied it, looking for some clue as to its purpose as I walked. Nothing. All manner of thoughts ran through my brain, like the time Carolyn James was summoned out of class to find out her father, an airline pilot, had been involved in a plane crash at the airport in Denver. Could something have happened to my dad? My mom?

The hallway took on a sense of the surreal. Was I only minutes away from finding out something that would change my life? Was there already a hole in my family that I would discover when I entered the office? I stood before the door, savoring my life as it was, before it could be inexorably changed.

I pulled the door open and went in.

"Mr. Daniels, the principal would like to see you," Mrs. Vincent said, nodding her blonde head toward his open door.

I stepped into Mr. Schmidt's office and stood there for a moment, letting him recognize me. He looked up from a file.

"Have a seat."

I sat in the familiar chair, my favorite, it seemed.

"I've been looking over your file. Despite the classes you rebel against, you are scoring well in others. In science, for instance, you're getting an A. In Art she says you are attentive and participate, though there was that problem with Jon earlier."

"That was Jon," I said.

"Yes, I know."

"So, no one's dead?"

"What?"

"Well, I usually know when I'm going to be called to the office. This is a mystery."

"Oh, no, sorry. I didn't mean to alarm you. I'm sure everything's fine."

"Then, what is it?"

"I saw you playing football this afternoon and a thought came to me, maybe if you had some other interests, you might be more willing to participate, even in the classes you don't like."

"You want me to join football?"

"I think it would benefit your education," he said, but it sounded hollow. "We're a new school and a lot of the talented players, even if they were supposed to come to this school, have opted to stay at Loveland High. There are recruiting considerations that the district has accommodated. In short, we need players, good players and you and your friends play hard. Coach Watson suggested he would be open to tryouts."

Schmidt didn't realize that as he talked, he contradicted himself. He said, initially that the thought came to him that it might help my education, but then he admitted that Watson suggested the program could use good football players. I didn't make an issue of it, but I registered it. It would dictate my response. I thought I might be able to leverage it in some way.

"I'll talk to the guys about it, the possibility, but you know, most of us have chores after school. We aren't like the average jock. People and animals depend on us."

Schmidt's head wobbled, as if wanting to brush that information aside and focus on how to achieve his goal, without accommodating ours.

"I don't know what I can do about that."

"Me, either, but it might not be a refusal, it might just be impossible to do both."

We sat looking at each other, thinking.

"Although," I said, "if you would establish a rodeo team, that might go a long way."

"A rodeo team?"

"Yeah. Poudre Valley has one, Fort Collins has one."

"Loveland doesn't," he said. "I don't think we can do that in this district."

"Well, I'll suggest it, but let's be honest, you don't want us to run the ball or catch it, you want us to play defense; to beat ourselves to death so your boys can take all the credit and get all the scholarships, right?"

I could see in his eyes that I was right, but he lied.

"No, I don't think that's it at all."

I walked out of his office feeling angry, hostile, mostly because it affirmed that even Schmidt thought of us as a bunch of rubes. We were big kids, muscular from hard work, not the gym. It was a term called "country strong" which, because we often used all of our muscles to move heavy objects, lift hay bales over and over when putting up hay, we were stronger than the athletes that focused on bench-press and building impressive muscles. It was why the best team in junior high, the school that won the state championship, was a rural school out in Eastern Colorado.

It wasn't so bad that he wanted to use us for our brawn,

but the fact that he wouldn't even consider a rodeo team to reward us for the blocking and tackling that would elevate their football team irritated me.

When I got back to study hall, I was met with a curious look from Mandy. I shook my head to relate that it was nothing and took my seat. I was fuming, sitting there, staring at the clock. She kept trying to get my attention, but I couldn't explain it to her in sign language, so I ignored her.

When the bell rang, I got up and waited for her at the door. I walked with her until we had to go in different directions.

"They wanted us to play football for the school," I said.

"That's good, isn't it?"

"No. Screw them, they don't want us to get anything out of it, they just want us to do the dirty work so they can take all the credit. Wouldn't even help us organize a rodeo team. It's bullshit."

I walked away.

CHAPTER EIGHT

The weather in Northern Colorado could change rather abruptly. Fall could feel a lot like winter in mere hours. It was mid-October and the temperature had dropped thirty degrees in just three hours. It was sixty degrees when I got off the bus; by the time I had finished my chores and changed the oil in the tractor, it was thirty degrees. I was just pouring the used oil into a barrel when I smelled the snow in the air. Minutes later, huge flakes the size of a quarter drifted down from the low-hanging clouds.

I stood in the middle of the yard, mesmerized by the large flakes falling to the earth. They melted on contact, leaving everything wet. It was Friday night. There was a country dance being held down at the fairgrounds, in the McMillen Building. Jon said he was going, but he wasn't home, yet.

There was a roast in the crockpot that filled the kitchen with the thick aroma of beef. All our meat was home grown, grass-fed and delicious. Not even the steakhouses in town served better.

Dad was in his office, doing paperwork, probably his expense account and I looked in on him.

"Hey."

Dad looked up at me over his reading glasses. He had short, black hair that was graying at the temples, but he still looked young, had always looked young. There was a picture of him when he was drafted at the age of twenty-one and he looked sixteen. I could not imagine the sort of life he had led, snatched up from the beet farm and dropped into Korea behind a machine gun. Korea was somewhat of a forgotten war. All anyone talked about back then was Vietnam, but Korea was a meat grinder.

How he bore up under the onslaught and the massive casualties of that conflict amazed me. There were residual after effects. Things that happened, reactions that seemed out of place. On occasion he would wake up screaming, but we didn't ask about it and he didn't offer an explanation.

"You get the oil changed?"

"Yes sir."

"How full is the barrel?"

"I didn't check. It didn't overflow."

"Go out and see. If it's full, load it into the back of the pickup. I have an empty barrel in the back, unload that either way."

"Okay."

As I walked back through the kitchen, I couldn't help but to lift the lid on the crockpot and use it to wave the aroma to me. I breathed it in.

Out in the snow, I went over to the oil barrel. I pushed on the top of it, but it wouldn't move. I shoved harder and it lifted very slightly. It was full. Dad knew that sort of thing. Without checking, he seemed to keep a running tally of how much the barrel held, how much oil had been emptied from different pieces of machinery, pickups, cars even the lawn mower and minibike, how full the barrel would be as a result. It was why he brought an empty barrel home that day. It was what made him good at his job.

"The big things are made up of little things," he would say when teaching us equipment maintenance. "If you take care of the little things, you might never have to deal with a big thing, but if you don't, everything will be a big thing."

I thought he was fanatical about it, but no one could argue with the fact that his rig was efficient and profitable. It was why he was promoted to rig manager. It was why he had the respect of his bosses; even the owners of the company dealt with him on a different level than most of their rig managers. It's also why I hardly ever saw him.

I knew when I went to work out there that I would have

to be as dedicated as he was. If I worked hard and saved, I would be able to buy my own place and raise children in the tradition of our family.

As the snow fell heavily in the yard, I started the tractor. I used a strap from the barn and wrapped it around the barrel. I hooked the end of the strap on the bucket of the tractor and lifted it up, the strap tightened on the barrel as it came off the ground. Snow was piling up on my shoulders as I worked. I lifted the barrel high over the pickup and set it down easily in the bed. I latched onto the empty one and lifted it over the side and plopped it down where the other one had been.

Dad had taken the tie down straps off the empty barrel when he got home and after I had parked the tractor, I climbed into the bed of the pickup and used the tie down straps to secure the barrel. Those were the sorts of details dad looked for to signify one's competence. Pleasing my dad was more than just trying to make him happy.

Whenever I would go out to the rig with him, it was clear that his employees respected him. He was more than their boss; he was their leader. To some of them, he was a father figure. Learning his ways, how he did things, why he did things could only make me a better employee, not just for him, but for anyone. That wasn't important to everyone, but it was to me, because I saw employment as a piece of the puzzle that, when assembled, spelled freedom. It would allow me to go anywhere and get a job, keep a job and advance. I wouldn't have to be tied to anywhere or anything because I was someone's kid or son-in-law or best friend. They could hate me and I would still have a job, if I learned from my dad.

I had forgotten to turn the fuel off on the tractor and was walking over to do that when Jon got home. The lights of his pickup landed on me as he pulled into the drive and I looked over at him. I heard the engine rev and saw wet gravel and snow spit out the back of the truck. Jon wanted me to jump out of the way, but I calmly walked to the tractor, stepping out of the pickup's path. It missed me by a foot or more and I saw him laughing behind the foggy side window.

"Asshole," I muttered affectionately.

I turned off the fuel valve on the tractor and looked back at the house. Jon got out of the pickup and slammed the door. We stood in the snow, appraising each other.

"What's for dinner?"

"Roast."

"What time's that dance start?"

"Eight."

He nodded and we walked to the house. I reached the steps first and he pulled me back by the jacket and stepped in front of me. He tried to open the door and get inside before I could recover, but I caught the door and held it open. We struggled for a while at the door, him pushing me back out and me pushing my way in.

"Knock it off!" mom yelled from somewhere deeper in the house.

We ate with grins on our faces, thinking about the struggle, planning other ways to challenge each other. Maybe at the dance I would find some way to better him, or him, me. I had to watch him, though. He would leave me at a gas station or a store, if he could, if I got out of the pickup. He had done it before and laughed all the way home; I know he did. The snow was a good sign, it brought me closer to my license, closer to independence.

There was something exhilarating about seeing the lights over the fairground parking lot shining in the darkness. They could nearly be seen from our place. After a couple of weeks of the endless cycle of school and chores, the dance was a welcomed moment of excitement. It was full of possibilities.

I rode with Jon to the dance. The snow had eased up some, but two inches had fallen, sticking on the grassy areas. The roads were wet, but not slick. Jon drove easily, casually through the streets.

"I don't care if you have a beer, or two, but if you get drunk…"

"I won't."

Jon nodded as we pulled into the parking lot. The lights reflecting off the wet cars made every vehicle look shiny and new. I had only been allowed to go to the dances for a year and I still had hopes that I would see something interesting or meet someone new. The dances never lived up to expectations, but that did not diminish the built-up anticipation of a young man wanting desperately to find someone who would make the love songs make sense. So far, I had found no one and the songs sounded insipid and ridiculous. How could anyone feel a broken heart? Over what? Some girl who decides to leave? Let her go, who cares?

The McMillen Building had an entrance way, a narrow hall that led to an interior set of double doors that opened out into the expanse of the building with a concrete floor. In that entranceway, they collected the five dollars cover charge to pay for the band and a little extra for the organization that held the event. I paid it as Jon walked up behind.

"He's got mine," he said.

"What?" I asked, looking over my shoulder.

"For gas."

"That wasn't five dollars' worth of gas!" I protested.

"You want to go back, or not?" he grinned.

That was Jon, my brother. I got into my wallet and pulled out a ten-dollar bill and took my five back. I knew he agreed to take me to the dance too easily. I should have been more suspicious, got the ground rules straight, but I thought for just a second that he was being decent, like a real human being.

"Asshole," I whispered again, less affectionate than the first time.

Jon reached back and punched me on the shoulder, but it was an afterthought and not well-delivered. The punch hardly moved me.

Through the double doors it was dark. One light shone on the far end of the building, casting just enough light to see. It was the perfect amount of light. The stage was lit up and the band members were arranging their equipment, getting ready to play, odd notes issued from the speakers as fingers drug across strings as they handled the instruments.

Cowboy hats worn by teenage boys were scattered about in pools, like bubbles floating on a pond, drifting from one group to another. I walked in behind Jon, who went up to Kevin Pulaski. Maybe they had gotten over whatever differences they had, or were about to go to blows. I slowed my walk until I knew which one it would be.

I went toward a group who had gathered some folding metal chairs into a circle and were busy chatting, laughing and spitting into pop cans. I arrived only to have Will Pulaski step out of the crowd.

"Hey, Lane, come here, man," Will said, grabbing me by the lapel of my jacket. I jerked out of his grasp but followed along to the restroom.

Once we got into the restroom, he turned around and pulled a bottle out of his jacket and handed it to me. I looked at it. It was a bottle of Everclear. Was he being a smartass, or did he think I liked making an ass out of myself and losing my driver's license for a month? I handed it back.

"I can't drink that shit."

"Why not?"

"I'm still diggin' out from the last time. Shit, man," I said and walked out.

As soon as I came out of the restroom I ran into Ronnie and Lisa. The band started playing a Merle Haggard tune, but no one was dancing.

"Hey," I said to Ronnie.

"Hey."

Lisa looked at me with an icy stare.

"Ronnie, come here a minute," I said, nodding to a spot a few feet away.

"What's up?" he asked, walking with me until we got out of Lisa's earshot.

"What do you say about me? To her, I mean?"

"Nothin'."

"She looks at me like I strangled her cat every time I see her."

Ronnie laughed.

"What the hell are you telling her?"

"It's nothing, she just doesn't like you."

"What did I do to her?"

"I don't know."

"Is she jealous of me, or something stupid like that?"

"I don't know," Ronnie said, laughing and I knew that was a lie. He did know why she didn't like me; he told her something, but why?

"That's bullshit," I said and walked off. I was going to have to go about it a different way. I might have to ask her. That would expose his lie, if I cared enough, which I didn't think I did.

I saw Annie Brewster across the room with a couple of her friends. Further along, Jon was talking to Kevin Pulaski. Vince Ciroli came through the door with his girlfriend and up to Jon. Vince had eventually been cleared of charges when the guy he had beaten up admitted responsibility, but it was touch and go for a while. The Gonsalez brothers were with their girlfriends and Zach Pritchard came in a few minutes later.

There were a lot of people I didn't know from different schools. Some might have been from Fort Collins for all I knew. There were girls I hadn't seen before and while the band got into a rhythm, I tried to build some courage. I was at a disadvantage, because I didn't understand the nuances inherent to the boy/girl dynamic. My experiences with Annie only confused the issue.

The first to get out on the dancefloor was Brad Romero and his girlfriend Julie Westerhaus. They were one of the few couples that came to the dances specifically to dance. They were good at it and it was obvious that they enjoyed it. Most of the others danced as a means of getting to know each other or expressing intimacy. For me, it was the only way I had to introduce myself to a girl and most of the time I didn't have the inclination or the courage to do so.

The first hour was when most of the boys and girls would partner up, some of it was pre-arranged, some of it was spontaneous, but there was only that first hour. I wasn't that fast, I couldn't sort it out that quickly, unless a girl came up to me, which is what I relied on. If that didn't happen, I would be alone the rest of the night. But, I still liked the music and the feel of being accepted, understood in that crowd. Someone would have beer and we would go out and drink it to take up some of the time.

I pulled up a chair to the group sitting in a circle. They were all listening to Stan Schiff tell some story. He and his cousin Doug Ham, who was twenty-one. They had a lot of adventures both in Loveland and Fort Collins, because Stan looked twenty-one and they could get into adult bars together. Sometimes they would go up to Cheyenne where the drinking age was nineteen. I didn't know if the stories were true or not.

Over the first hour the circle dissipated as each person paired up with someone, or went out to a car, or was involved in some brewing altercation. I wound up sitting alone, thinking. It was, no doubt, my biggest obstacle to socialization. I liked to think, to turn things over in my mind, to evaluate what I had heard over the course of the evening.

"Daniels," Stan called.

I looked up and Stan waved me over. I sat there, thinking, wondering if he was going to offer me whiskey or grain alcohol and I would have to refuse.

"Come on!" he yelled, waving again.

I got out of the chair and walked over to him.

"What?"

"You depressed or something? Someone steal your girl?"

"Naw, I was just thinking about shit, you know."

"Like what?"

I laughed; did he really expect me to tell him?

"Let's go have a drink."

"Of what?"

"Beer, whiskey, whatever."

"You heard about that shit over fair, right? It cost me my license for a month."

"Tell me about it on the way out."

I went with him, expecting Doug to come with us, but he never showed. We went out the door and into the parking lot. The snow was falling harder and we walked through the parking lot, large flakes sticking to our hats. When we got to Doug's big Ford pickup, it was running, the warm engine keeping the snow from piling up in the middle of the hood. Stan reached up to open the door and it was locked, he knocked on the window.

The foggy window rolled down and Annie Brewster looked out.

"Open the door," Stan said.

"What do you want?" Doug asked, yelling across the cab of the pickup at Stan.

Stan reached up and unlocked the door and jerked it open. He reached under the seat and brought out a bottle of whiskey.

"Beer," I said, over his shoulder.

"It's in the cooler, in the back."

I crawled up into the back and got a beer out of the cooler. I jumped down into the snow and walked around to the door. Stan took a huge drink of the whiskey and put the bottle back under the seat. He slammed the door and Annie rolled the window up. I heard the lock engage.

"She's only fifteen," I whispered. "Doug's twenty-one."

"That don't fuckin' matter, Doug ain't gonna do nothin'. It ain't like that."

I took a big drink of the beer, drinking it as fast as I could, so I could put the empty in the back of the truck and go back inside.

"You about done with that, or what?"

"Just a second."

I belched and took another huge drink. I felt pressure on the can and knew Stan was holding it up, so I couldn't bring it down and would have to drink it all. I started laughing and almost choked on it, but I got it down and we headed back to the dance.

"What do you mean, 'it's not like that?'"

"They're just friends. He likes her, but not like that, they just talk."

"Then, why lock the door?"

"They're weird."

I was feeling light-headed having to drink the beer that fast. But, that was good. I was probably too uptight to enjoy myself anyway.

"What happened at fair?"

"You didn't hear? I thought everyone heard about that."

"No."

"Someone gave me some hard stuff and it kicked my ass. I got so drunk; I woke up across the river under some huge cottonwood. I don't drink whiskey."

"Ah," he said, unimpressed, thinking that was fairly common after a night of drinking.

We went back into the dance and split up. I went back to the chair I had been sitting in and looked out on the dancefloor. I saw Jon dancing with someone I didn't know, probably some girl from the high school he went to, that hung around Vince and his crowd.

Thinking about Stan, I wondered what had happened. Why did he need me to go along? Something wasn't right there. Something else was going on. Was Stan making sure nothing was going on in the pickup that shouldn't, keeping Doug on his toes? I was turning it over in my mind when I saw Beth walking toward me.

"Aw shit," I muttered, I didn't even know she was there. Ronnie didn't warn me. He usually did when he had to bring Beth. Ronnie's mom often sent Beth with Ronnie to keep him from lying to her and going off with Lisa somewhere besides the dance.

Beth was very attractive and physically well-developed, even for thirteen, but when other girls saw me with her, they got the wrong idea. Then, I'd hear it from them; they would use it to ridicule me.

"Hi," she said, pulling up a chair. "How you doing?"

"Fine."

"Are you drunk?"

"No," I said, laughing. "Where did that come from?"

"Just asking. I saw you leave with that guy."

"I had a beer, that's all."

"Are you going to dance with me?"

"I don't know, I don't feel like dancing tonight."

"You always say that. Why do you come to a dance if you don't feel like dancing?"

"To talk to the guys and shit, have a beer, stuff like that."

Beth nodded, her big eyes staring steadily into mine. I kept looking down. She smiled at me as if she was thinking about something funny.

"What?"

"Stuff like what? Grown up stuff?"

"You're too young to ask a question like that."

"Come on, dance with me. Why not? Am I ugly? Is that it?" she asked, but she knew better, it was a ploy.

"Of course, not. You know that, I just don't feel like it sometimes. Dancing is a happy thing, right? I'm not always happy."

"So, you're sad?"

"No, I'm not sad," I replied, laughing. She did have a way of making me laugh.

"If you're not happy, you must be sad."

"There's a middle, you know. Neutral. I'm feeling kind of neutral right now, not sad, but not quite happy enough to dance."

"Come on, promise me you'll dance with me. It's why I came here."

It seemed like it was a goal she was trying to reach more than anything else. Like making me dance with her was a game that she could win. Did she have bets on it? Was it a means of making her feel powerful? Why else would she pursue it so hard, laying herself open to the rejection that I had to offer? I rejected her, that's what I did, it was predictable, at least initially, because it complicated my life and raised questions with girls my age and if I could get out of it, I would. Sometimes, I did. But, I couldn't break her heart, either. That was the trap she always set.

"Why don't you dance with some of the younger boys around here?"

Beth looked over her shoulder at some of the little kids, who had come with their parents and older siblings. The dances, aside from the goings on in the parking lot and occasional fights, were wholesome events that younger families attended.

"You mean, like that little guy in the red cowboy hat?" she asked, pointing with a painted fingernail at a boy about seven years old.

"You know what I mean."

"No, I don't," she said, acting confused and looking more attractive for it.

"All right, if it wins you some bet or something, I'll do it, but not, yet. Give me an hour or so," I said, hoping that in that hour Ronnie and Lisa might leave and take her with them.

"What? What kind of bet?"

"Yes, I'll dance with you."

"You promise?"

"Yes."

"Say it."

"I promise."

I laughed.

Beth got up from the chair, straightened her sweater and grinned a huge, dazzling grin. When she walked away, she was bouncing, almost skipping back to her friends across the dancefloor. Watching her, I did really like her. She was fun and we laughed a lot when we spent time together, but that didn't put years on her or take any away from me. Besides, I knew I was being conned somehow. The girls I had encountered weren't that open, that obvious about their intent and feelings. She seemed genuine, though. It didn't seem like a face she put on. That was how she was, every time. I rarely saw her mad, or depressed, just happy little Beth. I didn't get it. She never got anything out of me. I resisted her charm and made it tough on her. I didn't want to encourage whatever feelings she might have for me. It had nowhere to go. She would never be old enough and I wasn't going to be around anyway. When I was eighteen, I was gone. Some other town, some other state, maybe. It was pointless. I was comforted in the fact that when she got older, she would find a boy, or a boy would find her and those feelings could be returned, but I couldn't do it.

An hour later, after I had been out to Doug's truck a time or two, I walked back into the dance and Beth came up behind me and took me by the hand. Instinctively, I jerked my hand out of hers and looked at her, blinking, trying to figure out who had grabbed me. When I recognized her, I softened.

"Don't come up behind me like that, not here."

"Touchy," she said, grinning. "You ready?"

"Uh," I said, looking around, trying to figure out what song the band was playing. "To this?" It was a George Jones song, a sad one, a slow one.

"Uh huh, you promised."

I couldn't get out of it. Where was Ronnie anyway? Did he leave her here or what?

"Okay," I said, putting my hand on her shoulder, turning her toward the dancefloor.

We danced slow, careful, at a distance. She pulled me closer, but I kept moving back. I could feel other girls watching me, waiting for something they could use against me. She was Ronnie's little sister and I was being nice, damnit.

When the song ended, I walked her back to her seat, like a gentleman would and thanked her for the dance. She looked up with bright eyes and a big smile.

I was feeling the beer and I went to the restroom to relieve myself, telling myself that I was a good person, that, despite what people thought, I could be nice. When I came out, I thought I should dance with someone more my own age. If for no other reason than to keep the only dance I had that night from being with a thirteen-year-old girl. I walked through the crowd and saw Ashley Robertson sitting with her friend, Emily. Ashley was an attractive girl, with light brown hair, blue eyes and glasses. Emily was less attractive, slightly heavy, but was fun to be around. They went to Loveland High and I only saw them at the dances.

Ashley and I had a history. I had danced with her a time, or two and we had made out a little bit one night, but I shied away from relationships, so I let it go at that. There was some resentment for me, I knew that, but I wasn't asking her for her hand in marriage, just a dance and it took a few beers to get that far.

As I approached Ashley, I saw her lean over and whisper something to Emily. Were it not for the beer, I would have walked on by, but I had effectively killed my flight instinct with alcohol.

"Hey," I said, standing in front of her.

Ashley and Emily broke out laughing and looked at each other, then back at me.

"I say something funny?"

Ashley struggled to compose herself, lifting a can of Coke to take a drink from the straw.

"Hey," Emily said, mocking me and laughing.

"What do you want me to say, 'hi' like some retarded hippie?"

They burst out laughing again. The idea of asking Ashley to dance was losing its luster pretty fast, but there weren't a lot of other prospects and there was still the stigma of having only danced with Beth.

"Look, do you want to dance, or what?"

"I thought you were seeing Beth Flanders."

"She's Ronnie's little sister. She's thirteen for heaven's sake. I was being nice."

"You? Being nice? When does that happen?" Emily asked.

"All the time. I'm a sweetheart, ask anyone."

"I don't think so," Ashley interjected with some venom.

"Can I talk to you?" I asked.

"This isn't talking?"

"Alone, for just a minute."

They looked at each other, silently debating it. I nearly walked away; it wasn't worth the effort.

"All right," Ashley said, getting up from her chair, walking with me to the wall.

"I thought we were friends," I said.

"Friends?"

"Yeah, you know, we dance with each other now and then, that sort of thing."

"Make out? Is that what 'friends' do?"

"I was a little tipsy."

"So, you have to be drunk?"

"No, of course not. Why is this such a big deal?"

"You're an idiot," she said, walking away.

"I know that," I whispered, but I was feeling a little tipsy right then and I came up with a plan. I couldn't let Beth be my only dance.

I followed Ashley back to her chair and looked down at Emily.

"Would you like to dance?"

"With you?"

"No, I'm asking for someone else."

"I don't think so."

I threw my hands up in frustration, knocking my hat askew. I turned around and walked back to my chair, sitting down heavily. Where was Jon? Was he ready to go? I looked across the dancefloor. Zach Pritchard came over and sat down next to me.

"What's up?" he asked, pushing his glasses up.

"Do you understand these girls?"

"Not a bit."

"Me, either."

CHAPTER NINE

The snow started falling two days before I got my driver's license. Colorado snow comes in a couple of different forms, either small, dry flakes, almost pellets or light dry flakes or big, wet flakes that look like they were drawn by a cartoonist with detailed, complicated patterns; the December snow that fell was the latter. It covered the ground in minutes after falling and promised to be severe.

I stood on the porch, watching it cover my '68 LTD, as if symbolically smothering my dreams of freedom. The snow continued until everything in the yard was buried by it, retaining only the barest outlines of what was underneath. The traffic on the street running by our place had ceased completely by six that evening.

The haystack looked like a giant bar of butter covered with a white comforter. I was putting off feeding the horses until the snow lightened up enough that it wouldn't cover the hay as soon as I threw a bale or two on top of the already-fallen snow. I gave up at nine that evening and trudged through a foot of snow, the flakes tickled my face as I passed through them like walking through a curtain.

I went first to the barn and retrieved a scoop shovel before I approached the haystack. It would have been useless to arrive with anything else. I shoveled and shoveled until I exposed the green hay beneath and pulled a bale out of the stack. I grabbed it by the two loops of twine that held it together and lifted it. Wading through twelve inches of snow carrying a seventy-pound bale of hay was a struggle, especially because the snow on top of the bale added at least ten pounds. I scattered the hay on top of the snow, hoping it would be visible long enough to be eaten.

The tracks I made on the way out to the barn were hardly visible by the time I returned to the house. I was covered in snow, though I had been outside for no more than fifteen minutes. It wasn't very cold, but it was wet and weighed heavily on my shoulders. I shook off my jacket before I stepped up into the house. The only concern I had was how I was ever going to be able to take my test for the driver's license driving through a couple of feet of snow.

One day later, it was fifty degrees and the snow melted at an incredible rate; there was flooding in the streets. Our yard was a huge pool of water, despite being graveled, the gravel was over clay and drained very slowly.

When I did make it down to the DMV, the test went well. I had been driving for six years on back roads and our property, not only pickups, cars and tractors, but even a flatbed tandem-axle truck when I helped harvest hay on the Flanders place. The written portion was no more of a challenge than the driving portion. I had studied the material and I was good at taking tests.

The only problem came when I had received the license, held it in my hand and attempted to engage in the ironic insanity of having in my possession the perfect object of freedom and would use it for the first time, to go to prison, or what others called school. It was as close to being physically impossible as anything I had yet attempted. But, I did it.

The other side of freedom is responsibility. Being irresponsible was the sin for which I had been denied the license for thirty days and it would cost me as much if I acted irresponsibly again. The license was a test in a way, to see if I could possess freedom and still live up to my obligations.

I could not deny, however, that just sitting in the car, knowing I could go anywhere at any time gave me a sense of control over my own destiny that I had never experienced. Walking away from it, I kept turning half around to glance at the car. No, it was not a new car, not even close. It had been used to haul dirty men from work to home after a long day of filthy labor. They were sweaty and their hands and arms, even though washed, were marked with a heavy thread lubricant they used on the drilling rigs called "dope." Dope was among the most stubborn of substances to remove from a cloth interior, if anyone had tried. It gave the car an odor only found in the oil field, the mixture of diesel fuel, diesel smoke and dope. I did have thirty extra days to do the best I could, but even though I spent a lot of time scrubbing the interior of the car, I didn't get it thoroughly clean. It was mechanically sound, I made sure of that and to me it was an incredibly special car, but to any one of my classmates or friends, it would just look like a ten-year-old car. It wasn't even a muscle car. It was simply a car, but it was mine and it would take me anywhere I could afford to go.

It was several weeks of careful and responsible behavior before I stepped out of line. For a few months, I had no problem with health class. In it we learned about venereal diseases, good things to learn in the early stages of sexual discovery. There were a few other interesting or, at least informative, topics that held my attention. But, when we got to CPR and they were talking about using rubber dummies to practice mouth-to-mouth resuscitation, they lost me and I decided to ditch that day. I was getting an A anyway, so it wouldn't matter.

I walked out into the February sunshine that offered little warmth. The wind kicked up and I wrapped my jacket tighter on the way to the car. John Morales, a proud Chicano, who was guilty of contempt for our group of cowboys was walking along with me, but twenty feet away. I was dutifully cautious of what might transpire between us. The only thing about John was that we were in Science together and while neither of us cared for the other due to our social connections, we got along and even worked together on a couple of assignments. So, there was a degree of mutual respect even though he would eagerly call me a goat roper or shitkicker in front of his friends, surrounded by them and only a few of us to respond.

"Hey, Vaquero!" he said, calling to me using the Spanish

term for cowboy, so he wanted something.

"What?" I asked but didn't stop walking.

John altered his path to intercept mine.

"Que Pasa?"

"Nothin'," I said.

"Where you goin', vato?"

"I'm goin' to the store, get some gas and chew."

"Give me a lift?"

"Where to, the store?"

"No, my place."

"Chip in for some gas and I will."

"Come on," he said, rolling his head as if he were enduring some great imposition.

"Look, man, I have to earn that gas money, if you want to go with me, fine. If you want to go as far as the store and take it from there, fine. But, if you want me to take you all the way to your house, you have to kick in some cash."

"You ain't gonna make me walk in the cold, are ya?"

"I ain't makin' ya do nothin'. You either ride along or you don't."

We stopped and stared at each other, the wind lifting the collar flaps on our jackets. Natural antagonism from the conflicts we had shared showing on our faces. There were a lot more Chicanos (their preferred term) than cowboys and even being outnumbered we had been in fights on opposite sides. I never fought John, but he had been in the bunch of them that had surrounded us at a football game. It went no further than some pushing and exchange of epithets before the cops broke it up, but that was our history.

"All right, I'll ride along, where's your ride?"

"Right here," I said pointing to the LTD.

When we got to the gas station, I got out and put three dollars in the tank and bought a can of tobacco while John made a phone call. I assumed that he was arranging for a ride from there and I got back into the car and started to leave. I was pulling out of the parking lot when he came running to catch me. I saw him waving and resisted the urge to ignore him and stepped on the brake. He came up to the car and opened the door.

"I got you some gas money, dude. Take me home and I'll fill your tank," he said, not waiting for me to agree before he was sitting in the seat and pulling the door closed.

"Better not be full of shit," I said.

John met the implied threat with a look of humorous contempt. He thought he could kick my ass. I didn't know that before. Maybe he could, maybe he couldn't, but it wouldn't be as easy as he thought.

"Just go, dude."

"No shit, or you can get out right here," I said, holding my ground.

"Yes, yes, I got it."

I let off the brake and pulled the car out onto the street. We drove down Sixteenth all the way to Lincoln, up to First and we took that to Boise and turned north. When we got to the big apartment building, he directed me into the parking lot.

"I'll be just a minute," he said, getting out.

"I'll be here."

I had no idea what John had in mind. There was no loveloss between us and by his reaction to my threat, he didn't have as much respect for me as I thought he did. He might come out with a bunch of his friends and jerk me out of car and beat my ass for all I knew. So, I backed the car out of the parking spot and turned it so I had a clear shot out of the parking lot in case my fears were realized. I waited for a while and when I figured he had ditched me, I put the car in gear.

John came around the corner, was surprised to see the car wasn't in the parking spot. He searched the area until he saw me. I kept my foot on the brake as he approached. He pulled the door open and got in.

"It's cold out there," he said, shivering.

"Where's the cash?"

"Uh, we have to pick a dude up, he has it."

"Come on, John, what is this? I have to get back to school. I don't have time for this shit."

"Sorry, amigo," he said, seeming authentically apologetic.

"Where is this guy?"

"Just up Eisenhower, I'll show you."

We pulled out of the parking lot and started west on Eisenhower. I kept shaking my head as we drove further and further.

"How far is this place?"

"Just a little further."

"You said that a while ago."

"I know, it's just up here. Turn left."

I turned into a trailer park and followed the lane to spot number 26.

"This is it; I'll get the money for you. Mucho dinero."

"Yeah, yeah," I said, watching him get out of the car.

I thought I should just leave. He was with his buddy and didn't need me. While I knew that was the right move, that there wouldn't be gas money, I didn't. I didn't, because it would have looked like I was afraid to tell him straight out that I thought he was a cheat and a liar. No, if I was going to leave him, I would have to tell him to his face.

A minute later John came out with another boy, a skinny little guy carrying a box. John opened the door and pushed the seat forward so the other boy could get in the back.

"Wait, what the fuck's going on, John?"

"We gotta take this guy down to the pawn shop to sell a radio, then he'll give you your cash and we'll have the money for a party we got planned."

"We don't gotta do nothin'. I need gas, now."

"Please, last one, I promise."

I looked into the rear-view mirror at the boy in the back.

"You'll give me the money, right?"

"Sure, dude."

I still didn't believe it, but I was going through the three dollars' worth of gas I had put in and if there was any chance this would work, I had to take it.

We drove to the pawn shop through a back street, because my mom's fabric store was just around the corner from it and I didn't want her to see my car drive by. We pulled into the parking lot across from the police station and the boy got out.

When John and I were alone in the car I had my say.

"This has turned into a giant pain in the ass, John. Nothing you've said has been true."

"It looks like that, but it ain't, man. I've been getting' jerked around, too."

"That don't make it any better for me."

"I know, but he'll have the money in a second and we'll get you some gas."

"You had fuckin' better," I threatened, but this time he didn't have the cocky attitude he had the first time. He nodded and looked down.

It was taking a long time.

"Where is this guy?"

John looked out the windshield as if searching for him.

"I don't know."

That was when the patrol car pulled up behind us and stopped.

"What the hell's going on, here?" I asked, looking in the rear-view mirror.

John looked through the side mirror, then whipped his head around to look out the rear window.

"Cops."

"No shit," I said, at the same time the cop tapped on the window.

I rolled the window down.

"Get out of the car."

"Why, what's going on?"

"Get out of the car, both of you."

I looked at John, shaking my head as I got out of the car.

"What am I going to find when I look through here?" the cop asked, pushing the driver's seat forward and looking in the back.

"What are you looking for?"

"Stolen property."

"I don't have any stolen shit in here."

The cop came out with the box the boy had brought with him.

"What do we have here?"

"I don't know, that ain't my box, it belongs to the kid who went into the pawn shop. His buddy," I said, pointing at John.

At that time another cop came around the corner with the boy in handcuffs.

"It's his box," I said, pointing at the boy.

"Is this your car?"

"Yeah."

"Then you're in possession of stolen property."

"I didn't even know what was in the box."

"Put your hands on the car, both of you."

I looked across the roof of the car at John.

"Nice move, asshole," I said, handcuffed, before I got pushed toward the patrol car. I didn't know why they didn't just walk us to the police station a half a block away. At least they locked my car for me and brought me the keys.

When we got to the police station across the street, they put me into a room and shoved me down into a chair. I was still handcuffed and it made it uncomfortable to sit in the chair. I waited for what seemed like a half hour but was really only five or ten minutes. I kept thinking about the classes I was missing and if I could convince them that I didn't know anything about the radio being stolen, I might be able to get back to school before anyone noticed. It was still lunch hour.

The cop who arrested me came into the room and took a seat across the table.

"Lane Daniels."

"Yes, sir."

"What do you know about the individuals you were with?"

"Nothing. I have John in a class, science. The other guy, the one who had the stolen property, I've never seen before. He was a friend of John's. I was just doing them a favor by giving them a ride. I don't know nothing about any of what they did or what they had, nothing."

"Why do they say it was all your idea, then?"

"What!?" I asked. "That's bullshit and they know it. Now they're trying to pin it all on me?"

"So it seems. And, watch your language."

"My language?"

"Yes."

"I'm being framed for theft and you're worried about my language?"

"The stolen property was in your car, that's possession. You're not being framed."

"I don't go through people's pockets when they get in my car to see what they have and ask if it's stolen or not. The box was in the back, the kid was in the back. I wasn't in the back; I didn't have a chance to see what was in the damned box."

"I'm not going to warn you again about your language."

"Sorry, I'm pissed…angry."

There was a knock on the door.

"Yeah?" the cop said.

The door opened and another cop looked in.

"Wrap it up, we're cuttin' him loose."

The cop who had arrested me looked disappointed, but he got up and took my handcuffs off and led me out. As soon as we came around the corner, I saw my mother standing in the lobby, waiting for me. She looked upset.

Mom and I walked out of the police station and had gotten onto the sidewalk before she said anything.

"Thank you for getting me out."

"What on earth were you doing out of school?"

"I, uh, was going to get some gas and something to eat at the gas station and I gave this guy a ride and that turned into a big, complicated thing and eventually he was going to give me some money for gas. I didn't know that kid was selling stolen property, I thought it was his stuff."

"Well, I gave those officers a piece of my mind. They called me down here saying that you had stolen some radios. I knew better than that, so I came down and let them have it."

"You convinced them?"

"Yes, I did. I told them that no son of mine would steal anything and if they didn't let you go, I would sue them for false arrest and defamation of character. I would have, too."

"Thank you."

"You get back to school, right now. Understand me?"

"Yes, ma'am."

By that time, we had walked the half of a block between the police station and the parking lot, which was half a block from my mother's store. She continued on and I got into my car. I turned the key on and saw that my gas gauge was on the big, red "E". I didn't want to spend the five dollars in my pocket on gas. I had other plans for that, but I was forced to pull into the gas station across the street and put that in the tank. I would keep that in mind, next time I got into a conflict with John and the Chicanos. Then, we would put our cards on the table.

CHAPTER TEN

It was a long, cold winter that turned from 1977 to 1978, one marked by incessant conflicts between cowboys, jocks, hoods and Chicanos all trying to possess turf that did not exist. It was imaginary, a sense of place without substance, like a prison yard. The conflicts were a product of the forced habitation, trapped together in the school by deep snow, cold winds and negative temperatures.

Instead of being outside, where I would normally have been during lunch hour on a nice day, I was inside and had gone to the restroom by the cafeteria. I saw John Morales as I came in. The door was still closing, hampered by the hydraulic piston at the top, when the argument began.

"Where the hell's my gas money, John?"

"Pinche puto," he responded.

"Puto?" I asked. "I'm the puto?"

"Yeah."

I went at him, driving my shoulder into his chest, pinning him against the wall. His fists hammered my back and I felt his arm coiling about my neck. I bent over, grabbed his legs with both arms and lifted him off his feet, then let myself fall back and he landed flat on his face. I squirmed out from under his legs. He flipped over as I dove for his head, grabbing him by the neck. I lifted his head and slammed it down on the floor. He somehow got his knee into my groin and I loosened my grip on his neck. We scrambled for position, taking cheap shots at each other's testicles whenever possible and attempting to squeeze the life out of each other when we could get our hands on the other's neck.

The door opened for a second, then slowly closed as we

battled on the tiled floor of the bathroom, struggling to get a commanding position over the other. I had worked myself on top of him with my left hand clutching his throat as he swung his fist into my ribs. I reached under his left leg with my right arm and lifted it up, trying to push his head into the wall. He used the strength of his leg to pull me off until I let go and tried something else. That was when two of his friends came into the restroom and dragged me off him. They shoved me against the wall while John got up from the floor and pulled his shirt back into place. The door opened again and Ronnie and Zach rushed in and surveyed the situation.

"Let him go!" Ronnie yelled at John's friends as he and Zach neared John.

John looked like he had been through enough and must have felt that way, too.

"Let him go," John said, breathing heavily and looking at a cut on his arm.

I could feel the skin on my cheekbone swelling up and I had cuts and bruises here and there. I was breathing hard, too. I felt the rough hands clutching my shoulders and arms loosen and I pulled free. Ronnie, Zach and I withdrew cautiously from the restroom, each keeping a wary eye on the others as we left.

"What was that all about?" Ronnie asked as we walked toward a table.

John and his friends came out of the restroom and shot glances at us as they passed but said nothing.

"Leftover bullshit," I said, touching my cheekbone.

"That's going to swell," Zach said, pushing his glasses up his nose and looking me over. "I'll get some ice."

Mr. Schmidt came walking toward us as if to resolve something.

"What happened here?"

"I slipped in the restroom and smacked my head on the sink," I said. "You should put up some wet floor signs in there."

"What?" Schmidt asked.

"Lawsuit waiting to happen," Ronnie said, chiming in.

"What?" Schmidt asked, retreating to the restroom to evaluate the situation. He opened the door and went in.

"Let's get out of here," I said and we started walking to the hall to get around the corner.

Zach came running to catch up with an ice cube in his hand.

"Wait," he called.

When the first break in the weather came in March and the temperatures soared to sixty degrees, it was as if all the pent-up anger and agitation escaped through the open doorways like air spewing from a quickly deflating balloon. The freedom to go outside, breathe in the fresh air and remove the restraints of heavy coats fueled a sense of good cheer, acceptance and mutual tolerance.

I saw John coming up the long hall and he saw me. We looked away until we got closer.

"John," I said, staring him in the eye.

Morales returned the stare and nodded slightly in my direction as he passed.

We had managed to put it all aside in science, when we had to be in the same room, but we ignored each other. It wasn't until passing in the hall that we were at liberty to renew the battle. But, it was sixty degrees and we could go outside and what had happened before didn't seem all that important on a day like that.

To me, there was value in the fights; they taught us that we could have disagreements, even violent engagements, but we had to get over it. We could not fight each other every day all day long. The fights taught us to put our hostilities behind us and accept the fact that we had to offer each other a little respect.

I knew that all I had to do was to say "puto" instead of his name and the fight would be on; he knew the same thing. In that moment we mutually agreed that whatever had gone on between us was over. That could not have happened if I had walked out that day, if I had shown less resolve. John would have taken that as cowardice and whenever he wanted to impress his friends and needed someone to intimidate and humiliate, he would choose me. It was not speculation, it had been done before, to me, before I understood that there was no way out, but to fight back, establish the rules.

Teachers and principals, whose purpose it was to keep fights from happening in school for fear of legal liability, would say that fighting was not the way to settle issues, but it often was. They would prefer that a kid like me live in fear; run away every time they saw someone, like John, come around a corner; remain small and quiet to avoid attracting attention. I had long ago chosen to wear the scars on the outside of my body, recognizing that those wounds were not as deep and healed much quicker than the wounds of physical and emotional abuse. My brother, Jon taught me that. That's how I knew that taking a punch didn't mean much to me, as long as it was not the constant berating and demeaning that he was fully capable of dishing out.

When I got to study hall, Mandy was already seated at her desk. I sat where I usually did and leaned back in the seat. I closed my eyes for a minute, wanting to go to sleep.

"Why don't you ever have homework?" Miss Tanner asked.

I looked up at her. She was young and attractive for a teacher, but there was something cold and brutal about her nature that I didn't care for. After all, she was a teacher.

"Because I don't have any."

She looked at the other students feverishly working on homework, even Mandy had a book open and was casually taking notes.

"All of these other students have homework every day. How is it that you never have any?"

"I guess we have different classes."

"You all have the same classes."

"Maybe they're trying to impress someone and I'm not."

Miss Tanner had sleek, shiny black hair and pink lipstick

that highlighted her working lips that made her look like she was going to say something, but instead, she just stared at me with brown, hostile eyes. She was trying to argue with me and I wouldn't cooperate.

"Who would…why do…what…?"

I waited expectantly.

"Come with me," she said, moving toward the door.

I got out of my seat and followed her. When we were both in the hall, she closed the door.

"Can you read?" she said, trying to look sympathetic and kind.

"Of course, I can read."

"I would like to do some tests."

"What kind of tests?"

"We're here to help you, if you need it. We have tools that can help."

"Help me do what?"

"Help with comprehension."

"Are you out of your mind? I don't need any help. I probably read better than you do."

"Then you have nothing to be afraid of. The tests will reveal that."

There was a look of pity and superiority in her eyes, a look of demeaning benevolence. She saw what she wanted to see, which was a poor, dumb hick, unable to read well, rejecting school out of frustration, impotence and fear. Hostile toward the other children who could master the curriculum and rude to them as a means of deflecting criticism. It wasn't that she could not see me for who I was, but that she would not. I had insulted her, embarrassed her in some way unknown to me and that was her ultimate revenge. Maybe, my whole existence bothered her on some level, a living example of the stereotypes she had conjured up in her mind about rednecks; making the stereotypes real by applying them to me, whether I deserved them or not. She wouldn't let me have enough say to refute them. The only way I would ever be able to put the lie to her faulty assessment would be to take the tests and ace them, obliterate them until I removed any doubt as to my intelligence and ability.

The question that came to me as I stood there, looking at her vindictive expression, is whether I cared enough about her opinion to bother. I never had before. I didn't care what Mr. Schmidt thought of me, whether he considered me a hardheaded, but generally smart student, or an absolute moron and troublemaker. None of it mattered, because people like Mr. Schmidt and Miss Tanner only held power over people who were going to college, who would benefit from their good graces and acceptance or suffer from their wrath. To me, they were ridiculous custodians of classrooms and offices, emboldened by the power to affect someone's future, ransom it to a degree.

"Well?" she asked.

I wanted to say something clever, something that would set her back on her heels and make her reconsider her arrogant attitude, but everything that came to mind sounded desperate, as if I needed her understanding that I was more than I seemed, that all of us were, so, I didn't.

"Naw, I ain't gonna be your lab rat," I said and went back into the classroom.

Mandy was waiting for me in the seat next to mine. She was a gossip and liked to know all the goings on. I sat down next to her.

"What happened?"

"Nothing, she's an idiot."

"What did she say?"

Miss Tanner came back into the classroom and took her seat as if nothing happened, but I could tell she was furious.

We sat in silence for a while, then Mandy leaned close to me.

"I like cowboys, you know," she said.

I looked at her with skepticism that must have been apparent.

"I do," she whispered.

"Since when?"

"Always."

"I've never seen you at the rodeos or dances or anywhere else."

"Dances?"

"The country dances down at the fairgrounds."

"They have dances?"

"Yeah."

Miss Tanner looked at us, so we stopped whispering to each other, for a while, but Mandy started it up again.

"When?"

"When, what?"

"When are the dances?"

"Fridays, usually."

We were making too much noise, so we stopped again. We were supposed to be studying, or at least, not bothering the others who were. Mandy tried to start up again, but I shook my head; it could wait until after class. Mandy got up and went back to her usual seat.

I didn't know what Mandy was trying to pull, but I didn't believe that she liked cowboys. There were all sorts of things she could have gotten involved in if she did. She would have been around in the cafeteria or befriended some of the country girls, but she hadn't.

The class was about to end and I stood up. The bell rang. I avoided Miss Tanner's gaze as I walked to the door, but when I got close to her desk, she spoke up.

"Lane, can you stay after class for a moment?"

"No," I said, walking out. She had her chance. I sat there, right in front of her the whole rest of the class; she had all that time to talk to me, if she wanted to. She wasn't going to take up my time with her nonsense.

Mandy was the last thing on my mind as I walked down the shining hallway, but she caught up to me.

"Wait," she said.

I slowed until she came up next to me.

"Hey, so tell me about these dances."

"Down at the McMillen Building at the fairgrounds. All the cowboys and girls go there, it's kind of a big deal with people our age, too young to go to the 3.2 joints. Some of them are older, even families."

"When do they start?"

"Eight or nine."

"Really?"

"You ought to go sometime," I said, challenging her, knowing that she wouldn't and when she didn't, I could put the lie to her little ruse.

"I don't have a car."

"Bring one of your friends."

"I don't think any of them would go with me."

"How about your parents?"

"Oh, no, they wouldn't do that, not that late."

I was out of options and I shrugged my shoulders.

"Well, I guess you won't be able to make it."

We were at the part of the hallway where she had to go one way and I had to go another, so I stopped and looked at her, an amused look on my face.

"I really want to go. You can't think of any other way?"

"Where do you live?"

"West of town, in Shadow Hills."

"I think Zach Pritchard lives out that way, maybe he can stop and pick you up."

"I don't even know him," she said, her blue eyes reflecting doubt.

"Well, look, if you really want to go, I suppose I could stop by and get you," I said, doing the best I could to be helpful.

"I wouldn't go to some hick dance with you!" she literally screamed as if I had accosted her and stormed off while several girls stopped and stared. It seemed like everyone in the hall froze in place, their startled eyes fixed on me.

I didn't know what to say. I stood there, dumbfounded, trying to figure out what had happened. Then everything started to move again and I was being passed by crowds of kids trying to get to their next class.

I wanted to find Ronnie right then and ask him to explain all of that to me. Mandy exhibited every signal, gave every secret code for coming on to me and yet, it was all a ploy designed to humiliate me in public. What would Ronnie say to that? I got turned down and I hadn't even asked her out, I offered her a ride, that's all. Yet, to all the bystanders to the incident, it looked like I had made an unwelcomed advance on her that she had to strenuously reject.

I couldn't figure girls out and when they got to be women, they would be that much more of a puzzle, that much better at disguising their intent. I was lost and I knew it, why didn't Ronnie and the others respect that?

When it came to guys, I could sort it all out, see their devious plans to jump me, or sucker me into a bad position. I could see three hoods maneuvering to encircle me before they attacked and get my back to a wall to defeat their plans. But, girls outmaneuvered me every time.

CHAPTER ELEVEN

There had been some bumps during the school year, like when I got arrested and it was clear that I had been ditching school, but for the most part I had been able to act responsibly. I had effectively used my car to gain more freedom, not lose it by getting into trouble with it. I had gone to some parties and out to the small mountain town of Masonville to the little three-two joint out there that allowed kids my age inside to play pool, if we drank pop. The older kids could drink beer and there was some alcohol stashed in cars and pickups that we snuck into now and then, but I didn't let it go too far.

When the snow stopped falling, green grass sprouted on the prairie, trees filled with leaves, shade became possible on the large patches of grass out front of the school and school came to an end. My days then were full of time. Long hours spent at the house, nowhere to go and nothing to do. I didn't have the money for gas to cruise around town like some of the rich kids. I had been asking around for jobs but had no luck.

Two weeks into summer, Tom Wilson came back to town. Tom had lived in the big house, nearly a mansion, across the street from our place and further down. It was a section of town where the wealthy built small estates on several acres of land. They had decorative pillars at the entrance to long, graveled driveways leading through massive lawns, some of them tended to by gardeners.

I grew up with Tom, going to elementary school and part of junior high with him, but his father died of cancer and they stayed in the big house for a few years, but eventually his mother married a man from Kansas, a preacher, and they moved away. Tom's dad liked me, or tolerated me, but his mother hated me. She couldn't stand the sight of me and while she didn't come out and say it, it was apparent in everything she did, every gesture she made, that I was not welcome in her house.

The only reason I could see for her attitude was that after his father died, in the last two years that he lived there, Tom started to emulate me. He bought boots, jeans and a belt buckle. He secretly chewed tobacco and spent more and more of his time at our place. When he got caught with chew in his room, his mother exploded with anger and vehemence, denouncing me and berating him. I couldn't shake the idea that her move to Kansas had as much to do with getting Tom away from me as anything else.

So, when Tom was allowed to come back to see me that summer, I was surprised. During the discussions about his visit, it was clear that my parents considered him a part of the family and welcomed him as they would a returning sibling. Tom thought Jon was almost a hero and spent as much time with him as he could, but that still left us with a lot of time together. The good thing was, Tom had some money for gas so we weren't stranded at the house and with his help, we could do the chores in no time, leaving more time for us to carouse around.

Tom was taller than me, with dark, straight hair, green eyes and high cheekbones. Skinny. He wasn't used to the sort of physical exertion I was and got winded when putting up hay for an extended period, or herding cows by foot and having to run to keep them in line, or head them off.

Tom and I were sitting on the hay bales after having put up a couple of tons of the first cutting. We were sweaty and Tom was winded by the effort, so we were taking a break.

"What's Kansas like?" I asked.

"Screwed up, I hate living with my step-dad. He's a preacher, you know and strict."

"Not too many years left for that. You could move out when you're seventeen and no one could do a thing about it."

"Ha!" he laughed. "I thought you knew my mom."

I chuckled, too. I didn't want to say it, but there was

nothing that could hold me back if I didn't like being somewhere. The thought of mom being with some other man and me having to suck it up didn't seem possible.

"What about school, how's that?"

"Bad, a lot of tension between blacks and whites. I got the shit kicked out of me when I first got there by a group of black guys. I caught one of them in the bathroom a few weeks later and got my revenge, but you have to be careful where you go. There's places in town you don't want to be, if you're white."

"Same sort of thing happened to me, but it was just a wrestling match. I got a black eye from it and he had some bruises, but it got broke up before too much happened to either of us."

Tom nodded.

"Ready?" I asked, standing up.

"Already?" he asked, knowing it would crack me up. It did.

"Come on, only another ton to go. It'll be over in a jiff."

Tom stood and we went back to work. It was a nice day for it, not too hot. The snowy Long's Peak with blue sky as a backdrop made it pleasant, at least to me. When we were done and had time to catch our breath, I slapped Tom on the back.

"Let's go up to Masonville and play some pool, you wanna?" I asked. We hadn't been up there, yet.

"Sure."

We got into my car and rolled the windows down. As soon as we pulled out of the drive and headed west the warm mountain air poured through the windows. It was that thin, clean air of Colorado that I loved. What few times I had been at sea level, I felt smothered by the air, thick and odorous, as if holding the aromas aloft in its mass. The air at sea level had mass that the higher elevations did not and the thin air smelled fresh and crisp.

The area we passed through was lined with acreages with small, old houses or trailer houses on them and corrals or fences behind with horses, cattle or sheep restrained there. It was the area where my friends lived, most of them. Some lived by Masonville, or further up the mountain from there. I wheeled the car over the gravel roads, spewing a dust cloud behind. I let the rear end slide around more than I needed to, just to feel it.

Tom sat on his side of the front seat with his elbow out the window and a huge grin on his face. I don't know if Tom had ever driven a car, all I had known him to have was a motorcycle. The whole time he lived in Loveland, he rode his Kawasaki Enduro over to our place and we would take that up to the convenience store sometimes.

We pulled up to the highway. I stomped on the accelerator and spun the tires, leaving a black mark on the pavement as the LTD leapt into motion. We were laughing and having a good time. At the school, we turned right and started up the winding road that hugged the very base of the foothills. Waylon Jennings and Willie Nelson blared from the speakers.

As we went along, we saw someone on a horse up ahead; a girl. It was not an uncommon sight out there and I tried to make sure I had room to swing into the other lane when we got close so I wouldn't scare the horse. The closer we got, the more I recognized the person on the horse, it was Annie Brewster. I could tell by her long, blonde hair and the King Ropes hat she wore when she was riding.

"Who's this?" Tom asked pointing at Annie.

"Annie Brewster. You ever know her?"

"I don't think so."

"They moved out here about the time you moved to Kansas."

Tom nodded.

"Should we talk to her?"

"I don't know, that's kind of a touchy subject."

Tom shot me a strange look as we went by Annie. I looked up into the rear view to see if she had any reaction, but she kept riding, so I kept driving.

We pulled into the parking area in front of the Masonville store. It was half bar, half convenience store where local mountain folks could get supplies. The grocery store was further split between food and hardware items. Rural stores like Masonville were all the same, they had to stock items people might need in an emergency, but they charged for it, too.

There was a gas pump out front, but I didn't know anyone who bought gas there except in an emergency. They charged twenty cents more per gallon than the stations in town. The store's exterior looked like it was made of logs, but that was a façade. It did make me feel like an old-time cowboy, though, stepping up on the wooden slats of the boardwalk. The sound of my boots clomping on the wood gave me an eerie, feeling, a sort of Marty Robbins time shift. I pulled my cowboy hat down on my brow for effect.

The bell above the door jingled loudly as we entered, intensifying the old-time feeling of the moment. I felt like stepping up to the long bar and ordering a whiskey, but they didn't sell it and I had proved that I couldn't drink it. In my mind I could hear myself saying, "Set em up, Joe." But, there was no "Joe" and I wasn't even old enough to buy beer, so I went through the connecting door and into the store. I got a pop from the cooler and stepped aside so Tom could get one, too.

We took them up to the counter where Gladys waited on us.

"I need some quarters for the pool table, too," I said, laying a five-dollar bill down. Tom snuck his pop next to mine so I could pay for it.

"Hey, I'm not the rich one," I said, looking at Tom.

"I don't work for free, either," he replied.

Good point.

Gladys had short red hair, red lipstick and makeup as if she expected to go somewhere or meet someone important, but she always looked like that. She was heavy with age and wise to the shenanigans young boys might perpetrate. Gladys tended bar in the evenings and during Wednesday nights when they held pool tournaments. She was no one to fool with and no one wanted her husband Bill to get involved.

Bill was a short, thick character with curly hair and kind of a dumb look, but he was a Golden Gloves boxer and it was known that he could put anyone down if they got out of hand. It didn't matter how old they were or how tough they thought they were. The ones who didn't believe Bill was all that tough usually found out, the lesson paid in blood.

The pool table cost a quarter a game and I had a handful of them, so we went into the bar and set up along the wall. There were two racks full of pool sticks and one usually had to go through all of them to find a straight one.

We were in the middle of our first game when the door opened, setting the bells to jingling. The sunshine was a rude interruption to the cozily dark atmosphere, a rectangle of bright light into which Annie stepped, framing her shapely body for just a moment before she closed the door behind her. The bells jingled again.

Tom was frozen in mid strike and waited until his eyes readjusted to the darkness before he followed through.

"I knew you were coming here," Annie said to me.

"Hell of a deduction," I replied, feeling comfortable with her.

"Who's your friend?"

"This is Tom Wilson, he used to live by me, before he moved to Kansas."

"Hi," Tom said.

"He looks like a hood."

"Naw, they just don't have a lot of cowboys in Kansas and it's easy enough to get into a fight without egging it on," I said, in his defense, but he did wear tennis shoes and no belt, or hat.

"He, can speak for himself," Tom responded.

I took that for what it was and backed off. Tom had missed, so I nudged him out of the way as I circled the table looking for my next shot. That left Annie and Tom to consider each other, to size each other up. I was all for it, as long as the intense green eyes of the inquisitor weren't focused on me.

"You were the girl on the horse," Tom said.

"I was."

"So, you live around here?"

"Yep, just down the road."

"Can I buy you something to drink or a candy bar?"

I made three shots in a row, one very difficult one, but no one was paying attention. Tom and Annie were busy talking and I felt an odd sense of relief. She was a pretty girl, long blonde hair and green eyes that could flash with emotion, a narrow, straight nose and full lips. She had a body that fit well on a horse, molded from riding in a way. I don't know why I was cautious of her, why I felt better when her attention shifted away from me, or why I felt so uncomfortable when her attention was trained on me like it was that night at the party.

"I do, too!" Annie squealed. "That is so odd."

I missed my next shot and Annie went to the restroom in the back.

"Your turn," I said.

Tom looked at me like he had forgotten we were in the middle of a game and he probably had.

"Huh? Oh."

Tom went to the table and took a shot that looked like he didn't want to make it and didn't.

"Your turn."

"Surprise, surprise."

"What do you know about Annie?"

"As much as I know about any girl," I replied.

"So, not much," Tom countered.

We burst out laughing. I forgot how well he knew me. That was pretty much it for playing pool. I finished the game myself and then it was time for Annie to get her horse home and brushed down. We went outside with her as she left.

In Colorado, up in the mountains like that, it was not an odd sight to see a horse tied up at the Masonville store next to a car or pickup or even a Harley Davidson or two.

"Want me to ride your horse home for ya?" I asked.

"Cimarron," she said.

"All right, you want me to ride Cimarron home for ya?"

"How would I get home?"

"Tom can drive ya home and pick me up, easy."

Annie gave me an odd look. I didn't know what it meant.

"Okay, I guess that'd be all right."

I took the reins, reached up to the saddle horn and swung aboard the big thoroughbred, who tossed his head back when he felt my weight and could see Annie standing next to Tom. Cimarron was her horse and he felt like something untoward was happening, but Annie reached out to him and rubbed his nose to reassure him.

"You can drive a car, can't ya?" I asked Tom, having never seen him do it.

"Hell, yeah."

"Would you lie to me?"

"Hell, yeah," he said and we laughed.

It felt good, natural, for me to be riding away from the store on a horse, out in the mountains, like the mountain men who had once trapped and hunted along the Buckhorn valley. Even though it only took a few yards for Cimarron to recognize I knew what I was doing, he kept tossing his head around to see if Annie was somewhere near. Each time he did, I talked in an easy, friendly tone to ease his concerns.

"She's coming, don't worry. She's okay, just relax."

When I got to Annie's house I rode into the yard, up to the corral and got off the horse, the saddle creaking as I did. I opened the gate and led Cimarron in, then sat on the top rail and waited for Tom and Annie to show up. A few minutes later I saw the LTD appear around a corner in the road and drive up to the house. Man, I liked that car.

"Any problems?" Annie asked as she got out of the car.

"I didn't want to say anything, but he talked shit about you all the way."

"Uh huh," she said. "If anyone talked shit, it was you."

"Not me, I was nice as all get out."

"Only because he's a he."

"What the hell does that mean?"

"You know damn well what it means," she said, vindictive, but, I didn't.

I wasn't going to get into a "no I don't" "yes, you do" sort of argument, so I dropped it and went to get into the car. I walked up to the driver's door, expecting Tom to relinquish it.

"I'll drive," he said.

I threw my hands in the air in resignation and got into the passenger side. Annie was taking the saddle off as we backed out of the drive.

"I like this car," Tom said.

"Yeah, me too."

"Annie's going to meet us up there later," Tom said, putting the accelerator down and heading back to Masonville.

"What if we aren't going to be up there later? I was just going to play a game of pool, not spend all night."

"It won't be long, about an hour."

We rode in silence for a while as I got used to the idea of being held captive to Tom's plans.

"You seem to get along pretty well," I said, to break the silence.

"Yeah. We both like Meat Loaf."

"Meatloaf? How the hell did that come up? At what point did you two start discussin' favorite foods? That's just fuckin' weird."

Tom cracked up and started laughing so hard, I thought he was going to wreck the car. We were back to the store before he was able to speak.

"Not the food, the singer, you fuckin' hick. You've never heard of Meat Loaf?"

"The food, yeah. There's some dude calling himself Meatloaf?"

Tom cracked up again and I was starting to chuckle along in commiseration.

"*Bat Out of Hell*, the album. You haven't heard of that? Are you shitting me?"

"No."

"It's great, man, unbelievable."

"A great album is the *Outlaws* album. Now, that's music."

Tom just shook his head, he didn't bother to argue, because it was pointless.

We spent most of the rest of the night there at Masonville. Doug Ham and Stan Schiff showed up, having seen my car out front. They stopped by in Doug's Ford pickup to play some pool. Stan had taken up smoking somewhere along the line and bent over the pool table, smoke curling up into his eyes as he tried to shoot. He missed a lot.

Annie came up to the store about the same time as Zach Pritchard drifted in. The six of us played pool, drank beer out in Doug's pickup, then came back in to play more pool. Tom and Annie didn't play, unless they were on the same team. I studied Doug's reaction to Annie's interest in Tom, but the expected hostilities never developed, so, maybe Stan was right, they were just weird friends.

It was just a good time. No one got drunk, no fights erupted, Tom and Annie spent a lot of time holding hands, but not much more than that. I played some of the best pool of my life, but still not good enough to beat Doug, who had a pool table at his house. So, it was a real surprise when Tom and I woke up to banging on my door, with my mom saying that Tom's mom was on the phone.

Somehow, we never figured it out, Tom's mom heard that he was hanging out with me at bars, playing pool and getting drunk. As Tom went down to talk to his mom, mine cornered me in my room.

"What's this about a bar and getting drunk?"

"Absolutely not! We were playing pool at Masonville and while that's a bar, of sorts, Gladys knows me, that I'm too young to buy beer."

"What about outside?"

"Yeah, Doug's twenty-one and had some beer and stuff in his truck, but he could buy it in the store, too. This is really no big deal, mom," I said. "We were just playing pool. Tom met Annie there and they were hanging out, or we would have been home by six."

"What time did you get home?"

"Ten," I said, "still not late."

"Well, Marilyn is very upset. I don't know how she heard about it, but she did and she's livid."

"It was nothing," I reassured her.

Tom appeared at the bottom of the steps; his face looked like he'd taken a beating.

"I gotta go home. She has a bus ticket waiting for me at the station downtown."

"What for?"

"She heard all sorts of wild things about what was going on."

I drove Tom down to the bus station and waited with him until he got on. It all seemed so useless and stupid. It felt like a setup in a way, contrived, but they knew where we were and that he had been there till after dark.

Tom wrote down his address in Kansas and asked me if I could give it to Annie, which I promised I would. I didn't know what Tom planned to accomplish by writing to her or her to him, but I would accommodate it to the extent I could. I didn't know when I would see Annie again, anyway, but I put the address in my wallet.

Even when the bus pulled away, spewing a black cloud of diesel smoke, I still didn't understand what had happened. I felt stunned by it all, confused and irritated as I drove home.

CHAPTER TWELVE

After Tom left, I didn't have very much to occupy my time. Chores were still a couple of hours a day at best. None of the jobs I looked into materialized. Once I got my car, the Flanders stopped needing me to help out, supporting my notion that they were just trying to help me earn money for the car in the first place.

Then, a job that Zach Pritchard had mentioned only in passing came back around. Zach had arranged to take the job himself, but backed out at the last minute and asked me if I wanted it. It was a job on a hay farm up in Walden, a mountain town about a hundred miles up the Poudre Canyon and I think Zach got cold feet. It was a long way away and it lasted all summer with no breaks and no family around. To me, it was a Godsend. It provided everything I was looking for: money, work and a chance to see something new, go somewhere as an adult. I said I would take it, before I talked it over with mom.

I was packing my clothes into an old suitcase and getting ready to leave when my mom came up the stairs and opened the door.

"What's going on?"

"I'm leaving."

"Oh, no you're not!" she said.

"Mom, I got a job, I have to. You've been bugging me about getting a job, so I got one."

"I meant a job around here, a job that doesn't require a suitcase."

"I've been trying. Even when Tom was here, I still tried to get a job, but nothing panned out. Then Zach chickened out of this one and it opened a spot for me. It's either take this one or do without all summer."

"Where is this job?"

"Walden."

"Walden's more than a hundred miles from here. I think you better wait until your dad gets home, so we can talk about this."

"I can't wait. They want me available for tomorrow morning, which means I need to leave right now to get there before sunset."

"I don't know, what are you going to eat? Where are you going to stay?"

"At the job. It's room and board and salary, four hundred a month."

"Four hundred is not very much," she said.

"It is if you get room and board."

"Who are these people? Who do I call if there's an emergency?"

"I don't know. I have a phone number I'm supposed to call when I get into town and they'll give me directions out to the place. It's a hay farm, so nothing I haven't done all my life."

"Let me have the number, in case something happens."

I wrote it down for her and closed the suitcase. She stared at the phone number, her hand shaking a little. It was difficult to figure out what she was feeling, why she was being so hard on me about it. It was just a job and the distance would be good for me, the sense of having to take the job seriously.

"Well," she said, but didn't have anything past that.

"It'll be all right. I'll call when I get there."

I could tell she wanted me to hug her, but I just wanted to get going. It was still morning, but I had things I had to do before I left. I put my arms out and she hugged me tight and I heard her sniffle.

"It's okay," I said, lifting the suitcase and tromping down the stairs. I stopped in the kitchen.

"I need some gas money to get up there. I'll pay you back when I get paid."

Mom got into her purse, dug out a twenty and handed it to me. That would buy gas and something to eat.

"Thanks. See ya later."

I went out the door, my chest full of excitement as I put the suitcase in the trunk and got behind the wheel. I leaned over and rolled down the passenger window, then the driver's side. It was hot and I needed the airflow. I waved enthusiastically as I drove past her standing on the porch, waving with one hand and wiping her tears with the other.

I felt for her, I did, but that was my chance. The job was everything I had been dreaming about since I turned fifteen; it was freedom in ways I had not even imagined. It was a chance to test out adulthood. Zach said they weren't looking for people our age, really, but he got the opportunity as a favor and that's why he felt obligated to help fill the open spot. They were looking for people seventeen or eighteen, in other words, adults or nearly adults, but I would prove that I could handle it, even at sixteen.

I pulled out onto the street and up to Lincoln. I had to go through Fort Collins, so I got on US 287, which was Lincoln in town that went past the burger joint on Eisenhower, where I planned to get a hamburger. I was working it all out in my head, where I would buy gas, the route I would take to Poudre Canyon and everything. Once on Highway 14, I would be seeing things I had never seen before, because I hadn't been past the narrows. I had hardly ever been in Poudre Canyon at all.

At the burger joint, I was nearly vibrating with anticipation and excitement. It was all coming true, everything I dreamed about. I often made up this sort of scenario, only it usually involved the drilling rig. In my mind it was where someone got hurt and they needed someone to work for a few days and I had to be called out there and I worked so hard they figured out a way to keep me and my life started right then. But, I knew that wouldn't happen, that it couldn't happen. There were laws and social security numbers involved, checks that needed to have the right name on them to be cashed, but it was a fantasy that I liked a lot.

Sitting in the drive-thru lane, I imagined what it would be like at the hay farm. If it was big enough to hire help for the summer, it was big enough to have plenty of equipment to handle the hay. I took the sack of food from the guy at the window and the pop he handed out with a straw. I arranged the change in my pocket before I drove off, pulling out the fries as I maneuvered the car back out onto the street, headed north.

It was a clear, June morning that was edging toward noon as I passed through the first intersection on my way out of town. I rolled past the cemetery with giant sprinklers chattering as they sprayed big arcs of water over the gravestones and green grass. I was nearly done with the fries by the time I came around the curve that jogged to the intersection with Twenty-Ninth, the street that Loveland High School was on further west. From there, it was almost all farmland, some of it Schiff's land, with one gas station all by itself on the west side of the road.

Long's Peak was behind me and the lower peaks lingered on the west. I was finishing the hamburger when I got into Fort Collins proper. It was a big town, much bigger than Loveland and I had to watch what I was doing and what everyone else was doing as I rolled through the crowded streets.

I passed by the huge shadow-splashed lawn and ancient trees that made up part of Colorado State University. The huge building that emerged from the trees and came closest to College Avenue was a field house where indoor athletics took place. The university was largely hidden behind the tree-lined streets of downtown, but existed even further obscured in my mind. As often as I drove by, I saw nothing of the activities there. It was as if they were in my subconscious, a fake thing, a ruse made up by people who benefited from it in some way.

The whole area had the feel of something hidden, not only its physical existence, but its theoretical purpose. If there was little or no need for high school, if it served so little purpose that it taught nonsense, how could the university benefit? Even if I passed the classes in high school, I didn't see how that would prepare me for college, because it was only the grades that the college needed and I could have gotten them as I did in junior high, but they simply were not teaching important subjects anymore. It was a logical paradox that continued to plague me even after I had gotten into Old Town, where the streets narrowed considerably.

It wasn't until the road widened out and the traffic thinned that I felt I had made it safely through. Then, I relaxed and enjoyed the ride. I still had to get gas, but there was a gas station in LaPorte that I knew about and I would stop there.

LaPorte was another town named by French fur trappers in the previous century. It felt like a mountain town, where Loveland and Fort Collins just felt like any other city to me. LaPorte was small and rural, a lot of farms surrounded it, but just outside of town was Rist Canyon that, if followed, would bring one back into Masonville from the southwest. Northwest of Masonville was a road that led into the middle of Fort Collins passing Horsetooth Reservoir.

Just being in LaPorte felt like being at the beginning of the mountains and somewhere, at the end of a long, winding road was Walden. I filled up at the station in LaPorte and breathed in the air thick with the smell of pine, before getting back in my car and heading through town, around the bend and out toward the canyon.

Where US 287 and Highway 14 split up was another convenience store I had forgotten was there, or I might have waited to fill up. I turned left and started up 14, passing the missile sites off to the north, recognizable by the chain link fences and armed guards going back and forth in dark blue four-door pickups.

Then, the canyon started, the flat farmland slowly narrowing to high-sided, jagged walls. I felt a sense of adventure, of not knowing what would come around each corner as I powered the LTD along, swooping through the curves. Somewhere along the narrow part was a place called "Deadman's Curve" because it was deceptively sharp in the eastbound lane, bordered by the rock wall. Those racing down the canyon, having a few too many at one of the fishing and camping lodges further up, would inevitably miss the curve and plow head-first into the unforgiving stone. The westbound lane was bordered by the powerful, rushing waters of the Cache La Poudre River, big swells of water crashing into and flowing over gigantic rocks that had fallen from the sides of the canyon walls hundreds of years before, rounded by the constant flow and the spring runoff that put billions of gallons of water down the canyon in a year's time.

It was beautiful and pulled my mind back to when a couple of Frenchmen would be guiding their mules up the canyon, or riding along the rim a couple of hundred feet above, looking down into the deep gash in the surface of the earth, their mules loaded with pelts of beaver, muskrat, bear or mountain lion. They would have the whole day to themselves, no rush, no boss, just the undying need to be free and willing to risk all the possible dangers to know it, to feel it, to let that freedom swim through their bloodstreams, nourishing their souls.

For me, it was the last glimpse of freedom for a while. They needed me at the hay farm and I would be busy every day until the job was done. But, having a job didn't mean the end of freedom, it was more the understanding that I would have to live there, get my meals there that smelled of restriction and crept into my brain warning me of a trap.

It was still early, about two in the afternoon when I got to the top of the long climb of a couple of thousand feet and the sides of the canyon melted away into broader horizons. Tall pine trees lined the highway so thick they looked like a giant picket fence. It was a forest like I had rarely seen, even with all of the time I spent in the mountains. The pine were scattered somewhat sparsely in the foothills near Loveland compared to the forest at the top of the canyon. I marveled at it, becoming mesmerized by the individual trees flashing by, the sunlight filtering through leaving stripes of sunlight and shade on the road.

Then, I saw it, the most unexpected vision of all, an oil

drilling rig off to the right, way back in the woods, an oddity, it seemed. I stared at it trying to get a glimpse of it through the trees, then the trees thinned and I realized that the rig was actually in a more open space than it seemed as I approached. I saw what looked like a road leading back to it and having plenty of time to get to the ranch, I took the road and drove through puddles in the two-track lane. It had rained and the tire tracks that led to the rig were rutted by tires spinning through some of the deeper puddles, but it had dried since those tracks were made and I got through easily.

I pulled up onto the drilling site and parked. It was a rig about the size of the one my dad managed, maybe a little bigger, but not much. I just sat there looking at it, idling, then thinking about the gas I was wasting, I turned the car off. The air was cooler up there at that altitude and smelled cleaner, crisper.

With the engine off, I could hear the sound of the rig's engines roaring along as they powered the draw-works that spun the square pipe through the rotary table. The mud pump engine roared, too, pushing drilling fluid down the center of the pipe and back up the outside and into a pit to be recycled over and over. The lifting bales clanged off the swivel, the whole kelly pulsing with the surging motion of the fluid being pumped.

I sat back and listened to the familiar sound of it, having been out to work with dad numerous times when I was younger. Then, when he got the manager's job, I would go with him when he had to be out there to handle some crisis with the formation, the pump or the draw-works. It was at once familiar and foreign, the whole set up being familiar in its purpose, but the particulars of that rig being foreign. Their doghouse, where the driller performed his clerical duties, was smaller; the generator house, what they called a "lightplant" was bigger, having two generators instead of one; there were fewer pipe racks, because the drilling site was smaller; they had a round, upright water tank instead of the rectangular water tank beneath the doghouse on my father's rig. But, it was a drilling rig and I just liked being around it.

I watched it for a long time to see if anyone would come out and tell me to leave, but they didn't, so I started getting up the courage to go up to the doghouse to see what was going on. I developed fantasies of showing up when they were short-handed and getting a job there instead of at the ranch, all the time knowing that the laws that applied to my dad's rig would be the same for that one. It was federalized and removed any individual idea of right and wrong, it was the law and everyone had to obey, whether they agreed, or not.

I opened the door and got out. No one was walking around, checking things, which did not happen on the rig dad managed. There was most often someone out and about at his. I went up the steps leading to the doghouse. The handrails were filthy, so I kept my hands to my side and tromped up step by step. I got to the landing where the metal door stood open.

I looked in. It seemed as if the whole crew was there in the doghouse. The driller was standing at the "knowledge box" writing something in the forms. The other dirty-faced members of the crew looked at me when I came in. They said nothing, just stared at me. I walked past some lockers and looked out the open door on the far end of the doghouse.

"Just drillin'?" I asked, knowing the answer, but letting them know I knew something of what was going on.

"Finally," one of them said and they all chuckled, except the driller.

"How deep are ya?" I asked, imitating the sorts of things I had heard my dad ask when he came into the doghouse.

"Thirty-five-sixty-three," the driller said. "Lookin' for a job?"

"Not really, why you short-handed?"

"Naw, not right now."

"I got a job on a hay farm in Walden. I'm only sixteen."

They seemed surprised by that and I wondered if I couldn't have bluffed my way into a job. I would probably make more money working for them for a week than I would in a month on the farm, probably two months.

"Gotta be eighteen," the driller said.

"I figured."

"Didn't used to be that way," the driller said, irritated by the change. "We used to be able to do a little shuck and jive with the books and get a guy to work as long as he was a good hand. Pay him cash sometimes, if it worked out that way. Not anymore, though."

"If you could, I'd do it," I said. "I don't have any of my clothes with me, though."

"You worked rigs before?" one of the hands asked me, the derrick hand, I thought.

"Filled in some for my dad, just a day or so."

They nodded, understanding that from other experiences.

"Have a look around, if you want," the driller said. "Don't get hurt, though."

I passed through the doghouse and out onto the floor. It was only then that I realized how much different my dad's operation was from others. They had tools sticking out of holes in the top of the handrails, or pipe wrenches latched onto the handrails, the handles sticking out into the walkway. There was a leaking valve wrapped with rags and taped up so the gray drilling mud wouldn't spray all over the place, but it still made a mess on the floor under the valve that no one seemed interested in cleaning up, if even to just keep up with it.

It didn't look like a safe place to work. Hoses were scattered and looped up in the air; pop cans and sandwich bags were scattered around an overfull trashcan. I had enough and went back into the doghouse.

"Thanks, I better get to the farm. I enjoyed it, though."

"See ya," the driller said and the others nodded, if they did anything at all.

I went back down the stairs wondering how they could work in an atmosphere like that, nothing being taken care of and all of them sitting in the doghouse. It was vastly different from what I was used to.

I drove back down the narrow lane and met a pickup full of men coming the other way. It had to be evening tour showing up for work. We passed each other without acknowledgment and went on our way. I turned onto the highway and continued my journey to Walden. It was close to four when I got there and I drove around town looking it over, so I would know what was available and where to get it.

There were a couple of convenience stores, bars and outfitters on main street. A big inn sat in the middle of town, with a huge lobby. Four-wheel-drive pickups with steel grille guards covering the front were lined up and parked diagonally in front of the sidewalk. Some of them had tire chains looped around the grille guards for winter use. Walden was a town that was accustomed to deep snows and roaming wildlife. A little way out of town in all directions were barriers that could be swung over the roadway to close it when the roads were impassable. It had a rustic look, log buildings and old wooden, false-fronted stores.

I bought a pop and a candy bar at the convenience store where a pretty girl with dirty blonde hair worked. She had the look of a rugged country girl, accustomed to fixing her own flats and able to dig a car out of the snow. I could tell I looked different from what she was used to, with my straw cowboy hat, jeans and shirt. The guys roaming around wore their felt hats year-round, some of them wore coveralls with no shirt, some had shirts and they all seemed to revel in possessing that which had been worn out long ago.

"You new in town?" she asked when I paid.

"Yeah."

"I could tell."

I knew it was some sort of dig, some swipe at me for being a tenderfoot or something; for not being a hillbilly like the others I saw.

"How's that?" I asked, challenging her.

"In a town this small, anything new stands out."

"I suppose," I said, taking my things. "There a phone around?"

"Sure, outside, around the corner."

"Thank you."

"Any time."

I went out and called the number on the paper.

"This is Lane Daniels; I was supposed to call when I got into town."

Mr. Jeffers gave me directions to the ranch, which was down a block from the convenience store and all the way out, then on the left. I would see it, he assured me.

I went back around the front of the store to my car and got in. I looked through the window at the girl, nice enough, I guessed. I started the car and backed out, followed the directions and he was right, I saw it. It was the only thing on that side of the road for a mile or better out of town. I pulled into the drive, past the house to an open area across from a long building to the west of the yard. I pulled up next to a tractor and got out.

A group of young men were gathered in a circle, talking. I didn't want to interrupt, so I sat on the fender of the Ford and finished drinking the pop. The others shot glances at me and talked, then looked away and then back. A tall, dark-haired guy broke out of the group and came over to me while the others walked to the long building.

"You must be Lane, I'm Billy."

"Nice to meet you," I said, extending a hand that was gripped firmly and let go.

"I'll show you around," he said, waving me along.

I followed him to the long building.

"This is the bunkhouse," he said as we reached the door and went in.

The others were already on their bunks, or standing in the middle of the room.

"Four bunks, only one left on the top, put your things in this storage area," he said, pointing to sliding doors. "Bathroom is right there, only a shower, sink and toilet, but it works. Dinner is at the main house, or you can eat in town, if you got the money, up to you. We start work at six and get done when we get done, but we try to keep it at six, that's the plan anyway. Any questions?"

"Not yet," I said. "Might have some as we go along."

"You grew up on a ranch?"

"Small one."

"Know how to drive a tractor?"

"Since I was eight."

"Dale will get you started in the morning, show you where to grease. Grease every day, the tractor and the equipment. You'll be running a fluffer to start, then we'll see where we go from there."

I nodded.

When he left we made the introductions. There were two guys from New York, a sort of summer job arrangement with Kodak there in association to the one near Loveland. One of the New Yorkers was a big guy, over six feet with a broad chest and brown hair named Sean. The other one was blonde with blue eyes, shorter but just as stout named Cal. They looked like jocks to me, muscles puffed up by weight machines. The blonde was my height. The other fellow was an older guy, probably forty, named Jim. He was a former Merchant Marine. I didn't know what that was, having never been anywhere near an ocean, ships or any of that. I had rarely ever been at sea level. He said he helped supply the military on a cargo vessel.

We were called to supper at the house. It was a good meal of beef roast, mashed potatoes and gravy. Bread was passed around and we had tea to drink. I met Dale and his wife Ginny. Billy was their son, a veterinary student at CSU in Fort Collins. There was another brother, Paul, who would help if needed, but he lived in Steamboat Springs.

After all of the excitement, it wasn't hard to get to sleep and I had barely laid down when I drifted off.

CHAPTER THIRTEEN

I woke up to the sound of the others shuffling to get ready. It was after five in the morning and the unfamiliar surroundings confused me for a second or two. I got up, waited my turn, brushed my teeth and went out into the yard. The others were eating breakfast at the house, but I rarely ate breakfast, not since I was a kid. I knew it was said to be important, but I found it annoying and it left a heavy feeling in my stomach for most of the day ruining whatever lunch I might come across.

Meadowlarks were warbling as the sun poked up over the mountains to the east, which was an oddity for me, having grown up on the Front Range, where all of the mountains were to the west. Being surrounded by mountain peaks in Walden was disorienting. Without the sun in the east, I wouldn't know which direction I was facing.

Dew was heavy on the weeds surrounding the tractor with the fluffer attached to it. A fluffer was a piece of equipment with fingers attached to spinning wheels, that effectively gathered loose hay distributed by the cutting process and brought it into a tight row for the baler, saving hay and over several sections of land resulted in a massive benefit, two or three bales per forty acres.

I looked about the yard for a grease gun and found one lying on an old hay trailer, where pipe wrenches and crescent wrenches of different sizes were scattered. I checked to make sure there was enough grease, it was half full. It might not be enough; I would have to see. I went back to the tractor and started there. I checked the oil and fuel before I started greasing in the pattern I was accustomed, which was to start in front of the left rear tire and work my way clockwise around the tractor from there.

I ran out of grease by the time I got around to the rear hitch where numerous pivot points were. Some of the others were starting to come out of the house, so I pulled the plunger out of the back of the grease gun, moved it into the notch and unscrewed the top. I figured I would have it ready by the time someone arrived to tell me where they kept the replacement tubes, but no one came walking toward me; they all went back to the bunkhouse. I looked at my watch, it was five-forty. With nothing else to do, I wandered over to a small shed, the wood was weathered and gray, the door hung by rusty hinges that creaked when I pulled the door open. There was a trash can just inside the door and I dropped the used tube into it as I looked around. Inside were a number of other tools: shovels, saws, picks and the like. On a shelf was an open box of grease tubes. I reached in and grabbed one, pulled the plastic cap off the back and inserted it into the grease gun. I pulled on the metallic ring, exposing the grease. Every time I did that, it reminded me of the small cans of pudding that had the same sort of lid. I licked the pudding top, but didn't think of licking that top; I dropped it in the trash can. There was a box of rags on a shelf and I grabbed one to wipe the grease off the zerks.

I returned to the tractor with the grease gun reassembled and ready. I pumped on it a few times to get the grease to come out of the flexible hose, then knocked the grease off on a weed. Dale came out of the house and angled toward me when he saw I was greasing the fluffer. He carried a brown paper sack in one hand.

"See you got an early start."

"Just getting this out of the way while I waited." I said, straightening.

"You know we serve breakfast, too, right?"

"Yeah, I don't eat breakfast much."

"Here's your lunch, take it with you."

I took the paper bag that had a sandwich, a bag of potato chips and a can of pop that would be warm by the time I could open it.

"Thanks."

Dale looked the tractor over, a disappointed look on his face.

"We wipe the zerks off around here," he said.

I pulled a rag out of my back pocket.

"I wanted to leave the grease until someone had a chance to make sure I got them all. It's a new piece of machinery, I could miss one the first time around."

Dale looked at me surprised at the thought I had put into the act. He inspected the job more thoroughly after that, searching for a zerk that I missed. He found three, one on the tractor and two on the fluffer. I wiped them all down after that.

"This tractor starts on gasoline, but runs on diesel."

I had never heard of that.

"It has oil and gas; I didn't check the diesel. New one on me."

"It's right here," he said, pointing to a fuel cap just behind the gas cap. I thought they went to the same place. He opened it. "Needs diesel, there's a can over there."

After fueling the tractor, getting it started and taking a test spin around the yard, he turned me loose on a field a half mile from the house. He showed me how to raise the fluffer when I was just driving from one place to another.

Dale was a tough boss, I could tell. After all I had done, before work even started, he didn't mention that I had done a good job, or anything. I didn't expect it, but it would have been nice to have been recognized as knowing what I was doing.

I drove the tractor to the field, let down the fluffer, engaged the PTO shaft that spun the wheels with the long, metallic fingers and started going over the path of recently cut hay. That was it, that was my job. I was supposed to do that field and the one across the ditch. The only excitement of the day came when I was crossing from one field to the next and the tractor tire slipped on some loose ground and the rear tire went into the ditch. I had to put the tractor in low gear to get out and maneuver cleverly around so the tire on the fluffer didn't go into the same hole.

It was a long day of following the trails of hay. The sun was brutal at that altitude without the atmosphere to block the UV rays. Walden was four or five thousand feet higher than Loveland and Loveland was at forty-five-hundred feet. I could feel my face was sunburned and I kept pulling my hat lower and lower on my head to cast a shadow over my face. I might have to wear my cap instead.

I didn't know how long I was supposed to work. They said something about twelve hours, but six was fast approaching and I only had a little more to do. I didn't know where to go after that, so I kept working until the field was done, then drove the tractor back to the yard. Billy was waiting for me. It was seven.

"Where have you been? You almost missed dinner," he said, when I turned the tractor off and closed the fuel valve.

"I only had a little more to do and it seemed a waste to go back to the field I was working on when I could start a new one in the morning."

"You got them both done?"

"Yeah, that's what Dale wanted."

"I don't think he expected you to get both done. I think he expected you to start on the second one, but that's all."

I shook my head, how was I supposed to know?

"We work 'til six," he said.

"That sounded like a general idea, not a solid rule," I replied, feeling like I was being chastised, like I had done something wrong and feeling the need to defend myself.

"We need to eat before it gets cold," Billy said, walking toward the house, leaving me to follow along. "Wash up before you sit down."

There was only me and Billy at the supper table. We met the rest coming out when we went in. As I was finishing, I looked up at Billy. I had come to the conclusion that he was mad at me for making him wait to eat.

"Don't bother waiting for me," I said. "Go ahead and eat,

I'll be along, or I'll get something somewhere else."

Billy didn't know that I usually didn't eat breakfast and I didn't like lunch at school, so I was used to eating only supper most days and that was done at seven or seven-thirty a lot of the time.

"Stop at six and I won't have to wait," he said.

I didn't want to argue, but it went against everything I had been taught to stop work only an hour or so away from finishing a job. I didn't think I was capable of doing that. At our place, we were sent to do a job and unwelcome at the house until that job was done and done right. I don't know what sort of things went on at the Jeffers place, but that was how I was raised.

When I got back to the bunkhouse, it was the first time I had a chance to socialize with the others aside from the initial introductions. I went in and waited my turn to take a shower.

"Where were you?" Sean asked, bare chested, holding a towel.

"Finishing a field," I said, digging in my bag for my shower kit.

"We stop work at six."

"So, I heard."

"You tryin' to impress the boss, or what?"

"I'm trying to do my job."

He studied me for a minute as he hung his towel up on the end of the bunk to dry.

"They said you were raised on a ranch."

"That's right."

"That make you something?"

"Makes me a ranch hand, I guess."

"And, we're not, because we're from New York, is that it?"

I straightened up, recognizing that I was going to have to put up with Sean and Cal and I didn't need to have a conflict with them right off the bat, so I figured that I would have to set some things straight.

"I don't care what you are or what you do. I try to do the

job the way I'm asked to do it, that's all. I don't look at what someone else does and make a comment on that one way or another, because its none of my business. If you do a great job, the boss will know; if you do a lousy job, the boss will know. I don't see myself anywhere in that equation and I don't intend to insert myself into it, either."

That was how my dad wanted it; how he taught his boys to be. He did not have the time nor inclination to listen to one of his boys talk about the other and whether they were doing their jobs or not. I found that out the first time I complained about it. He was pretty insistent that I never mention that sort of thing again and it stuck. I did what I was asked, to the best of my ability and the rest of the world could go to hell for all I knew.

"You tryin' to say something, cowboy?" he asked derisively.

"No, I pretty much said what I meant."

Cal came out of the restroom drying his hair, wearing his jeans and flip-flops.

"Cowboy, you're alive!" he said, before he recognized the tension in the air.

At least they were calling me "cowboy" instead of shit-kicker, or goat roper.

"Still kickin'," I said, on my way to the restroom with my towel and shower kit. I knew they would get together in my absence and figure out how to attack me from then on. Sean wasn't used to being stood up to and he wouldn't let it go at that.

Sean and Cal thought they were dealing with some idiot who had not been through the fire like I had. They would try things that worked back home, but I had seen it all; all the ways of demeaning and ridiculing me; all the ways of goading me into a conflict. I could brush them off with standard retorts for a while and it would take them a lot longer to get under my skin than they thought, because I could smell a trap. I already knew how they would go about it. They would continue to ask me leading questions and try to put words in my mouth until they felt like I had gone far enough that they could take offense. If they only knew how worn out and tired those tactics were, they would leap right to the confrontation.

I stripped down and stepped into the warm shower. The water turned muddy as soon as it hit my body. It washed thirteen hours of dust out of my hair and off of my body. I scrubbed my face and another wave of dirty water cascaded down, swirling into the drain. I didn't stop lathering up until the water cleared to crystal clean. I couldn't reach my back and felt like it was probably still dirty, a fact I confirmed when I dried it off and the towel turned a slightly brown color.

When I came out of the shower, I could see that they had had their first powwow and had established that I was to be challenged, not accepted the way Cal had when he came out of the shower. There would be no more light-hearted teasing.

I put on a clean shirt, feeling their eyes on me the whole time, looking for something to ridicule.

"You play any sports?" Sean asked, sensing the answer would be no and he could ridicule that. It told me that he did play sports, probably football or baseball and was likely good at it, too.

"Just rodeo."

"Rodeo ain't a sport," he laughed, nudging Cal.

"It's the only original American sport," I replied, getting ready to leave. I had a car and they didn't. I could drive into town to get away from them and I would. I certainly wasn't going to play their game, by their rules all night.

"What about football?"

I had had this argument before with jocks at school. They did not understand that I had been through all of it before. They thought they were original in their derision and they weren't, so they were at a disadvantage, not me.

"Football is played with a ball and therefore a derivation of every other ball-oriented sport," I said, getting to the part I liked the best, the one that drove football players nuts. "In that way, it's not much different from bowling."

"Bowling!?" Sean screamed. "Bowling!?"

I thought he was going to hit me right there.

"It's played with a ball, right?"

"Well, yeah, but it's nothing like bowling."

"Is there any ball in rodeo?" I asked, waiting for a second. "You don't know anything about rodeo, so I'll answer, no, there is not. Is there a ball in bowling? Is there a ball in golf? Baseball? Basketball? Rugby? Tennis? Bocce Ball?"

"Bocce Ball, what's that?" Jim asked.

"An Italian game played by old men," I said, enjoying the look on Sean's face. I had researched to topic. "Rodeo, was invented by cowboys in the American West and involved the skills they used in their daily work, breaking horses, roping steers, like that. Absolutely, one-hundred-percent American sport."

"It ain't a sport," Sean said, sullen.

I shrugged and dug my keys out of my pocket. I looked at both of them.

"You can say it all you want, but pitting your skill against another human is ordinary, pitting it against a raging bull is an act of courage."

I walked out and to my car, knowing that we had just concluded round one and that there would be many more to come, but I didn't have to put up with it for hours on end. I could drive into town, even if I did nothing other than sit at the park, I would find it better than listening to their nonsense.

As I got into my car, I wished that Mr. Schmidt could have been there to witness public speaking in real-time and understand my contempt for a class in oral communications.

I drove to the convenience store where the girl worked and bought a can of pop.

"You're back," she said, when I put the can on the counter.

"Never left," I said.

"You live here, then?"

"Sort of, I'm working for the summer."

"Oh."

I went outside as the sun was setting. It was cool. The

temperature fluctuations were significant at that altitude. I stood by the car and watched the activity in town. Pickups were the most common mode of transportation. People walked from place to place more frequently than they did in Loveland, largely because nothing was more than three blocks away. I walked down the street, looking at the different stores and came upon a laundromat and checked to see how much it cost to do a load of laundry. I watched a couple walk from the inn across the street to the bar. Cars would pull up to the little store and several people would get out, as if it was an outing more than a casual stop. Tourists would come through on occasion and were easy to spot after noting the earmarks of the locals for a while.

It was about ten when I got back to the bunkhouse. I pulled up into the yard and killed the lights so as not to wake anyone up when I pulled in. I was careful not to make any noise as I entered, stripped out of my clothes and got into bed.

I lay awake, staring at the ceiling for a long time, thinking about things and wishing I could read a book. I brought the one I was reading with me, but there was no light by which to read. An hour later I drifted off to sleep.

CHAPTER FOURTEEN

One day stretched into the next at the farm. I forced a routine that eliminated Sean and Cal from my life as much as possible, making the job a lot easier to enjoy. After supper every night, I would get into my car, drive into town and park in a wide area where semis sometimes parked. I would roll down the window and read my book, letting a cool breeze pass through. I didn't read very steady, other things would catch my attention and I'd stop and focus on that. Sometimes, I would talk to the girl at the little store for a few minutes. Often, there would be friends of hers loafing around inside the store, talking to her while I was there and I would pay and leave.

All of this confounded not only Sean and Cal, but Billy, too. They kept wanting to know where I went and what I did when I left every night. They were starting to make up things, trying them out in passing.

"You got a girl in town?"
"Nope."
"You go to the library?"
"There ain't no library."
"A museum?"
"Nope."
"You have friends in town?"
"Nope."

If pressed, I suppose I would tell them that I left to be gone, with nowhere to go and nothing to do and it didn't matter, because I didn't have to listen them talk. But, I saved that as a last resort, because it would start another round of accusations and insinuations, trying to goad me into a conflict. As it was, the not knowing bugged them and that was enough.

One night, three weeks into the job, I was getting low on money and gas and decided to stay at the bunkhouse instead of going into town. I recognized that it would cause trouble, but I had every right to be in the bunkhouse as much as anyone else.

I ate with the rest and took a shower, then with all of us in the bunkhouse, I climbed into the top bunk. There were some books and magazines kept at the bunkhouse, not generally things I would read, but I picked one of the books, a Western by Zane Grey. I read it while Sean and Cal played a board game on the card table in the middle of the room. Jim was dozing in his bunk below me; I could hear his heavy breathing for a while, then he would wake up and say something to Cal or Sean, then the heavy breathing would resume.

Instead of talking directly to me, Sean and Cal had developed a habit of talking about me loud enough for me to hear without having to endure my rebuttal. They could get out of it by saying that they weren't talking to me.

"I think cowboy got dumped by his girlfriend," Cal said, moving his piece.

"I think her boyfriend finally got wise and threatened to kick his ass, so he's hiding out."

"Cops might be looking for him."

"A loan shark, maybe," Sean suggested.

"Do they have those in this hick town?"

"Good question."

I read the book and ignored their attempts to get me talking. Billy came in, looked at me in the top bunk.

"Lane, can I talk to you for a minute?"

I got down off the bunk and followed him outside. We walked away from the bunkhouse and he turned around.

"You haven't been around much, so I haven't had time to talk to you."

There was nothing to respond to, so I waited for him to continue.

"Are you having trouble with any of the others?"

"No."

"There's no problem?"

"No. I'm used to deciding who I spend time with, it's not forced on me like it is at the bunkhouse, but that's a condition of the job, so I'm doing the best I can with it."

"They haven't threatened you, or anything?"

"Not at all."

"Okay, I just wanted to be sure."

His duty done, Billy went back to the house and I went back to the bunkhouse.

"What did he want?" Sean asked when I got back into the room.

"Nothing."

"He called you outside for nothing?"

"Yeah."

Sean's skepticism beamed from his face and he rolled his eyes.

"Hey, cowboy, you got a girlfriend?" Cal asked.

"No."

"No?"

"That's what I said."

"I think he does," he said, addressing Sean. "I think he's too ashamed to show a picture of her, because she looks like your uncle Fred."

They laughed uproariously, enough to wake up Jim for a moment. I ignored them and got up on the bunk. I picked up the book and opened it.

"You wanna see a picture of my girlfriend?" Cal asked.

"What for?"

Cal was pulling his wallet out and looking through some photos that he had.

"You might want to see what a real girl looks like. They don't look like sheep, or these cowgirls with cow shit all over their clothes."

Cal held a picture out to me. I took it and looked at it. She was a pretty girl, but then, I figured that much. Sean was a good-looking kid, even I had to admit that, but Cal seemed sort of ordinary. He had a good-looking girlfriend, so he must have been all right.

"Pretty," I said, handing it back. "Blonde, though."

"Yeah, what about it?"

"Blondes are bitches," I said, not really believing it so much as exerting it as an opinion that would drive him crazy. If he was going to get into my space, he was going to pay for it.

"She is not! My girlfriend isn't a bitch, is she Sean?"

"Sweet girl," Sean said.

"See there! How can you say that? You don't even know her."

"I know blondes," I said.

"Take that shit back, she ain't a bitch."

"I didn't say she was. I said blondes are bitches."

"But, she's blonde," he puffed.

"Then I gotta wonder."

Cal was red-faced angry over it all, but more so, because I didn't care if he was angry, or not. He kept trying to make me denounce my opinion, as if it mattered, but I wouldn't, because I was entitled to an opinion and I stuck by it. His only purpose in showing me the picture was to prove his superiority over me. I had no girlfriend, or an ugly one and he had a pretty one. That was the message he was intent on making, but I was used to jocks employing that tactic.

"Daniels, what kind of car do you have? Some ten-year-old piece of shit Ford ain't it? I have a new Camaro, wanna see a picture?" It was the same thing over and over and Cal was no different.

When he realized he was getting nowhere with me, he dropped it, but I had insulted him and it wouldn't die that easily. The next day, I was working on a field two miles south of the farm. It was an eighty-acre field and would take me most of the day. The sun was beating down on me and I pulled out my can of tobacco and took a pinch. It felt odd between my fingers and when I put it in my lip, I could tell something was wrong. I looked into the can and it was filled with coffee grounds.

"Huh," I said, putting the lid back on. It would have to do in a pinch, no pun intended.

An hour later Dale came by with the paper bag lunch that I left at the house. He brought it and a jug of water out of the pickup.

"Forgot your lunch," he said, handing it to me.

I shrugged, because I hadn't forgotten it, I just didn't take it. I was getting sick of sandwiches and potato chips every day and thought I would skip lunch and wait for supper. I drank heavily of the ice water, though, having inhaled dust most of the morning.

"The thing I could use, if you don't mind, is a dip."

"What's wrong with yours?"

"Someone filled the can with coffee grounds last night. No big deal. They didn't take my wallet and it was in the same pants. I'll get another one tonight, but I could use a pinch right now."

Dale tossed a can to me.

"I've got more at the house. You can pay me back later."

"Thanks."

Dale drove off and I spent the rest of the day finishing up that field and started on another, but I wasn't going to be able to finish it, so I stopped at six like I was supposed to. When I got back to the farm, I parked the tractor and went into the bunkhouse. Sean and Cal weren't back, yet, so I got into the shower first and was combing my hair when they appeared at the open door of the bathroom, shoulder to shoulder, as if to block my exit. I looked up at their faces in the mirror. They stared at me with hard eyes of hatred.

"How was your chewing tobacco?" Sean asked.

"Coffee grounds, funny shit," I said. "I laughed for about a half hour." I put the comb back in the shower kit. "I had to borrow a can from Dale, but he had more, so it was no big deal."

"You ratted us out?" Cal asked.

"You did that? I thought it was Jim."

"What if we did?" Sean asked, making the direct challenge.

I looked in the mirror at both of them and chuckled. When I was done, I turned around and pushed my way through them, leading with the shower kit. They let me pass, I hadn't expected that. The same thing had happened at school a few times, but the hoods didn't let me out, they beat the hell out of me. Other times, they shoved me around for a while. The New Yorkers did nothing.

I could see how it was going to be from then on, though. Their little prank didn't have the desired effect, so they would try bigger and bigger things until they got the response they wanted, which was for me to give them an excuse to beat the crap out of me. Eventually, they would get around to the car and that would set me off, but I'd have to fight them both, sooner or later. If they had an inclination to take me alone, they would have done that. It became clear in the restroom that they'd team up.

I hadn't liked living with them from the start and then it escalated to where I would have to subject myself and my stuff to their pranks. If the job had been something I loved or it paid better than it did, or the pay arrangement was better, I would have stayed, but I decided that the job wasn't worth the crap I was going to have to take and I would eventually get fired for getting into a fight, which had already been explained to us as a group.

At the end of the meal, when we were finished and getting ready to leave, I looked up at Dale.

"I'm gonna need my pay, boss," I said.

"What? Why?"

"Aw, I don't wanna be rude, let's just say I have better things to do."

Dale was alarmed, it meant losing an employee that did as he was told, worked hard and took care of the equipment. But, maybe, they should think about better living conditions. It was a lot to ask people to work all day and be forced into tight quarters. There was a lot they could do to make it a better place to work, but bringing any of that up would be rude in my mind.

The New Yorkers looked at each other, then at me, then at Dale, who was staring at them, a flush of anger rising in his cheeks.

"You're gonna leave me short, right in the middle of the season?"

I shrugged. "As far as I know, I come out, work hard and do a good job," I said. "That ought to be enough."

"That's right," Billy said. "Can you explain this?"

"I could," I said, looking at Dale and his wife, "but I ain't gonna sit at someone's table and complain. You all have been good to me. Let's let it go at that."

I stood up, because if I stayed, we would just go over it again and again and I didn't want it to turn into what it naturally would, which is me detailing what I didn't like about the job, them getting angry about it and saying rude stuff to me in return, to which I would get more explicit and more offensive.

"I'll get your pay, minus your draws and meet you outside."

I took my plate to the sink as usual, washed it off and set it on the counter. When I stepped out into the cool, evening air, it was as if I had not taken a full breath in weeks. The air filled my lungs with the sudden promise of freedom and I sucked it in. I knew it wasn't a good thing to quit a job in the middle and I felt a twinge of shame over it, but there were no surprises about what was going to happen if I stayed. I knew they thought it could be worked out somehow and keep me around, but the only way to settle things was to fight it out in the bunkhouse, then, we would all get fired, so what difference did it make?

Dale came out with cash in his hand.

"Lane," he said, to get my attention.

I turned around to face him, looking him dead in the eyes as I was taught to do.

"Here's what I owe you, it's only two-hundred, but the figures are right."

"No doubt," I replied, knowing him as an honest man.

"I wish there was some way you could stay. Tell me, though, is it the New Yorkers? They were the ones who messed with your chew can, right? Is that what this is all about?"

"Mr. Jeffers, that's only a small thing. I didn't quit over that. I quit, because I would sooner or later beat the crap out of one of them and the other one would jump me from behind. I know that like I know where I am. I'm not guessing here, I've been through it, before. I appreciate your concern and I wish it didn't have to be this way, but…"

"What if I got rid of them?" he asked.

"Then, you'd be two short instead of one," I replied. "I've thought this out."

Dale handed me the money and I walked away with the satisfaction that he considered getting rid of both of them to keep me, but it wasn't enough. I would still have to endure the living conditions that I found annoying at best. I would still want to get away every night.

I drove out of the driveway and into town. I put a few dollars' worth of gas in the car to get me where it was cheaper in Fort Collins and left Walden behind. That night, driving through the towering pines that lined the highway, I plugged in an eight-track tape and turned it up loud. The country twang of Merle Haggard poured out of the speakers and echoed off the trees.

I could see the spire of lights from the drilling rig that was still at the same location as when I had come almost a month before. They must be having trouble, or the formations were harder up there than they were near Greeley, where my dad's rig drilled most of the time. His rig was hardly ever on the same location for more than a week. I felt a desire to stop and check the rig out again, but it was a nostalgic thing, with no purpose behind it, so I didn't.

In the dark, on the empty canyon road, I drove swiftly along, feeling the weight of the car shift as I went around a corner; I could hear the slight squeal of the tires at times. The river flowed heavy with water, fluorescent in the moonlight. My hands gripped the wheel tight, prepared to swerve if a deer or elk leapt into the road. I had passed several deer already, munching on grass just beyond the asphalt.

Outlines of cabins slid by the side windows and occasionally a house with a light on in the kitchen, but otherwise dark. Stores and lodges were dark. Nothing was open, not even at eight o'clock. There was a bar about halfway down the canyon and it looked like an interesting place to be: cars and pickups were parked outside, the neon Coors and Budweiser signs beckoned and I could see in my mind the events taking place within. I imagined it as an adult Masonville, with real drinks, tourists mixing with locals and a jukebox playing favorites over the crack of balls striking each other on the pool table; grizzled men with pool sticks clutched in their dirty hands and beer foam on their mustaches.

I thought of Masonville after passing the bar and imagined it as it was, with teenagers roaming around, pretending to be older, acting the part of the actual goings on in the real bar. Masonville was a pretend sort of place in my mind, practice for being older, learning how to drink and act in public without making an ass of oneself. And, that made me think of my friends, Ronnie, Zach, Juan, Frank, Brad and my brother Jon, all of whom would take a turn at Masonville from time to time. It wasn't a place that one would go every day or even every weekend. There was much more to do, there were dances and parties out in the hills at abandoned stone quarries where the earth had been hollowed out almost a century before, leaving gaping holes in the side of the foothills where we would build a fire and consume beer and liquor with older cowboys and girls.

The night wore on as I drove, cognizant of Deadman's Curve up ahead somewhere, ready for it, like I was ready for deer to jump out, but still putting the accelerator down, feeling sure that there would be no cops up there to give me a ticket and the faster I could go, the sooner I would be out of the canyon and back on familiar ground.

I thought about Tom, too, back in Kansas, working at a restaurant as a cook. That seemed strange to me, since the only sorts of jobs I had ever had were like the one I had just left. I wouldn't know what to do in a restaurant, but Tom told me about working there as a dishwasher the year before and word had gotten back, that he was working there again as a cook. I thought about Annie, too, what she was doing, how she felt about Tom leaving. What was the attraction? How easy it was for them to find each other, how quickly they had become comfortable. The times I had been with girls, it was awkward and even contentious to some degree, not like it was with Tom and Annie.

Lost in thought, I mechanically moved the wheel, following the snake-like double yellow line in the middle of the road. Then, Deadman's Curve. I didn't know where it was, but I knew it when I got there. It looked like all of the other curves in the road bending away from the jagged rock wall, but Deadman's Curve turned sharply, much sharper than the rest. It was the lulling effect of all the others that made it so dangerous. The LTD leaned over, the weight pushing to the right-front corner of the car, the tire digging in and starting to slide just a little. There was no time to brake, I took my foot off the accelerator at the start of the corner and that was all I had time for, I was in the middle of it, struggling to keep the car on the pavement in a second. The front tire hit dirt and slid, then the back end started to come around. I worked the wheel with short, jabbing attempts to get the front tire out of the shallow ditch at the side of the road, as it threatened to guide my car into the rock wall. Then I was out and back on the road, my heart beating like that of a rabbit after a chase; my breath came short and shallow.

I drove through LaPorte and Fort Collins at night, something I was unaccustomed to, with unpredictable traffic and unfamiliar landmarks, but I made it to Loveland and through town out to our place. It was eleven by the time I got there and the house was dark. I pulled into the yard. Dad's company pickup was there and so was Jon's. I didn't want to wake them up, so I snuck around to Scott's room and tapped on the window. Scott came to the window, startled and surprised when he saw me. He pushed the window up and I crawled in.

"What are you doing here?" he whispered.

"That didn't work out," I whispered back. "They had some New Yorkers working there and we had to live together and that was just a fight waiting to happen. I just got tired of it."

"You should let mom and dad know you're home."

"Shhhh, no, 'cause I'm not. I'm just stopping by to see you and let you know what I got planned."

"You're not staying?" he asked, his face registering his disapproval.

"No. I've had a taste, a sample of the freedom that's out there in the world and I want more of it. As long as I can work, I can do whatever I want, be wherever I want to be. This is what I've been waiting for and thinking about for years, the idea of living life the way it is. I don't have any fantasies or stupid dreams about it. It's full of hard work and saving money to pay for things like rent and food, I know that, but just the idea of being somewhere, because I want to be there, instead of having to be there, because I can't get away, is pushing me on.

"All the way down the canyon, I kept thinking about life, about even reading a book in a place I pay for, in a town I want to be and walking to the refrigerator to get pop or milk that I bought and make a sandwich from ham and cheese that I put there with my money from working my job. All of that, as simple as all of that sounds, is what I want. To be free from coercion; to not do anything I don't want to do, without parents or anyone telling me when to go somewhere or when to come back is it, the magic that I need right now."

"Because you don't want to be told what to do? That's why you're leaving?"

"It's more than that, it's proving to myself that I can make it on my own. It's proving to the stupid principal and that arrogant Miss Tanner that I can do it already, that they have nothing left to teach me. Any skills I need to survive on my own have already been learned and applied. Their classes are all nonsense. Their value does not exist and I can prove it by taking this chance and doing it myself. It puts the lie to their stupid world, their made-up world of academics where one letter in a box is somehow worth hours and hours of reading boring, monotonous rambling words and another letter is punishment for not doing it. It puts the lie to the idea that they can control my future by which letter they put in the box, because that's all they have as leverage over me, that letter and the belief that it makes a difference."

"Well, you can't get into a good college with shitty grades," Scott said.

"That's the point!" I said, too enthusiastically, too loudly and I quieted my voice, whispering again. "It only matters if you're going to college and I am not. I have no interest at all in more school. I just don't. On top of that, I love to work, especially outside, away from offices and halls. I've had enough of that already and it feels like prison. Going to college would only ensure that I remained there for the rest of my life, chained to a desk, pale from fluorescent lights, trapped by happy-speak to avoid resentment and anger from the other inmates of that insane future. You can see that, can't you? You're like me, you can feel the same things, right?"

Scott wavered and I realized that I had never asked him what his future would hold, what he wanted to do. I considered work on the ranch and on the rig as the only reasonable goal, the only thing that would make me happy and therefore him, too. But, I hadn't talked to him about it.

"Are you thinking about college?" I asked.

He didn't answer, but I could tell that he was. He saw value in that future, that he had some vision for his life that was benefitted by higher education.

"You might not feel the same, I understand, but I can't deny how I feel any more than you can, so I'm leaving in pursuit of my future, my world where things make sense."

CHAPTER FIFTEEN

I left that night, having gathered a few more of my things from my room, sneaking up the stairs and silently going through my drawers, carrying clothes and useful trinkets down in the dark to keep from waking anyone up, then climbed out of Scott's window and out to my car.

I knew I was going to Kansas, though I kept that thought buried while I pretended to be giving consideration to every other state in the nation. It was the only way to be fair to my future, but I went east, eliminating several states by that act alone.

There was a sense of nostalgia as I passed by my grandfather's old farm on the east side of town. The barn was still there, standing solidly, but out of place amid the industrial park that had consumed most of the farmland he once owned. Highway 34 had taken over the smaller roads that led him from Yuma to Loveland in the 1940s and just being on it brought back visions of his old Model T and everything they owned on it or in the trailer towed behind.

I was mentally saying goodbye to my past in Loveland with the intent to leave it all behind. I had no plan in mind, no set amount of time I intended to be gone. I assumed that I might not come back, except for some family gathering, a wedding or funeral. Who knew what I would find out in the world, or who?

That thought jumped me to another consideration. Was I so discouraged by my prospects in Loveland that I had given up on finding a girl there? Is that what it was all about? On a subconscious level, deep inside my brain, had I come to that conclusion and everything else was built around that? Was my demand for freedom really a desperate attempt to find love?

Those thoughts came to me as I drove in the dark along the highway, several other taillights and headlights were the only things moving with me through the dark. That didn't feel right. I hadn't consciously come to that conclusion; I didn't feel like I had exhausted all options in Loveland. There were girls, there were possibilities. I felt confused by girls, especially after Mandy pulled her little trick of leading me on only to shut me down publicly. That still puzzled me, not knowing if I was misreading what she wanted from me, or if my inability to take a hint had, along the line, angered her to the point that to save face, she had to reject me and to do it in a way that restored her self-esteem.

It was, in fact, about freedom; the ability to be somewhere where I was the only occupant, where I would not have to share a bathroom, or shower, or dinner table. After my Sophomore year, I was completely sick of people and didn't understand the depths to which that was true until I got to the bunkhouse. I had used up all the tolerance I had for them.

Greeley passed by the windshield and I was out in the farmland again, driving past farms visible only by the big yard lights that illuminated the wide areas in front of the houses. Dots of light on a black horizon, islands of humanity amid a sea of crops.

I was deep inside Kansas by the time the sun rose, blinding me as I drove east. I had worked my way down to Interstate 70 through the night, taking different roads that angled south or east. The speed limit was a mind-numbing fifty-five miles an hour, the result of an effort to save gas in reaction to an oil embargo in the early '70s. It didn't help that the scenery beyond the windows was as bland and uninteresting as the darkness. All of that added up to the fact that I was getting tired, having started work the day before at six and having not slept since. I could stop anywhere, my future was my own, but I kept driving, letting the fuel gauge dictate when and where.

It was exploration. I had never been east of the state line before and until the sun rose, I could not differentiate between

Colorado and Kansas. When the sun did rise, when that great, orange ball edged up over the horizon and spread rays of light across the fields of sunflowers lining the interstate, it was different. I felt new, no longer restricted by my family's past or my perceived future. I was just Lane Daniels, a kid, driving east in search of solitude, privacy, independent thought and individual choice.

Tom lived in a town called Fort Scott on the eastern edge of Kansas. It was as good a place to start as any, at least a visit, then on my way if I didn't like it. That was the plan in mind when I turned south at Salina, where the trees began after long stretches of nothing but sunflowers, wheat and cornfields. I angled down to Wichita, a map on the seat to confirm the route, but mostly relying on road signs pointing the way to towns and cities in sequence. Salina, Wichita, Andover, El Dorado and once I was headed toward Eureka, I would just have to follow US 54 into Fort Scott.

Interstate 135 down from Salina was just like any other, four lanes, median, periodic exits to get gas and go to the restroom. Except for the marked increase in vegetation, especially trees, it was unremarkable, but it was also where I began to feel the air grow thick and feel the precipitation held within its greater mass. The air felt wet, even more so than it did when it rained in Colorado, because once the rain was over, the sun would come out and wispy streams of evaporation would climb up from the ground and into the air, but in Kansas, the air felt so encumbered with moisture that no evaporation could take place, there was no room to put it.

Once on US 54, I started passing through small towns and could get a sense of what Kansas was about, what life there was like. Little restaurants with names like "Mom's" and "The Rusty Nail" and "Joe's" passed by, depressing little tire shops selling used tires and promising to speedily fix-a-flat, but the employees looked like it might take longer than advertised. I judged by their appearance. All of the buildings looked rundown, lacking maintenance, the wood heavy with moisture and rotting.

The newer stores, the chain stores made everything else look dilapidated and suspicious, but also homespun and intimate like the services would be provided by someone known to their customers since birth, related in some tenuous way back along a nearly forgotten lineage. It was dirty and the streets were populated by loud cars and ancient pickups, two-wheel-drive pickups that were hardly ever seen in the mountain communities of my experience. These were towns dominated by the farming community, implement dealerships more populous than car dealerships, grain elevators, farmers clogging up traffic as they moved their tractors from one field to the next over the paved roads and men wearing bib coveralls instead of jeans; women in threadbare dresses as everyday attire instead of sparkled dresses for special occasions that I was used to back home.

Then, I was close to Fort Scott, the sign said twelve miles further on. I started thinking about what I would do, where I would go first. I knew Tom worked at a place called "The Kitchen" on the south side of town, but that was all I knew. I liked it, not knowing for sure where I was going, just going. I came to a bridge and passed over the Marmaton River and a Co-op gas station and grain elevator on the south side of the river, then the street was paved with red bricks making the ride rough. I passed through the older part of town where interesting architecture was abundant and bars were plenty. The street led out to what must have been the south side of town long ago, where huge houses and enormous lawns sat amongst the protection of massive trees not quite forming an arbor over the street, but protecting the cracked sidewalks from the sun. Past that, it was as if the town began again. After the brief interlude of shade and comfort was the noisy, metallic rush of cars and trucks following highway 69 through modern stores and restaurants with the classless and utilitarian design of a shoebox. I knew "The Kitchen" had to be somewhere amongst the depressing urban construction. I saw it on the left, wooden frame, big sign, part of a chain of such restaurants nestled in one corner of the parking lot of a department store set back away from the street. I pulled the LTD in and parked in line with a number of other cars. I was covered in sweat from the long drive in the smothering heat and felt my shirt stick to my back as I leaned forward to get out.

The air was so thick, I expected to leave a hole in it as I walked to the door of the restaurant. I pulled the door and was met by cool air that was attracted to the wet spots on my shirt. I stood there for a moment, in the stream of the air conditioner and looked the place over. There were booths along the north wall, a counter like in an old-time diner, then an open dining area behind a partition of heavy wooden balusters. I didn't know if Tom was working or not, I couldn't see into the kitchen.

Other people were coming into the restaurant, so I moved along, out of the stream of cold air and took a seat at the counter. A nice-looking girl with brown hair, light brown eyes and a cute little nose was working the counter and I waited to get her attention. She served as the cashier as well, so I wasn't her first concern. She seemed bashful, something I hadn't expected of a waitress, starting and stopping a few times before she got to me.

"What'll you have?" she asked, pen poised for my response.

"A coke is fine," I said, hearing the cook flipping burgers in the back by the sound of metal scraping metal, then the hiss of the burger on the stove. "Does Tom Wilson work here?"

She pointed with her pen to the kitchen.

"You want me to tell him you're here?"

"Naw, I'll wait to see if he recognizes me."

"Suit yourself, sure you don't want some pie, or somethin'."

"I'm fine, thanks."

Moments later she set a glass of Coke in front of me, I didn't really mean a Coke, I was using it as a euphemism for pop, or cola, but that's what I ordered. I saw slivers of Tom's head when he moved into the open rectangle in the wall that separated the kitchen from the counter and dining area. Other waitresses, older waitresses came around the ends of the counter and up to the rectangle to stack plates on their arms, or to hang new pieces of paper with orders on them up on the circular metal ring.

"Kitchen special," they would holler into the rectangle.

"Order up!" would come back when several plates had been placed in the rectangle.

If I could have sat there long enough, I probably would have been able to recite the whole menu.

I saw Tom look out, duck back out of view, then stick his head back out to look at me. He stood there as if unsure whether to trust his eyes or not. Then, he came out from the kitchen and up to me.

"The hell you doin' here?"

"Long, long story," I said, "but, I'm here."

"Oh man!"

He looked at me for a minute, just soaking me up, then jumped, remembering something in the kitchen.

"Gotta go, I'm done at five," he said, backing away. "Shit."

I drank my coke and stared at the girl, the badge on her uniform said Barbara. It was a solid brown and brown plaid outfit made to look like a skimpy country-girl type thing. She was my age or a year older from all I could tell, but the more I stared at her, the redder she got, so I kept doing it.

She came over to me, leaning on her stiff arm planted on the counter.

"What are you staring at?"

"You."

"Why?"

I shrugged in response, because I didn't want to tell the truth, which was between looking at her and the stainless-steel milk dispenser, I chose her.

But, I stopped staring at her and started looking out the window at the broiling parking lot and watched people, dragging children out of cars. It was too hot to leave the windows up so they didn't. I paid for another pop and almost fell asleep, halting only when my head snapped back and I had to steady myself on the stool.

Barbara gave me a concerned look, but said nothing. I waited for Tom to get off work and when he came out of the back, he took up a seat at a booth on the north side of the room and called me over.

"Have a seat, this is the employee's booth."

I sat down across from him and looked at him.

"Wow, I didn't expect to see you here."

"I didn't expect to be here."

I told him about the job in Walden and the New Yorkers, the living arrangements and everything up until that time.

"Just drove here," he said, wagging his head.

"Yeah, what the hell. Figured I'd give this place a shot, see what's happening, then maybe move on. I got a couple of months before school starts, might as well see what I can until then."

"I called Annie a couple of times," he said, shrugging.

"Yeah?"

"Yeah, but you know how it is. There's girls here, too and she's a long way away."

"So, the weddings off?" I asked, making him jump in surprise.

"Wedding? Did she say something...?"

"Calm down, I was joking."

Tom relaxed, but he had a strange look on his face that made me think he might have made some promise somewhere along the way.

"Barbara asked me if there was something wrong with her or with you that you kept staring at her."

"It made her blush, that was most of it. But, other than that, she was a lot more interesting than the milk dispenser or the glass rack. At least, she moved."

"You don't find her kind of cute?"

"Kind of. Cuter than the others," I said and he laughed.

"She's a ditz sometimes," he confided, shot a glance at her as she rang up someone's bill and made change while the family waited, the little children, a little girl and boy, drifting over to the candy dispensers by the door.

"Get away from there," the mother scolded and took them by the hand.

"So, what now?" Tom asked.

I shrugged.

"I need to get a shower and some rest."

"Looking for a job?"

"Yeah."

"We might have an opening; the dishwasher wants to quit. Gave his two weeks' notice, but he'd like to split."

"I guess."

"My mom's still pretty pissed. She'll probably let you stay with us for a day or two, but I don't know how long."

"What was that all about anyway? We didn't do nothing wrong."

"Don't even get into it," he said, holding up a hand. "Just apologize to her and promise not to do the same thing here."

"Do what? I didn't do anything there!"

"You wanna place to stay, or not?" he asked rhetorically. "You can follow me home, I got a motorcycle, but don't come in. Let me talk to her, first."

"All right."

I followed Tom on his bike back toward town, then a few side streets and we were in the rich section, with well-kept lawns, sculptured hedges and the like. I pulled up to the curb as he swooped into the garage and parked his bike. He entered the house through the garage. I got out of the car, because it was too hot to sit in it. I leaned on the fender, waiting.

Tom came walking out, looking like it had gone poorly.

"Come on in, she says you can stay for a little while, as long as you work and try to find a place. No drinking."

"Of course, I'll get a job. What else would I do?"

"Be humble," he said, waving me to follow.

The shower felt great. I could feel the dried perspiration flaking off as the jets of water beat on my back and cascaded down my body. I scrubbed hard, in case there was some of the hay dust and dirt left over from the ranch. I came out wearing just my jeans and went down the hall and to Tom's room. The air conditioner sent a chill through me and I dug in my suitcase for some clothes to put on.

I fell asleep on the floor. It was dark when Tom woke me up and guided me over to a place where a big, heavy comforter was laid out on the floor with a light blanket on top and pillow at one end. It was where I was to sleep. They had to have had at least two extra bedrooms, but she disliked me that much.

I could hear her saying in my imagination: "make it too comfortable and he'll never leave," like I was some sort of mooch. My parents said nothing about Tom, were glad to have him and treated him better than they treated me, which is how I was taught company ought to be treated, not like some bum, but that was how she insisted on seeing me.

CHAPTER SIXTEEN

I woke up at seven in the morning, when Tom got up to get ready for work. I talked him into letting me brush my teeth first, before he occupied the bathroom for too long. I took my shower kit with me to the bathroom down the hall, passing an open door with a bed and dresser, but no sign of occupancy and I shook my head.

I followed him back to the restaurant.

"I have to get started working, but as soon as I get a chance, I'll talk to Morty for ya."

I nodded, went in and ordered coffee at the counter. Barbara wasn't there, but a woman in her thirties was. Sylvia, by her badge. Long, dark hair, almost black, nice face and heavy, the look of women who have had a couple of children.

"You're a friend of Tom's?"

"Yes ma'am."

"You from Texas?"

"No, ma'am, just country."

She looked at me, squinted one eye and turned away.

I had left my cowboy hat in the car, choosing to wear the International Harvester cap in Kansas, where I had seen no sign of cowboy hats all the way through the state. Not that I had to fit in, but I didn't want to stick out, either.

"You're not from around here," she said, refilling the cup with black coffee for the third time. I wasn't sure how much more coffee I could drink.

"No, ma'am, Colorado."

She nodded and went to work as a cashier for a spell.

"No breakfast? Growing boy, like you?"

"No ma'am."

"Okay, knock the 'ma'am' stuff off, you're making me feel old."

"Okay."

I sat there for an hour. I did relent to a sweet roll and a glass of milk, just to feel like I was a buying something and to put a stop to the endless coffee.

"Hey, Lane," I heard Tom call and looked to see him waving me over to a door at the other end of the kitchen. I got up and followed him down a hall to an office. Tom guided me into it and went back to work.

Inside, sitting at a desk was who I assumed was Morty, who motioned me to a seat.

"You're looking for a job?"

"Yes sir."

"You ever work in a restaurant?"

"No sir, but I've worked every other kind of job there is, I'm sure I'll catch on."

"What other kind of work?"

"Well, just got off from putting up hay in Walden, Colorado. I've worked building corrals and tending horses, cattle and building and repairing fences."

"This work ain't that hard, but you have to be fast. We can't be waiting for dishes when food needs to go out."

"No sir, I can see how that would be bad."

"Very bad." He looked at me. "Tom's a good worker and he says you are, too. I hope he's right, I just let my dishwasher go. You can start today, right?"

"Right now, if you need me."

"Tom will show you how to run the dishwasher. Do not run me out of dishes."

"No sir."

"Get in the kitchen and get started. No hats."

I took the hat off my head and looked at him, holding it out.

"Just set it on the chair," he said, irritated.

I dropped the hat on the chair I had been sitting on and

went into the kitchen.

"Easy shit," Tom said, pulling me by the sleeve toward the dishwasher. "The waitresses clear the table and put everything into these bins. They might bring them back to you, they might put them under the counter out there, either way, when you get done with one, find another, but when it gets busy they'll pile up here," he said, pointing at a stainless steel alleyway leading to the dishwasher. It looked like three bins could be in a line on it. "You take these bins, wash off all the plates here at this sink with the disposal, then stack the dishes in this tray and push them in, close this door," he said, pulling a handle down that was attached to a square piece of metal that fit into some guides. "You push this button and it goes through a cycle, when it's done, this light comes on. You open it, stack the dishes and restock all the places around the restaurant, all the cups, all the silverware. Got it?"

"Yep."

"You're sure?"

"Easy shit," I said.

"Any questions, come ask me."

"Right."

Tom went back to cooking and I went to work. I hadn't even filled out an application. It was a little rocky to start. I couldn't get the dishwasher to run, because I hadn't pulled the door down far enough to close a switch. I didn't know all of the places where plates, cups and silverware were kept, so some spots got low and the waitresses complained, but that was easily fixed. I didn't know all of the places where they would put bins full of dishes, until the waitresses complained, but it was another easy fix. By the end of the day, I was out of bins, the dishes were all stocked and I started to bus tables to have something to do.

"Good job, man," Tom said, slapping me on the back.

"It ain't stackin' hay, but I got the hang of it."

"I told 'em you were a good worker, at least you didn't make a liar out of me."

We went out and sat at the employee's booth to relax. I didn't need to relax, but Tom worked a lot harder and his job was more stressful than mine, so I sat with him. He pulled out a pack of cigarettes and lit up. I had never seen him smoke and sat with wide eyes. He caught my stare.

"Everybody smokes here," he said, holding up the cigarette. "It ain't cool to chew."

I nodded. Deciding that I would just have to be uncool.

"You get a free meal every day, but at night, you can only order off the lunch menu. You want somethin'?"

"I guess," I said, not having eaten lunch, only the roll in the morning.

Tom got up, went to the cash register, reached underneath and brought out an order pad. He tossed it in front of me.

"Just write down whatever you want from the lunch menu, drinks and all that and give the ticket to one of the waitresses."

I took the big, laminated menu out of the holder and looked it over.

"The hell's a Ruben Sandwich?"

"You don't know what a Ruben is?"

"No."

"Well what should I expect from a guy who doesn't know what meatloaf is?"

"I know what meatloaf is and it damn sure ain't some guy."

We chuckled at each other's quip.

"But, really, what is a Ruben sandwich?"

When we got back to Tom's house, his mother was waiting for us. She stood in the kitchen. We came in through the garage.

"How did it go? Did he get a job?" she asked, as if I wasn't there.

"Yep, did a great job, too. Everyone was impressed."

That was news to me, but it was probably a lie to get his mother off his back.

She looked at me in her perfectly styled, reddish-blonde hair and fashionable earrings. Her lips tight, a smudge of lipstick the color of faded pink rose petals across a marble face, as if a smile would crack and shatter it. A gold chain hung from her neck with a gold cross hanging from that. Two of her fingers and left wrist were encircled in gold, real gold. Her cold blue eyes registered surprise at the news, but no hint of kindness.

"I take it you've eaten?" she said, looking at me, simply because she wouldn't make me a meal if she could get out of it.

"Yes, ma'am."

"Good, I only had enough steak for the three of us. I'm sorry, I went shopping before you came. Tom, your plate is in the oven, nice and warm."

"I'll just take a shower, then," I said, starting toward the hallway.

"Please remove your boots, it's hard on the carpet."

I nodded, went to the door, took off my boots and walked down the hall in my socks. After all, I was a guest and I was obliged to do as I was asked, resisting the urge to state that it must be particularly cheap carpet if boots can ruin it. Anything I could say would hurt Tom and I didn't dislike her enough to punish him. I took my shower and went into Tom's room to wait for him.

"I'm sorry," he said as soon as he closed the door.

"I should have taken my boots off."

"I mean about the steak."

"I don't care, Tom. I'm lucky to have a place to sleep."

He nodded.

"They really were impressed, especially Morty. He thought he was going to make you fail, but when you caught on as quickly as you did, it kind of disappointed him. He wanted to have something to hang on me, but you showed him."

"It's like you said, easy shit."

"Well, they're used to some of the dumbshits around here, so that's what they were expecting."

"I've always benefited from low expectations."

We talked for a while, quietly whispering, because Tom said his mom often listened at the door. It was not the sort of freedom I was looking for when I came and his mother seemed hellbent to make sure it wasn't.

Tom got up from the floor and went to the door. He opened it and looked out, then he came back and sat down on my "bed" close to me.

"I have this girlfriend, she's eighteen and lives across town. I'm going to go see her tomorrow, so we're not going to come back here after work, okay? I don't want you to come back without me."

"So it looks like we were together, right?"

Tom nodded.

"All right, but what the hell am I supposed to do?"

"She has a friend."

"Oh no, not that. I'll find something to do, drive around or something, but not that."

"Why? She's cute, blonde, nice figure."

"No man, not me. You know how I am with girls, especially ones I don't know."

"Man, you gotta get over that. You're sixteen, gonna be seventeen."

"I don't understand 'em. It's like they're talking a different language. They drop all these hints and I don't get it, then they get mad, because they think I'm ignoring their hints and it all goes sideways. Just leave me out of it."

"You've never even been laid?"

"Yeah, but that was just as screwed up as anything else, so you don't have to save me from virginity or anything. I just don't get it and I don't like it. There'll be a time, there'll be a girl, but not now, not like that."

"Okay, but you'll kick yourself if you ever see her."

"I'll risk it."

We went to bed, Tom on his nice, fluffy one and me on the floor, but I went right to sleep. I hadn't been able to go to sleep as easily as I did on the floor of Tom's bedroom. Of course, we didn't have an air conditioner at our house, it wasn't needed as badly as it was in Kansas, spitting distance from Missouri in the middle of the summer. It probably had more to do with the stress I had been under the past few days, but I enjoyed it.

The next day at the restaurant, there was a new waitress, at least I had never seen her before. Rae. It was clear that Rae and Barbara did not get along, so I assumed that she was not new to the restaurant, just new to me, who had only worked there for one day.

Rae was short, my age or a little older, attractive in a way, but there was something wild, something crazy about her. Little actions betrayed her, a look would come into her blue eyes that sparked with vengeance or stubbornness without cause, at least nothing I could discern. Rae brought the bins into the kitchen more often than any of the other waitresses, who might bring one a day, if that. Most of the time, I went out and got them, so I didn't know if the hostility between Barbara and Rae was over that, or what.

I tried not to let any of them bring in bins. I felt like that was my job and if the boss saw them bringing them to me all the time, he would think I was shirking my responsibility. So, I was more vigilant about checking to see if there were any full ones under the counter, but it was like before. Then, I noticed that Rae would bus the tables and bring the bins back to me directly from there, not putting them under the counter. That made me feel better, but that wasn't her job.

"I'll get 'em, just put 'em under the counter," I said, when Rae brought me another one.

"Why would I go through the hassle of putting them under the counter, when I'm already carrying it?"

It was a good point. I hadn't thought of it like that.

"The boss'll think I'm not doing my job," I said.

Rae's eyes sparked with knowledge and rebellion.

"I'll take care of Morty," she said and it was just one more example of her behavior that I caught from the start. It was like she knew things and had a way about her that kept everyone off balance. She had the upper hand in most things and made sure it stayed that way. She had already gotten the upper hand with me and I could see where Barbara might have reason to dislike her.

As soon as I emptied the bin, I walked over to Tom.

"Hey, what do you think of Rae?"

Tom grinned a sly grin and looked at me out of the corner of his eye.

"Why?"

"You think she's trying to get me in trouble?"

"Why?"

"She keeps bringing me these bins and it feels like I'm not doing my job. She always does that, I guess, huh?"

"I've never seen her bring a bin back to the dishwasher before."

"Huh."

Was there a woman anywhere in the world that would make sense to me? Would I ever encounter even one that did not get my head spinning with confusion the first moment I met her? Maybe she had just realized the foolishness of putting the bin under the counter when she could bring it through the door and hand it to me. I didn't know and couldn't figure it out, but it did give me something to think about while I was washing dishes off and stacking them and unstacking them, so I owed her one, I suppose.

When we got done for the day, I waited for Tom to finish explaining the status of dishes to the other cook, an Iranian, who attended some college during the winter and worked at the restaurant in the summer.

I was going to eat, but figured that would be something I could do while I was waiting for him to come back.

"You have to drive me over there," he said. I want to leave the motorcycle here; in case she drives by to see where I am."

"What about my car, how do you explain that being gone?'

"I'm going to say we went shopping for shoes in Joplin, but I couldn't find any. She won't let me take the motorcycle out of town."

I didn't want to say it to my good friend, but I would have told my mother to take a leap if she tried to keep that tight of a leash on me. I wasn't raised that way. We were allowed to do just about anything that came to mind as long as we were honest about where we went and what we did. My parents hardly ever asked me what I did. That was why getting drunk and not coming home at the fair was such a big deal to my mom, it broke the trust she had in me. Getting arrested didn't help, either, but that wasn't my fault and she knew it. Ditching school was, though.

"All right, let's go," I said, pulling the keys out of my pocket.

We drove back down Main, halfway through the old part of town to a convenience store where we turned right, went down under the highway and over the tracks, then a few blocks further and turned right. We stopped in front of an old house with several numbers on it. It was basically a tenement.

"What number?" I asked.

"Number three, why?"

"In case I have to pull you out of there, so I can go to sleep."

"It'll only be three hours. That's how long it takes to get to Joplin and back anyway."

"All right."

"You can't go back to the restaurant; she might see your car and know I'm lying."

"It just keeps getting better and better."

"I'm sorry, but…"

"Just go, will ya?"

Tom looked at me, saying thank you without saying it and got out.

I drove off angry, well, tiffed is a better word for it, because I understood where he was coming from. Mrs. Wilson, or whatever her name was after she remarried, was a terror, a possessive woman determined to control everything about her son's life: who supervised what he saw, what he did, where he went and knowing that made it easier to see why she hated me; I was a loose cannon that did just about whatever I pleased and that challenged her control, making her goal of total dominance that much harder to achieve.

I drove down by the river, parked in the wide space by the Co-op and got out. I walked over to the bridge and sat down on some concrete pilings to watch the water flow muddily by. I realized that my book was in my suitcase at Tom's. Maybe they had a library somewhere, or maybe there were books at the department store, but I didn't think I should go to that end of town. The convenience store might have some, but they would all be insipid nonsense that I didn't like to read.

I got up with renewed purpose and drove back down Main, looking for the library and there it was, a big square brick building with white corners that made it look like a courthouse. I parked in front, but it was closed. So much for that, so I drove back to the convenience store on the corner and went in.

There were a couple of black guys talking to the black girl behind the counter. They looked startled when I came in, like something was going on, but I kept on, back to the cooler where they kept the pop. I got a can and walked up the aisle toward the counter. They were all watching me, like they expected me to do something. One of the guys, taller than me and older stared at me.

"What you doin' in here, man? This ain't yore store."

"I know it ain't my store," I said, holding the can of pop out so they could see what I was doing there.

"Then, what you doin' here?"

"Buyin' this."

"You don' buy that shit in this store, whitey, go on, get outta here. This is our store; we say who buys what here."

"Your store?"

"That's right," the other one said, glaring at me.

"Her store, ain't it?"

"Go on, mister. Keep the pop and get out of here," she said, almost pleading.

I pulled a dollar out of my pocket and dropped it on the counter, watching for any signs of movement like they were going to jump me, but they seemed content with insults and demands.

"Your store?" I said, walking out. I got in my car and drove away. I'd have to file that one away for the future. Tom told me about some racial tension in town, but I hadn't noticed it until then. Of course, I had only been in town a few days. I hoped it wasn't going to be that way. I didn't have anything against anyone, but I didn't take to getting bullied.

CHAPTER SEVENTEEN

It was ten after nine when I pulled up to the curb in front of the tenement. I waited, leaning back in the seat and closing my eyes. I jerked awake, looked at my watch and decided that enough was enough and it was time to go home. Walking up to the house it was clear that whoever owned it was sitting back, collecting rent for as long as he could, before they condemned the place and made him shut it down. Maybe it was a woman who owned it, property left to her by a father or dead husband and she didn't know what to do to keep it up or was simply miserly and would not fix the tree scraping a hole in the roof, digging deeper every time the wind blew, or the paint which had mostly fallen off from lack of care or supplemental coat. It seemed like whoever the owner was, they might be able to arrange to have the grass cut, at least.

I opened the screen door and the wooden door behind it. The stairway leading up to the second floor was dark and smelled of rotting wood. There was no light either at the top of the stairs, or at the bottom and I made my way up stomping on the steps as I rose, trying to alert Tom that I was coming, but it felt like my foot might go through on some of them, so I lightened my step.

At the top of the stairs I turned left, the only way to go and looked down a dark hall, not a lightbulb lit anywhere. There was a door standing ajar to the left and another door fully closed to the right. The one on the right had a metallic looking number four tacked in the middle of the door. I turned around. Number three was on the other side of the hall and standing slightly open. I heard voices erupt, angry voices. They were having some argument and I didn't want to interrupt. At the end of the hall was a bathroom, the door standing open, a sink and part of a toilet visible through the opening and the darkness. I walked down the hall, went into the restroom and pulled down on the cord. A dim light bulb illuminated above and I closed the door. I would give them the time it took me to use the toilet, then I would have to knock on the door. Nothing good would come of upsetting Tom's mom.

I finished, flushed and left the door open as I yanked down on the chain and was enveloped in darkness, but for the shaft of light from the open doorway spilling out onto the floor and up the opposing wall. I crept closer, listening, but intentionally not hearing what they were saying, instead listening for a gap in the dialog through which I would enter.

As I listened, I realized that it was not Tom's voice that I heard, but someone else, some other man. Was Tom there, or not? I listened with more intent, to hear some news about Tom.

"Yeah? He had it coming, damn him!"

That was enough for me, something had happened. Not knowing what I would see, I burst through the door, caught hold of the man by the throat and threw him up against the wall.

"Where's Tom?" I asked, then beat the guy's head against the wall a good rap. "Where is he?" I demanded. I felt tiny fists beating me on the back and heard the girl screaming something that I didn't understand through my rage. I pulled the guy's head away from the wall and rammed it back again, but this time he went limp in my grasp and the weight of his unconscious body slumped to the ground, slipping from my fingers. I turned around.

"Where's Tom?" I asked, seeing the girl that had caused all of the trouble, a beautiful brunette with a pale complexion and large, blue eyes standing in front of me, shaking her little fists.

"Leave him alone, you..."
"Who's this asshole?"
"He's my husband."
"Husband!?"
"Yes, now leave...please."

"What happened to Tom?"

"He caught us together and hit Tom really hard, knocking him down, but he got up and ran out. That's all."

I ran out of the room and down the rickety steps, bursting through the doors at the bottom and got in my car. I looked all around, tried to find Tom walking back home, thinking that's the best place for him to go, or back to the restaurant to get his motorcycle, which was more likely. I drove slowly along peering into the darkened sidewalk, branches of huge trees hanging down, obscuring it with leaves, cars parked along the street made it difficult to see. I was looking for any motion at all, but the neighborhood was quiet.

I drove back to the restaurant and Tom's bike was still there. I drove back along a different route, hoping to find him. I drove to his house and passed slowly by, but the window to his bedroom was unlit. I drove back to the house, paying more attention to the bushes and places a person might be hidden. Then, I came to the stop sign at the end of the block and the passenger door to my car flew open and Tom dove in.

"Go, go, go!" he screamed, pulling the door shut. "Go, damn you, go!"

I stepped on the accelerator, the car leapt away from the stop, across the tracks, up the hill, onto Main and down. I kept going, though slower through town and out onto highway 69, then I took a side road and went a mile or two before I stopped.

"What the hell?"

"Kathy's husband came home early, he caught us having sex and beat the crap out of me."

I turned on the dome light and had a look at him, he didn't look too bad, a swollen jaw.

"I feel for ya, I do, but you were doin' his ol' lady while he was at work? Holy shit, man."

"No, he's in the Navy, he wasn't supposed to get home until next week."

"Ah," I said, but I still didn't approve. I couldn't help but feel like he did have it coming.

"He's going to kill me, I know he is," he said, worried, looking out the back window as if some creature were out there in the night, stalking him.

"No, he won't."

"You didn't see how mad he was, geezus!"

I couldn't help but chuckle a little.

"What did you expect? Holy crap."

"He'll track me down, bust up my bike or something."

"He won't mess with ya."

"Yes, he will."

"No, he won't."

"How do you know?"

"He won't want to mess with you, because he won't want to mess with me and I already took care of him, so don't worry about it."

"What?"

"I went lookin' for ya. I told you I'd pull you out of there when it was time to go home, right? Well, that's what I went to do, but then I heard him arguing with her and knew it wasn't you, so I went in to find out what happened."

"What?"

"I slammed his head against the wall a few times. Don't worry about him, he knows he'll get us both if he tries anything."

"You hit him?"

"No, I banged his head against the wall a few times."

"I gotta get home!" he yelled, realizing he wasn't out of the woods, yet. "Take me back to get my bike."

I drove him back, the mental mess that he was, first worrying about the husband, then about his mom. He kept trying to alleviate his fears through me.

"We'll just show up at home like nothing happened."

"She might see your jaw, I'd keep your left side out of her sight, if you can."

"Right, but she might not be up," he said, as if convincing me would make it true. I knew better and so did he.

"Just keep your right side facing her."

"Right," he said, fidgeting, his head darting first left, then right, trying to see something that was only in his fears.

I followed him back to the house and parked out front. He pulled into the garage and waited for me. We went in together.

"Where on earth have you been? Let me smell your breath," she said, closing in on him, sniffing the air.

"We were shopping for shoes, I need a..."

"Where?"

"Joplin, didn't I tell you?"

If she had asked me, we were in bad shape, because I wouldn't be able to lie. If she had ever bothered to know me, she would know that and use it against her son, but she was busy ignoring me, except to cast those angry little eyes on me from time to time in accusation.

"You are not supposed to ride that motorcycle out of town!" she screamed.

"I didn't, we took Lane's car. We just got back."

"Why didn't you tell me you were going to be this late? I was out of my mind with worry."

"I didn't know, we got hung up looking for shoes and it got late on us."

"Where are they?"

"I didn't find any, that's why we kept looking."

"You seem pretty calm," she said, looking at me with suspicion.

"I didn't do nothin'." I said.

She glared at me, but it looked like it was going to work, then Tom lost track of what he was doing and went to grab something, a newspaper advertisement for the shoes to prove he had been searching for them and turning around he revealed his left side to her, that, in the well-lit kitchen, revealed a growing bruise on the side of his face that I couldn't see in the dim light of the car or the garage.

I braced for it, but still I was not prepared for the explosion of emotion, anger and mistrust that burst from her small, fragile-looking frame. A bony finger came aggressively toward me, berating my very existence as the cause of everything vile and rebellious her son had ever done. It was me, not the pressure-cooker life she had devised for him, the constant surveillance that she subjected him to that caused his occasional escapes from custody out into the wider world. I was the one who had led him astray, taught him the wicked pleasures of disobedience.

The whole lie came undone as he tried vainly and with no corroboration to explain how shopping for shoes caused him to get a bruised face. He kept up what parts of the story he could, but admitted that he had been messing around town instead of in Joplin. Yet, no matter how bad it was for him, it was worse for me and unlike him, I could not receive a pardon.

"You!" she screamed, "you get out of my house, right now!"

"Mom, he has to shower, you have to let him do that at least."

"I don't have to do anything, that boy is nothing but trouble, never has been anything else and never will. I don't see why you can't see how smooth your life is, how easy, when he isn't around to talk you into these things, drag you down into the gutter with him."

"Please, mom, let him take a shower so he's ready for work tomorrow.'

"I'll give him one half hour to clear out, what he does with it, I don't care, but not a minute more, not even a second more." She looked at her gold watch to mark the time.

I hurriedly got my stuff shoved into the suitcase, all but a clean shirt, underwear and the shower kit. I took a shower and got out of that house, before anything else could go wrong at my expense. At first, I didn't know where to go or what to do. I decided to go to the restaurant and park there, behind the building and look at the map.

I might not have had a place to stay, but I did have a job.

It was more than a start, it felt like the beginning of something and I didn't want to lose it, because Tom's mom hated me. If I could figure out a way to take a shower, I could stay in my car until I got my first paycheck, which should be on Friday. I didn't have time to ask when I got hired, I assumed we would be paid weekly, so I could stay in my car for a week, easy. With the thought that I would tough it out, I was met with a sudden realization that I had finally achieved my ultimate goal of freedom, complete and whole as at no other time in my life. In my poverty, with no place to live other than my car I inhaled the greatest and most valuable air, free air, as valuable as oxygen itself to a man who is being held down and smothered by a dominating and controlling society. The car became a world unto itself, supportive and protective in many ways, but also mobile, free to leave and to return, move from one place of inhospitality to another of gentle welcome, flowing as the Marmaton River.

One might be depressed and fearful, captured by the uncertain future of lost friendships, lost comfort, lost support, but it was there in a different form if one bothered to evaluate it as such; if instead of counting the losses, they recognized the opportunities that that loss revealed. While convention would dictate that I should be confused and afraid, I was not. The punishment Tom's mother tried to heap on me slid off, because I would not carry it; I would not own shame that was undeserved.

In the comfort of freedom, I relaxed and got hold of the book, Sal in San Francisco. I read until I fell asleep, then woke up at one and again at three but went back to sleep both times and woke up for good at seven, when the heat was starting to build in the car. I stretched and straightened my clothes that were wrinkled, but no one thought too much of my attire as it was. I woke with only the thought of the day ahead, one day closer to my pay when I would voluntarily accept the chains of rent and food, but they would be chains I agreed to wear and could abandon whenever I chose.

I heard Tom's motorcycle pull up and I got out of the car

to meet him.

"I'm really sorry, Lane, no kidding, what can I say?"

"What's there to say?" I asked, thinking about letting him have it, making him feel as bad as he should for putting me in the position of having to take all that abuse from his mother for doing absolutely nothing wrong, except to do as he asked. But the taste of freedom was still on my lips and the idea of not going back to his house was a blessing of sorts, a favor that allowed me to see the freedom that surrounded me.

"I'll talk to some of the people and see if I can't find you someplace to stay."

"Don't bother, I'm fine."

"You found a place?"

"In a sense."

"What does that mean?'

"It means to let it go, it's not your responsibility. I came here on my own, I was not invited, so thanks for the few days of comfort, but I'll be fine. I got it worked out."

Tom went in to work and I stayed outside long enough to brush my teeth with what was left of a can of pop. It was certainly not the best thing to use to brush one's teeth and it tasted weird, the combination of toothpaste and carbonated soda. It double fizzed, too.

Work was my salvation, no matter what it was or where. There was nothing wrong with the hay farm as far as a job went. The job was the only thing about the place I liked, it was afterward, living with others that I detested.

I settled into a routine of working all day, eating a Ruben or a patty melt at night after work, though I was supposed to get a lunch break, I couldn't see a reason to do so. All that accomplished was to get me backed up at the dishwasher when it was over. Whereas, I could keep working and keep up comfortably all day. Breaks and food didn't mean much to me, never had as I grew up. I was raised on job completion, that was all that mattered. There were plenty of breaks between jobs. After work and after supper, I would sometimes drive to the library and get the last hour out of it before it closed, just to be somewhere. I did find books there, but I was still reading Kerouac. Eventually, I would wind up back at the parking lot and walk to the department store. Tom would stop by and we would talk for a while or I would go back into the restaurant and drink pop.

After the restaurant closed and everyone had gone away, I would wait until twelve or one in the morning and sneak into the fenced off area where they kept the trash. There was a water hose there, used for washing down the sidewalk or spilled waste. I would take the water hose, jam it between two slats of the fence and turn it on. I would strip naked and lather up under the water hose, shampoo my hair and get dressed again. I would go back to my car where I had made a good bed out of the backseat. I did that for a couple of days until it was Friday and I waited expectantly to get paid. I looked for signs from the others that they had gotten paid, but saw nothing obvious.

Toward the end of the day, I asked Tom about it.

"Do we get paid today, or what?"

"No, we get paid next week, its every two weeks."

"Oh."

"Why? You need money?"

"Naw, not yet, but no one told me."

I didn't want to let on that I was crestfallen, to me it would give someone an opportunity to ridicule me or use the fact that I needed money against me. It wasn't the sort of opening I was accustomed to revealing to anyone, ever. The fact was, I didn't need the money, not to survive, not to stay in my car, but if I wanted to get a place, I would need every bit.

I was enjoying my freedom, nonetheless. A place could wait, it would be a chain around my neck when it came, so I wasn't too anxious to get it anyway. But, I did have plans, plans that would have to be put aside for another day. It would have been nice not to shower amid the trash, is all.

CHAPTER EIGHTEEN

The day before payday, I was busily doing my job at the dishwasher when Tom came back into the kitchen and called me over.

"Morty wants to see you after work."

I blinked and stared at him.

"Is there any more?"

"No, he just wants to see you."

I went back to the dishwasher wondering what he could possibly want to see me about. I had heard nothing about the job I was doing, except that it was okay. No one complained, but a lot went on in the restaurant that I didn't know about. It was the same way everywhere I went, there was a subtext to everything that, because I kept to myself and did my job, was hidden from me. I don't think people intentionally kept me out of the loop, but they recognized that I didn't care about the politics. I didn't engage in gossip and when people started to gossip around me, I found other things to do.

The day wore on and Rae came back into the kitchen with a bin of dishes. She had stopped doing it all the time, but still brought one on occasion, along with some sexual innuendo that she took great pleasure in, but that I didn't care for and refused to participate. I wasn't good at that sort of thing and hearing it made me feel uncomfortable, I didn't know why. It seemed to be the opposite with others, like Tom, who was good at it.

"It's hot out there today," she said.

I nodded, because I didn't know if it was, or not. I was stuck in a kitchen that was always hot.

"It makes me want to take all my clothes off and stand

under a water hose."

Did she know something about how I had been taking a shower? Is that what she was getting at? Was it supposed to embarrass me? I looked at her dumbly blinking my eyes trying to figure out what she was saying, what the message of that was.

"You ever feel that way?"

"No."

"You don't? You don't like the feel of cool water flowing down your naked body?"

"Not from a water hose," I said, to which she wrinkled her brow and walked away.

Were there rumors going around? I was pretty cautious about when I took a shower and what time it was and that sort of thing. I had never even had a close call when I thought someone might have seen me, so I was confused after talking to a girl. Big news, that.

When my shift was over, I went into Morty's office and sat down. I looked at his office, pictures of his annoying daughter were everywhere. For some reason, Morty's daughter thought the fact that her dad owned the restaurant made him some sort of financial guru, or important part of the community and played the part of the princess to the employees. I avoided her at all costs, because I didn't know if my tongue could be held long enough to escape with my job.

Morty had some bowling trophies high up on a shelf, I couldn't read the reflective plastic plates, so I didn't know what they were for, but he had them and seemed proud of it. Nothing wrong with that, people were proud of being football players, too. None of it meant anything to anyone around them, not in a material sense, like knowing Albert Einstein or Neil Armstrong, where unique and special knowledge or understanding might be found. They did something good one day, good for them. I rode a steer one day, won seventy bucks and I had nothing to prove it, not the money, not the score emblazoned on some plaque, I didn't even get a buckle. I got seventy bucks and I got drunk.

Morty came in a few minutes later. He was balding and had grown a goatee since I first met him. He was heavy, but not obese and wore a suit, every day a suit. I couldn't figure out why, when a guy owned his own business that he would dress like that, but he did. He fingered his tie while he looked at me, studying me like he never had before.

"Is it true you're living in your car?"

I studied him back. Where had he heard that? Some cops stopped by one day and asked me my business and I told them that I had gotten kicked out and I was just waiting to get paid and would get a place. The cops came to the restaurant all the time, but why would they talk about me? If they had a problem with what I was doing, they could have run me off and I would have had to find some other place to park, that's all.

"Well?"

"Yeah."

"You don't have a place to stay?"

"I will when I get paid, I've just been waiting to get my first check."

"I thought you were staying with Tom."

"I was, but I got kicked out."

"What for?"

"Some hassle Tom had with his mom and she blamed me for it."

"When was that?"

"A couple of days after I got here."

"Two weeks?" he asked, his eyebrows arching up.

"Almost."

"Why didn't you tell me?"

I failed to understand why I would. I stared at him. Had I done something wrong? At least as he saw it?

"Was I supposed to?" I asked. "I'm technically in the department store parking lot."

"You weren't supposed to, but why didn't you come to me?"

"For what?" I asked, confused. Was I in trouble, or had I

violated some etiquette?

"To help you find a place."

"I didn't have money for a place, even if I found one." I said and it was his turn to sit there, blinking trying to figure out how to respond.

"We could have worked something out."

"Why would you bother?"

"Because, I'm a Christian and I like to think a good boss."

"You are a good boss, but I don't see why you would care where I slept as long as it didn't interfere with the job. I mean, I'm not really an employee until I get to work."

"You're a difficult young man," he said. "I want you to get a good night's sleep, so I'm willing to give you fifty dollars to get a motel room tonight and something to eat."

"Payday's tomorrow, right?"

"Yes."

"I can wait it out, it's just one more night."

That was not what he wanted to hear. I don't know if it bothered him from a personal point of view, or a spiritual point of view, or if he was somehow embarrassed by the fact that one of his employees had to sleep in his car, but it bothered him.

"Listen, it's important to me that you take this money and sleep in a bed."

"I don't need fifty bucks."

"How much?"

"Twenty-five would do it."

I didn't tell him that I still had twenty-five in my wallet, more than that, but I wouldn't spend my own money to sleep in a motel for one night when I could get my own place the next day, with money I earned, keeping the twenty-five for something more important.

He handed me the money and I stood to leave.

"You can come to me, if you have problems. I know people, I can help."

I nodded, but that is not something I would ever do. He was a stranger and if I did ask a favor, it wouldn't be from someone I didn't know. That was a personal thing with me, not a casual thing. Even then, I would want to trade it off for something I could do for them, so that no one was in debt at the end of it. Debt was something my father avoided at all costs and debts to friends was not considered. Borrowing money from a bank, with a set interest rate as a standard of commerce was one thing, but asking a friend for a loan was another.

On my way out of the restaurant, I fell in with Rae, who was on her way out, too.

"What did Morty want?"

"He found out I was sleeping in my car and gave me some money to get a motel room. You know of any cheap motels?"

Rae looked at me with eyes that glossed over for a second, lost in thought, then looked up from under her brow as if I had made some sexual comment.

"Why do you want to know?"

"'Cause you live here and I don't. I could drive around and ask everybody, but if you know a place, it would save some time."

"Oh, come on, follow me; I'll show you one," she said, seemingly disappointed in my sexual innuendo quotient.

I got in my car and followed her big Chrysler out of the parking lot. She was a small girl, short, but she drove a huge Chrysler and it looked funny following her. She didn't look old enough or tall enough to drive it.

On our way down Main, we passed Tom on his motorcycle and I saw him turn around and follow us. We went back into town and turned down a street, a block further on was a motel and Rae pulled in, our little convoy following suit. I pulled up to the office.

"How much is a night?" I asked the elderly man behind the counter.

"Thirteen dollars," he said, as if I didn't have it.

I put the twenty on the counter and took a key.

"You gotta sign," he said, holding out a pen.

I pulled the LTD in front of the room and opened the

door. I got my suitcase out of the car and put it on the bed. Rae came in and lay down on the bed, pushing my suitcase over with her foot. Then Tom came in and plopped down in a chair.

"So, got a room, huh?"

"I guess."

"Where'd you get the money?"

"Morty gave it to him," Rae said, grinning.

"Gave or loaned?"

"He said he wanted to give me fifty bucks, but I said twenty-five and he gave it to me."

Rae laughed

"He'll take it out of your pay," Tom said.

"No, he won't. I didn't ask for it, he offered."

"It doesn't matter, it was a loan."

"You'll see, tomorrow," Rae said.

"Well, that's bullshit," I said, looking at them as they nodded. "Glad I didn't take the fifty and stay in a nice place, buy dinner and all that. As it is, I still have twelve bucks. I ought to throw it back in his face. Some Christian."

Rae grinned.

"He pulled that, too?" she asked.

I nodded and brought another chair over and sat down.

"I didn't want to spend money on this shit, or I would have done it already. Hell, I had twenty-five bucks."

"Morty likes to feel like a big shot, making out that he did a good thing, but when you look at it, he didn't do a damned thing," Rae said.

"Except take the credit," Tom added. "He'll talk up how he saved you, put you up at a nice hotel at his expense until you got on your feet. His church will bless him and look on him as a paragon of virtue and it's all bullshit."

"If he wanted to do something, he could have given you a voucher for dinner," Rae said.

"Yeah," I said, chuckling, realizing how he had conned me.

"How did he know, anyway? I'd been there nearly two

weeks and no one said a thing."

"Found out somehow," Tom said, "he called me into his office to see if it was true."

"Did you know?" I asked Rae, still working on the puzzle from earlier.

"Nope," she said, but I thought she was lying. She was good at it.

It was silent for a while, each of us working on thoughts of our own.

"I've gotta go," Rae said, stretching and yawning.

"Me too," Tom chimed in.

"Thanks for everything," I said, watching Rae swing her short, shapely legs off the bed, planting her tennis shoes on the floor and standing up in her little waitress outfit.

Tom followed her out and closed the door. I was alone. I sat in the chair, looking at the television. It had been some time since I watched television, before I went to Walden. It was something to do, but what could possibly be on that I wanted to watch? Nothing, that's why I had not missed it. The book was more entertaining than the television.

I got up and went outside to get the book. I opened the door on the car as a flatbed pickup bounced up and into the parking lot. Some blonde-haired local with no shirt and bib overalls bounced off the back and walked up to me. He was taller than me, but skinny and not too smart.

"Where is she?"

"Who?"

"Rae. I saw her car parked right here a minute ago."

"She left."

"What were you two doin'?"

"Nothin'."

"Don't lie to me, boy," he said, puffing his chest out.

I shut the car door. Staring at him. He didn't know that accusing me of a lie went straight to my heart, set a fire there that was usually only doused by someone's blood. I had endured too much pain from telling the truth, paid numerous costs, because I considered a lie to be the same as cowardice. I owned up to what I did and it was painful, but I did it out of a dedication to honesty, something pounded into me by my parents and my brother. A lie was the greatest sin.

"Why the fuck would I lie to you?"

"To keep from getting' yore ass kicked."

I laughed.

"Call me a liar again," I said, getting ready, looking at the driver and the other fellow on the back of the flatbed, sitting on a bale of hay. I was calculating whether they would be a threat after the blonde guy went down. It was something I had gotten used to at school, measuring the threat, preparing for the worst, knowing that taking one guy didn't mean the end of anything.

"Then, what was she doin' here?" he said and I could see his resolve drain away.

"Showin' me where it was."

"That's all?"

"That's all."

"That better be all," he said, walking back to the flatbed and leaping onto the back, like a cat.

"Or what?" I asked, walking toward the flatbed, the threat pissed me off. "Or what?"

"You'll find out," he said as the flatbed pulled out of the parking lot and away.

I got my book and went back into the motel room, slamming the door. I could not enjoy myself at the motel, knowing that I was coerced into paying for it. I could not enjoy having a meal on the remainder, knowing that it was my money that I would be spending and if I had wanted to spend my money that way, I would have. The experience reinforced the way our family went about things, which was not to ask for help, not to accept charity (which is what I had done and it was clear that it was a mistake), remain self-sufficient and in control of one's own destiny as much as possible. Those were things passed down through demonstration, they weren't vocalized to us.

That night, having been one of the very few times I had

ever stayed in a motel, I opened the drawer to the nightstand to see if there really was a Bible as television shows had often portrayed and I was astonished to see that it was all true and when I opened it, it did say that it was a Gideon Bible. It seemed like a considerable expense to print all of the Bibles and deliver them to motel rooms all across the nation in an attempt to do what? I doubt that they did much to deter extramarital or premarital sex that seemed rampant since the introduction of the birth-control pill. I recalled images of the "free love" movement and the whole hippie revolution I had witnessed from afar on our little ranch and only through the portal of television, except that the existence of men with long hair persisted and had increased since then.

I flipped through the Bible and came across some red letters, so I stopped, curious as to what they had to say and try to figure out why they were in red. It took some reading, but I figured out the red letters were supposed to be the words of Jesus and the black letters were the stories told by others. Of all of the things I read, figuring that out, none of them seemed like something Morty would endorse, not when he acted the way he did. I wondered if Morty actually read the Bible or just professed faith as a means of doing business or because he was supposed to profess faith in that community.

I put the Bible back in the drawer and thought about my own faith. I didn't know that I had any particular faith of my own. We had gone to church as children, but our pastor left and we got a new one that my mom didn't care for, so we stopped going. The only thing that spoke to me about the church experience is that the Ten Commandments seemed like a good general outline to follow and I tried, my whole family did. Beyond that, I don't know that we thought about it a lot. We tried to be moral, I guess.

I woke up the next morning and packed my things. I looked the room over and took the key to the office to check out. It was nice to have a place to sleep in comfort, with the air conditioner going after all those nights in the car, but it still seemed like a waste of money. I was anxious to get my paycheck and see how much I could expect to earn, knowing then how much I could afford to spend on a place and set a budget for food and gas. The paycheck would tell me a lot about how I would be able to live while in Kansas. I was also choosing the words I would say to Morty, because I could not let him do that to me without some comment. I had to choose the words, because my natural response to such things had caused trouble in the past, offhand comments could deeply offend people like Miss Tanner and the Taylors and I had no reason to believe that Morty was any different.

It was a good, bright morning as I got into the car and rolled down the windows. There was a deep blue sky above, only traces of white clouds high up in the atmosphere and though it was already growing hot enough to soak my shirt in the short trip to the office and back to the car, I had a good feeling about the day. It was payday and all of the efforts I had put forth would bear fruit. I could stop pulling slivers from the savings I held jealously against privation and loosen up a little, maybe buy a burger at the joint where Main met up with Highway 69.

Hard at work, not thinking about very much, except clearing the backlog created between six in the morning when we opened and eight when I started, I saw Rae a time, or two, but did not have a chance to talk to her.

Tom was busy cooking breakfast, his face glowing with sweat, dark hair hanging down over one eye, moving as efficiently as he could, moving hash browns that were almost done to a cooler part of the stove, rolling and chopping the egg mix until it resembled scrambled eggs, cracking a few and moving them expertly further up and away from the center, where he flipped sausage patties and thin, cheap steaks.

The day wore on, closer and closer to the end when I would get paid and ultimately get a place of my own. I had a newspaper stashed in my car for that very purpose. I got caught up on the dishes and restocked the plates and cups. Rae walked toward me with a bin of dishes and I met her at the counter.

"Met a friend of yours last night, blonde guy, skinny, he was worried about you," I said, taking the bin.

She rolled her eyes and turned away. So, I guess it was something we weren't going to talk about. I went into the kitchen with the bin, there were only a few plates and some coffee cups. I unloaded it and waited for more before I could run the dishwasher.

At the end of the day, I got my paycheck. I opened the envelope and looked at the deductions, there was twenty-five dollars listed as an advance. I thought, having thought about it that I had dealt with the emotions of it all, but when I saw it actually listed as an advance, I realized that I had not dealt with it well enough. I looked at my watch and it was after five, all the banks would be closed.

Tom picked up his paycheck while I was standing there.

"I need to cash this," I said, hoping he had a solution.

"Take it to the grocery store, they charge fifty cents, but they'll do it."

Still, it was only one hundred and seventy-one dollars with the advance taken out, so my typical pay would be two hundred every two weeks. Out of that, I would have to pay rent, which meant I could afford to pay a couple hundred on rent, but would still have to eat most of my meals at work, where it was free. Two hundred a month wouldn't buy much in the way of an apartment. The hay farm in Walden paid more, all things considered.

I went out to the car and got the newspaper. I couldn't afford to drive around to check the places out, either, not until I found something. I came back into the restaurant and sat down at the employee's booth and opened the paper. I ordered a coke.

Barbara got off work and sat down next to me, counting out her tips. I scooted over to give her room.

"What? Do I have cooties, or what?'

"I was takin' up too much room."

"Whatcha doin'?"

"Lookin' for a place to live," I said, folding the paper in half lengthwise, then over again horizontally, focused on apartments for rent. I started reading. One month in advance. First month due immediately. I didn't have enough money for a whole month. I had not thought of that. Ad after ad, they wanted a month in advance. All told, I did have enough, but I had already dipped further into savings than I wanted to and I wanted the job to pay its way. If I couldn't make my bills on what I earned, I would have to look for another job. Also, I was supposed to be putting some aside for when I decided to leave, if I did. I came across one that said fifty dollars a week that piqued my interest. I could afford that, barely, but it could be done. I looked at the address, it was out on highway 54.

I nudged Barbara and nodded that I needed to get out.

"You can't wait a second?"

"What are you going to do, lose count?"

"I already did, damn you."

CHAPTER NINETEEN

I drove out Highway 54 until I went past the address, then came back and realized that it was a motel. A couple of old cars were parked at the east end of a long building with numerous doors marking individual units. I went up to the office and asked about a weekly rate.

"Fifty dollars a week and you have to ask for new towels, we don't clean those rooms, but once a week until you leave, but if you mess them up, we won't renew your rental," an elderly woman said, her thick glasses magnifying her eyes.

I gave her one hundred dollars in cash and waited for a receipt. She handed a key over along with a yellow slip of paper showing that I paid. I parked in front of number eight and got out of the car.

"Home," I said, inserting the key and taking a deep breath to see what I had purchased. It wasn't bad. An old television was high up on a ledge across from the bed. The bed was covered by a cheap almost plastic-like bed cover, some sort of polyester and thin, weak pillows. I had better in my car. The bathroom was outdated, the faucets were rusting and the shower curtain was stained a sort of yellow like people had been pissing on it. It was clean enough for me, though. Out of curiosity, I opened the drawer, sure enough, a Gideon Bible.

I went out and got my book and suitcase. I had about seventy dollars left from my paycheck. I was working on thin margins, so I had to be careful. I thought about everyone back home and what they might be doing right then, but it was just depressing, so I opened the book. I read for a long time, until the sun started to wane. I went outside and sat on the trunk of the car, watching the darkness edge closer and closer. Cars and pickups sped past on the highway, sometimes a big truck would pass. A breeze picked up and cooled the air for a moment, then the heat came back. The nighttime sound of insects began to grow as the light faded and they crowded around the light bulbs in the sockets spaced out on the overhang that shielded the doors from the weather and provided a porch, of sorts. Some of the more permanent occupants further along had lawn chairs setting next to their doors as a place to sit and watch the traffic or weather. It was tornado alley, after all. Lightning bugs illuminated for a short second and went out. I hadn't seen them before and was mesmerized by them for a time.

It occurred to me in that moment that I hadn't thought about beer in a long time. It was not something I could afford and had no way to obtain, but it should have been in my thoughts. As much as it seemed to play a part in my life at home, I had not missed it at all. That surprised me. But then, I had no need to socialize. I got more attention at the restaurant than I was accustomed to getting in a month back home.

The car was getting low on gas and I needed to fill the tank. If I was going to have to drive to work every day, I would need to have some gasoline. It was better to fill it up at the start of the week, so I could see how much that was going to cost. It was all part of making a budget and sticking with it.

I drove to where 54 intersected 69 and took 69 to the restaurant where a convenience store and gas station was only a bit further down the road. In my head, I knew I should have waited until Monday, when I would go back to work, but it was Friday night and even though I had not earned enough to cruise town, I wanted to be out. All the kids my age cruised town in their cars and pickups and it just felt good to be among them for a moment.

Freedom seemed elusive then, because with all of my freedom, I was the one who could not participate in the endless loop of automobiles and those held captive by parents or spouses were zooming back and forth as they pleased. It was harder to see how I had gained anything for all of my sacrifices, except that I knew I could be out there in that parking lot all night and no one would ask where I had been. I could get involved in some bad deeds, sins or crimes and no one would have a say other than perhaps the police, but I would shame no one but myself. The practical aspects of freedom resisted easy comprehension in those circumstances, but I was convinced that they existed far and above anything the other kids my age experienced and I was proud of it.

So, I sat on the hood of the car and watched the flashy cars drive by, the ones that had been jacked up in the back, hood scoops applied, fat tires fitted and new paint sprayed. Loud pipes verbalized the existence of massive engines under their hoods. Once in a while, a pretty girl would drive by with friends in the car and I would fantasize an encounter that even in the depths of the fantasy, reality persisted, overpowering it, forcing me to recognize the impossibility. Then, as time wore on, I began to feel foolish and childish for sitting there watching life literally pass by without the money to participate. I had always been an outcast, but I felt it more acutely then than ever before. I wasn't even from that town, had no connection to it at all, except Tom, a friend I was forbidden to visit.

I got up and sat in the car for a while, watching it pass through the windshield. I drove back to the room and parked in front of the door. It was going to be a long weekend without food or entertainment. The worst part of the job was that I couldn't work all week, because Morty wouldn't pay the overtime. Without working every day, I was unable to eat every day. I could get a pop out of the machine by the office, I had enough for that, but nothing else, because I could not afford to drive to a convenience store every time I got hungry for a candy bar or some other cheap filler.

I flopped on the bed and stared up at the ceiling. The weekend seemed like an eternity stretched out before me, unfathomable and unrelenting. Panic set in when I considered that I might have made a mistake, that the freedom that meant so much to me was an illusion. I felt free, but trapped in a motel room that consumed half of all that I earned. Freedom did not fill my stomach or put gas in the tank. At home all of my money could be spent on recreation, pleasure, beer and gas. None of the money I earned paid for rent or food. Those were paid for in exchange for good behavior and obedience to the rules. In Kansas I had no rules but those of finances and budgets which seemed at the time to be the greater forces of bondage, so what had I accomplished, really?

My mind raced, working through it, weighing the illusion with the reality, the different kinds of restraints, those imposed by others and those imposed by finances. There had to be some value achieved that was worth the sacrifices I had made, the privations I had suffered. Wasn't there?

That question remained on my thoughts all weekend, through the fishing shows on a local channel where the images separated and hung ghostlike over the other image, back and forth, rarely solidifying into one discernible image long enough to decipher the action taking place. It remained with me when I went outside and listened to the eight-track player emit Ronnie Milsap songs through the speakers, especially the oddly rock and roll vibe of *Honky Tonk Women*, that in my ignorance of rock and roll I did not identify as the Rolling Stones tune, but a weird aberration of the Milsap brand. It remained with me when I purchased a pop from the machine and looked up into a broiling sky of dark clouds infused with a white swirling mass and barely made it back to the room before hail pelted the car, jumping off of the surface of the roof like spring-loaded white beans. The hailstones piled up like snow three or four inches deep all across the parking lot, then began to move as one, sliding down the slope to the ditch lining the highway.

At the end of the weekend, when I got back to work deep inside the kitchen at the dishwasher, I was able to distract myself from the question that vexed me by clearing up the backlog of dishes that awaited my arrival. As soon as I had gotten the dishes cleared and the bins emptied and replaced out front, I ordered my usual Monday morning huge breakfast of sausage, eggs and pancakes, pacing while it was cooked, doing anything to distract my attention from the stove where Tom prepared the meal. I ate hungrily and incessantly until I could put the plates and silverware in the rack and wipe my mouth.

Rae came in with a bin that had only one coffee cup in it. I stared at her as I took the cup out and put it in the rack.

"I saw you parked on Friday night," she said, letting the bin dangle from her delicate, fine-boned hand.

I waited.

"You looked lonely and sad."

I chuckled.

"I would have stopped, but I was with a friend."

"Blonde skinny dude?" I asked.

She looked at me with an air of disgust, rolled her eyes and turned away without answering. I followed her out and looked behind the counter to see if any bins were full enough to let me run the dishwasher, but they were empty and I went back to the confines of the kitchen.

After the lunch rush, in the midst of the pause between then and the early supper crowd, I walked over to Tom.

"How much you payin' for the new place?" he asked.

"Fifty a week."

"Sounds like a lot."

"It is, I wish I could get some extra hours around here, but I'm already at forty."

"Yeah, not much chance of that."

I nodded. I heard sounds of tables being cleared, so I went out to get the bins and get back to work. I could carry two at a time, something that helped move things along. The job wasn't hard and only the mornings kept me as busy as I wanted to be all day, but it came to an end and I went back to the room.

The smell of grease and food stuck to my clothes and I could hardly wait to take a shower every day. I stripped out of my shirt, boots and socks. I dug in my suitcase, that I hadn't bothered to unpack, for some clean underwear. There was a knock at the door. I approached it with caution, not knowing who it could be. I opened it and looked out.

Rae was standing there in a T-shirt, jeans and tennis shoes having changed out of her work uniform.

"Hey," I said, looking behind her and to the sides.

"Hi," she said, a light-hearted giggle in her voice.

"I was just about to take a shower," I said.

"Want some company?"

"Yeah, give me a few minutes, okay? I'll be right out."

"You're gonna make me wait outside?"

"I guess not," I said, stepping back, pulling the door open for her.

She came in, looked around and took a seat on a chair.

"I don't have anything to drink, or eat," I said, explaining my scant hospitality.

"It's all right."

"I'll be out in a minute," I explained as I backed toward the bathroom.

I closed the door, wondering what she was doing there. We hadn't talked about her coming over, or even where I had moved to. It was part of her tease that she pretended to be interested in me, would make sexual remarks, the sort of things that were designed to embarrass me or get me to chase her, which I was not going to do given the fact that I met her boyfriend in the parking lot of the other motel. My natural sense of conspiracy led me to wonder if she wasn't setting me up for him to come in and beat the hell out of me the way I had treated Kathy's husband. The way Kathy's husband had Todd. I had to consider that a possibility as I showered.

The truth is, I didn't know anything about Rae, except that she was a year older than I was, had a little girl by someone who was no longer around. I had knowledge of her boyfriend not only in the parking lot, but that was who she had been with on Friday night, that much was clear. What were we going to talk about? Was there anything at all that we had in common? I wasn't good at talking to girls as it was and I was sure to make her mad within a few minutes, so what was the point?

I dried off with the scratchy towel supplied by the motel owners, kicked my dirty underwear into the corner, put on the clean ones and pulled my jeans up over them. I thought I ought to pick up the underwear in case she needed to use the facilities after I got out, so I did. I held them in my hand, thinking out the moves I was going to make so as not to draw too much attention to them as I got dressed. I wasn't used to having anyone in my room, much less a girl and it threw off my patterns of behavior.

I opened the door, saw that she was no longer in the chair and thought she might have left, until I opened the door further and saw that she was lying on the bed naked, except for pink, fuzzy socks. She was grinning at me with her left hand propped under her head, her right leg angled over the top, obscuring her pubic area while her small, white breasts sloped toward the bed, small mounds only slightly falling out of form. I stared at her, still trying to figure out what it meant. I tossed the underwear at the suitcase on the dresser and stepped up to the bed. As I looked down at her, taking it in, her eyes closed softly like a cat's eyes when it's being stroked. She liked being looked at that way.

I reached down and ran my hand down her side, feeling how rough it felt against the soft skin stretching over her ribs and wondered how that could feel pleasant to a girl, a woman, the callouses from throwing seventy-pound bales of hay up onto a stack rubbing abrasively against her skin. She reached around my leg with her free hand, high up on my thigh, close to where it counted and pulled down on the loose fabric there. I straightened up, undid my pants, let them fall, stepped out of them and sat next to her on the bed.

I leaned down and kissed her on the cheek, her ear and up on the forehead as my hand slipped down into the hollow between her ribs and her hips, then up the smooth side of her hip. Rae reached up, pulled my head down onto the bed as she scooted backward, giving me room. I laid down, staring up at the ceiling until her face hovered over me as she straddled me. She kissed me aggressively, backed up, pulled my underwear down to my thighs and moved back up and over me.

She slid on top of me, over me, put one hand on my chest and began to rock back and forth, smoothly at first, then faster and rougher, emitting a chirp from her lips in a rhythm with her backward stoke. I finished a second or two before she did. She shuddered, her eyes closed tight and her fine, blonde eyebrows knotted as she licked her lips and collapsed on top of me. Then, she hummed, pushing back against me, rocking slightly back and forth. She pushed up and away from me, looking down into my eyes with a crazy, desperate look, kissed me quickly, then got off and went to the end of the bed where her clothes were piled. She had no underwear, but pulled her jeans on over her bare bottom, put her shoes on as she pulled her T-shirt over her bare breasts and looked at me for a second as I lay there, underwear still pulled halfway down my thighs, my pubic hair glistening.

"I really gotta go, I have to get home," she said, walking out and closing the door.

I pulled my underwear up to cover myself and stared at the ceiling, realizing that whatever had gone on was just for her. It was something she had wanted to do from the first day, probably, and waited for me to get a place, but it had less to do with me than her. I didn't even have to exist as a human being. I felt like an empty box that had been checked somewhere in her sexual ledger. At least with her, I didn't have to wonder what it would all mean in the bigger picture of school, or dances or parties; whether she would expect some sort of relationship to take hold, or expected me to call her every day after school or what. I was just fucked. Nothing else, no emotion involved in it, a biological thing had taken place that very day all over town in bedrooms and living room floors all through the day and night between consenting men and women.

I enjoyed it, it was the sort of romantic relationship I could handle at that age, that didn't come with all of the other baggage of affection normally associated with the act. But, it was empty, too. Lifeless, in a way; unfulfilling. She meant nothing to me, I did not cherish her, would not die to protect her or work my entire life to sustain her, provide for her. Our times together would never be precious or gentle, the sort of luxurious stroking of a loved one, basking in each other's adoration. Just sex. The only kind I had ever had. Not usually so abrupt or callous, but still, the same, hurried and meaningless sex.

The next day at work, all hell seemed to have broken loose. There was a huge fight raging between Rae and Barbara, something that had been brewing for a long time. I stayed out of it, even though each of them would come back into the kitchen and corner me at the dishwasher.

"That little whore just called me a bitch! Me! A bitch!"

What could I do, but stand there shaking my head in commiseration? I took the bin from their hands, often empty, but giving them an excuse to come into the kitchen. They had been brought back into Morty's office and told to keep it down and not to disturb the customers over it and they toned it down quite a bit, but the undercurrents were strong.

Rae came into the kitchen and threw me against the dishwasher with all her weight, which was still only about ninety pounds, if that.

"She called me a whore! But, you know that's a lie, don't you Lane?"

"Yes ma'am," I replied.

I didn't think I would be able to make it to the end of the shift. Tom got it as much as I did and nearly got sucked into the argument, but I saved him with a clever defense.

"What's this all about?" I asked, because Tom was much more privy to the goings on than I was.

"I don't know and I don't want to know. I'm just praying that I don't find out before I can get out of here."

CHAPTER TWENTY

Things had gone along fairly peaceful for three days, until Friday, when I was called into Morty's office after work. I went in, sat down and waited. I had never met his daughter and only seen her a couple of times at the restaurant, but I could tell from the photos that I wanted nothing to do with her or her boyfriend, who were caught in all manner of poses. Looking around at the walls was like looking at a cheesy montage of a television rock band trying desperately to be the Beatles with edgy photos of them taken in different settings making faces at the camera.

Morty came in and sat down heavily in the chair.

"Whooo," he said, "it is hot out there." He wiped his face with a rag he carried in his hand. What hair he had was wet with sweat, beads of sweat forming in place of those that had just been wiped away. "It's good to be inside."

I looked at him, hoping that whatever he wanted to say wouldn't take too long.

He looked at me, studying me, looking for signs of something, but I didn't know what.

"I hate to do this, Lane, but I gotta let you go."

I blinked, uncomprehending. What did that mean?

"Let me go where?"

"Out, into the world. You can't work here."

"Why?"

"You're the cause of all this strife between the girls and getting rid of you will solve a lot of problems, it'll cause a few too, but fewer than it solves, so I have to let you go," he said, handing me an envelope with my last paycheck in it.

"What?" I asked, none of what he was saying made any sense. How could the strife between the girls have anything to do with me? It wasn't possible. Rae is the only one I had anything to do with and that wasn't love or a cause for jealousy, by either of them. There had been no secret meetings at the dishwasher or anything in the past couple of days. No one could have known what happened by our actions, because there was nothing. I wasn't even sure anything had happened; it hadn't been acknowledged by either of us and might have been a dream for all I knew.

"I gotta let you go, I'm sorry."

"I don't get it; I don't have a job?"

"No."

"Because a couple of the waitresses are fighting?"

"Fighting over you," he said.

"That's not possible," I said, shaking my head. "I'm not seeing either one of them, they both have other boyfriends, don't they? How the hell am I involved?"

Morty didn't have any of the answers and it didn't matter, he wasn't going to change his mind. I wasn't even sure it was true and I didn't know who would tell me the truth. If I asked either of the girls, they would deny it to my face. I knew that. So, I took my last paycheck and went out to my car and leaned against the broiling trunk as I tried to figure out what I was going to do. I stood out in the parking lot, stunned. Then Barbara came out and walked up to me.

"Heard you got fired."

"Yep."

"What are you doing for dinner?"

"Don't know."

"Come with me to dinner at my house, okay?"

"Sure," I said.

"I get off in half an hour."

I nodded my head and watched her walk back to the restaurant. She did have kind of a nice rear end, after all. I thought about trying to get her to tell me what actually happened, but not unless I thought I could get the truth out of her. I would have to ask at a moment when her guard was down and we were being nice to each other.

Barbara and I had never exactly gotten along. We would have, but she thought my staring at her meant something when I first got to Fort Scott and it didn't. I just liked to watch her blush. Ever since then, we had bickered like a brother and sister would, affectionately disliking each other. The invitation to have supper at her house, to me, was an admission of some sort of guilt. Maybe Barbara lied to Morty, telling him that I was the problem to hide the real reason the girls were arguing with each other.

When she came back out, I followed her in her Datsun pickup all the way to her parent's house. It was something I normally wouldn't do, but I thought she had something to do with my predicament and that she owed me supper. What other reason would she have for inviting me? She had never invited me to supper before, she had never really talked to me at all, unless it was to annoy me at work.

I met her mother when I got there. She was an attractive older woman with a nice figure and kind face who welcomed me as I assumed, she would welcome one of Barbara's boyfriends, but I thought she got the wrong impression of who I was and why I was there. Her dad was out working in the shop.

"Maybe, I ought to go out and help," I offered, thinking that it would be a better place for me than sitting in the house with the women, who talked about subjects of which I knew nothing, on which I had no opinions.

"No, he'll be along," Barbara's mom, Jane, said with a stern voice that I wanted to obey.

I nodded and drank the iced tea offered to me when I came in. The two of them could have been speaking a foreign language and I would have understood them better, been able to pick up on sign language and an encouraging nod of the head. But, Barbara and her mom talked about things I could not even grasp.

"No, the one with the pink bodice," Jane said, arguing with Barbara.

"But that's so old-fashioned looking," Barbara objected.

"That's the point, dear."

I had no idea; I wouldn't know a bodice from a bratwurst. When was the old man going to show up and talk about cars?

It was closer to six before I met Jim and I was relieved to do so.

"Yeah, what were you working on out there?"

"Aw, the emergency brake was stuck, I just had to pull the wheel and WD-40 the spring."

"Don't wanna get that on the pads," I said, grinning.

"Oh, hell no," he said, chuckling at the thought.

Then, we sat down to supper, saying grace before we started, which was different from our house, where supper was somewhat of a free-for-all and we only said grace at Thanksgiving and Christmas. The Zimmers did it every meal.

"Sound like you know your way around cars," Jim said, chewing on some bread.

"Equipment more than cars, but cars, too," I replied, taking a drink of tea. "I haven't overhauled anything, but I've done some push rods and ground some valves for dad, he's the real mechanic, used to work for the Ford garage when he was younger, after Korea," I said, realizing I was telling Jim more about myself than I had ever told anyone. If they didn't know my dad's story, I wasn't the one to tell them.

"Korea?"

"Yeah."

"Don't know too many folks from Korea, mostly World War Two. I was in Vietnam from sixty-six to sixty-seven," he said, looking down.

I nodded. The supper table was not the place to discuss such things.

Jane put her hand on his shoulder, rubbing it.

"What do you do for a living now?" I asked, feeling obligated to change the subject.

"Mechanic, down at the Co-op."

"Ah," I said. "I bet you got a nice shop out there,"

"I take on some side jobs now and again," he said.

We finished supper and I went outside with Barbara to say goodbye. It was awkward, what were we going to do? Kiss? That would have been weird. Jim came out as I opened the door to my car, ready to get in.

"Lane, you ought to go down to the Co-op in the morning, go up to the office and tell them I told you to fill out an application."

"I will," I said, then looked at Barbara. "Thanks for supper, first meal I had that tasted like someone cared in a long time."

"Mom's a great cook."

I nodded and pulled the door closed. I backed out of the driveway, waving at Jim as I passed the shop. Then, I was on my way back to the room, my head swimming, struggling to figure out what everything meant. The day had been so full of lies and deception, of things that could not be true, or were odd and unexpected, that had hidden meanings and unknown definitions. I had to get a dictionary from somewhere to find out what the hell a bodice was.

Jon and I loved words. Whenever either one of us heard a new one we would bring it back home and tell the other and sit around for hours trying to figure out what it meant. We recalled to each other the sentence it was used in and since he was older than me and had gone to school longer than I had, he taught me a lot of words that way. Any new word we heard on television would go through the process of working out what it meant. We weren't trying to increase our vocabularies, they were puzzles, but increase our vocabularies we did. A bodice wasn't in them.

I got up early the next morning and drove down to the Co-op and found the office in the building behind the gas station where they fixed cars and did all the tire work. That sort of service station was going out of style and more and more convenience stores that sold gas were popping up.

I walked up the stairs that led to the office above the feed store. I met a receptionist who asked who I was there to see.

"I don't know, I'm just here to fill out an application, Jim Zimmer said I should," I added, hoping it made a difference since

I had no job.

She handed me an application and a pen. She showed me to a conference room. I sat down at the long table and filled out the application. There wasn't a lot of information to put down. I didn't put down that I worked at the hay farm in Walden, what difference did it make? I put down the restaurant, hoping Morty would give me a good recommendation if they called him. I put down Jim Zimmer as a reference. I handed it back to the receptionist and was told to take a seat in the room.

The boss came in wearing a shirt and a tie with my application in his hand. He read it over while I sat there. He would stop and look at me after reading something and go back to the application.

"You put Jim Zimmer down as a reference."

"Yes sir."

"Who's that?"

I blinked and tried to figure out how he could not know his own mechanic.

"The mechanic at the gas station," I said and a knowing look came into his eyes.

"You know Jim a long time, have you?"

"No sir, just met him last night. I know his daughter Barbara from working at the restaurant."

"Uh huh," he said, arranging his tie. "It says here, you're from Colorado."

"Well, that was the only address I knew, I'm living out at the motel on fifty-four."

"All by yourself?"

"Yes sir."

"You're sixteen?"

"About to be seventeen," I said.

"What are you doing in Kansas all by yourself?"

"Working."

"Parents know you're here?"

"Yes sir."

"And, they're okay with that?"

"Well, I don't know that they're okay with it, but I'm here and they didn't tell me to come home, so, I guess they are."

The boss looked at me for a long time, thinking.

"I don't think I should give you this job," he said. "I think you should go back home and go to school."

"Well, sir, I'm not going to, even if you don't give me the job. That just means that I'll have to find another job somewhere else, because I've made this decision and I will not go back home, because I couldn't make it. I would rather stay here and starve to death than that."

He thought some more.

"You're honest, I've gotta say that for ya. Okay, you got the job, go tell Jim you can start tomorrow morning."

"Thank you, sir. I'll work hard, you'll see," I said, getting up to leave.

"You know how I know you're honest?"

I thought because I made it a policy to always tell the truth and that the fact of it would shine through, but I wanted to hear how he knew.

"How's that?"

"Because that's not Jim Zimmer, it's Jim Crandall, so you could not have known him any longer than last night. Had you said you knew him for a year, or even a month, I would have known you were lying."

"But, his daughter's name's Zimmer."

"Step-daughter, Jim married her mother two years ago."

"Ohhhh, thanks for letting me know," I said and left.

I stopped at the station and told Jim I got the job and I would be there in the morning.

"Any reason you can't work today?"

"Not really, but the boss said tomorrow."

"I'll talk to him. You might as well learn what to do. Kevin, get this boy a time card and show him how to punch in."

I worked the rest of the day pumping gas, cleaning windshields, checking oil and putting air in tires. It was much better than the restaurant and a lot of the people who stopped there for gas were country folks, farmers and farmer's kids, people I identified with on a basic level. I went to the room that night dirty, needing a shower. My clothes smelled oily but they didn't stink of french fries.

I took a shower and laid down on the bed. The gas station paid more than the restaurant, too, plus I got to work every other Saturday, so I would make more money. Things were starting to look up.

I heard a knock on the door, but it didn't sound like my door. I looked out the window and saw Barbara standing at the door next to mine. Maybe she got confused and was trying to find me. I cracked the door open and saw her go into the room next door where a guy was also renting by the week. He drove a pickup and worked for some sort of construction company. I closed my door again.

A few minutes later, I heard the bed next door working, then it started banging against the wall. I could envision what was taking place, but I drove that thought from my mind and turned the television on. I didn't want to hear the panting or squealing that would inevitably result.

Could that have been it? That when Barbara came to meet her boyfriend, she saw Rae's car and assumed that Rae was with her boyfriend? That she got the room numbers mixed up or didn't recognize my car in her anger? I chuckled at the thought of it.

It made sense in a crazy sort of way. Could it have been when Barbara called Rae a whore, Rae took it wrong and thought she was being attacked for being with me? That before the two could work out what was going on, Barbara let it be about me, rather than to own up that her boyfriend lived next door? She threw me to the wolves to put Rae off the scent of her boyfriend, knowing Rae might just get even by sleeping with him, too. The way Rae went about it, I had no doubt that she could do it.

Without admitting a thing, Barbara assuaged her guilt by helping me get a job with her stepdad. That did a couple of things, too. Since I knew she got me the job, I wouldn't betray her to her father, as if I would. That was none of my business.

After piecing that puzzle together, the only question I had left was whether Barbara intentionally came to see her boyfriend when she knew I was there and had sex as loudly as she could to exert some power over me, or trying to make me jealous, or she just get a little kick out of doing it, knowing that I could hear it, demonstrating what I was missing by not taking her seriously.

I was getting a whole different perspective of who I thought she was. She seemed a little bit kinky to me after that. But, not working at the restaurant any longer, I had no reason to see her, unless she came to the station; even then, our relationship was at an end. We weren't friends and I was just another guy working for her dad.

What I did not know and would find out later through discussions overheard at the station, was that Kathy, Tom's girlfriend, who was married to the Navy guy I knocked unconscious, was Barbara's sister. They looked nothing alike and it was not something I ever would have linked on my own.

While I kept my mouth closed and didn't engage in the gossip that went around at the station, I heard a lot of it. I heard more of it at the station than I did at the restaurant and that surprised me. There were crosscurrents flowing every which way in that town. One of the guys I worked with at the station was the father of Rae's daughter. I found that out, too, by keeping my mouth shut and letting other people reveal their secrets while protecting my own. It seemed more and more like a good policy as the months wore on.

The months did wear on, though. In time, all of the kids went back to school and I started filling up cars for high schoolers and students at the community college. The well-dressed, clean shaven boys in their new cars would pull in and I would dote on them and their vehicles like anyone else, at the same time enduring the familiar sneers of people of that class.

In September, Kevin, Jim's actual son, who worked at the gas station as a mechanic asked me to move in with him. He had a nice two-bedroom house on Main that he rented and his roommate had just moved out. I was sick of the motel by then. It was eating up all of my pay and I didn't have any way to keep food cold or heat it up when I wanted to. I wound up living on cold soup out of the can and potato chips. The rent at Kevin's was only one-hundred and seventy-five a month and, despite the fact that I hesitated to live with someone I worked with, the events of Walden still fresh in my mind, I did it.

    I moved into a bedroom off the kitchen. I was making more money, paying less in rent, could afford and was able to keep stuff to make lunch meat sandwiches, fried egg sandwiches, scrambled eggs, toast and bacon. I learned how to make omelets at the restaurant and ate those occasionally. It was a whole new world from where I started.

CHAPTER TWENTY-ONE

It was about the time that I settled into Kevin's rental house that Roger showed up. Roger was a former roommate of Kevin's who had worked at the same restaurant that I did, who was friends with Tom when Tom was a dishwasher there. He came back to town from some college somewhere in the state. He was there to visit and I steered clear of him, because he did not come back to visit me, but rather Kevin and I liked to keep my distance from anything personal with Kevin.

Then, one Friday night, while Kevin was on a date with his girlfriend, Roger tapped on my door.

"Yeah?"

"I thought you might like to come out and talk for a while. I'm all alone out here with nothing to do."

I should have stayed in my room, because I sensed Roger was one of those people who couldn't stand to be alone. He was the sort to talk to some random person at a bus station or in line at the grocery store or would even sit down next to someone on a bench and strike up a conversation. It's not that that was bad, or wrong, but it was so totally opposite from me that I could tell we would really have nothing to talk about, except his experiences, his thoughts, his ideas and dreams. People like that can't stand for silence in a conversation and I lived for it. I liked the uncomfortable look people had when I refused to talk. I did that, because I got tired of hearing my own voice after a while and I would shut down, but that wouldn't deter them in the least. I felt like Roger would carry the conversation and I went out to have a chat.

I followed Roger out into the living room where he felt most comfortable sitting on the floor close to the stereo. I knew then that I was going to be in for a lecture on modern rock music, the evolution of the soul since the Beatles white album and the medicinal benefits of marijuana. Every one of them thought that, being a cowboy, I hadn't heard of their rambling patter before, that they were educating me, enlightening me, when, to me, it all seemed like self-deception to put a healthy, creative nuance to doing dope and listening to the stereo. I don't know if any of them actually found a deeper meaning through chemicals, or just deluded themselves into believing it as a means of continuing self-destructive behavior. It didn't matter to me, because I didn't do it and I didn't care if they did.

Roger sat cross-legged near the stereo so he could change records with ease to emphasize one point or another, during the evolution of rock lecture, but what he should have been doing is paying a little more attention to his weight and lack of physical activity. The thing I noticed about drugs was they made people lazy and maybe that was because they were so busy inside their own heads that they couldn't get up and go to work, but what did it matter? The outcome was the same.

Roger pulled a little pipe out of his coat pocket and a small bag of weed. He started packing the weed into the bowl of the pipe.

"I don't know if you should do that in here," I said, not knowing how Kevin felt about it.

"Oh, yeah," Roger waved me off. "Kevin and I used to smoke all the time, no problem."

I didn't believe him, but that was between those two, not me. He wasn't my friend. I didn't bring him in, Kevin did. Roger dug a lighter out of his pocket and lit the pipe, took a big hit and held his breath. He exhaled slowly and reached the pipe toward me.

"Naw, that ain't my thing."

"What ain't your thing?"

"Dope," I said.

He grinned.

"What ain't your 'thing'?" he mocked, "enjoying life ain't your thing? Digging deeper into your subconscious ain't your thing? Being with it, ain't your thing? You're too fuckin' provincial, man."

I shrugged.

"You're cheating yourself, ya know? And, pot ain't the half of it, do some LSD sometime, if you really want to expand your consciousness and understand the intricacies of reality, man, like go down a rabbit hole, ya know, like wonderland. I can turn you on if you wanna see what you can't see from your limited scope, your Protestant, straight scope."

He lit the pipe again and inhaled deeply, holding it and letting it out. The smell of burning weeds filled the air. I wondered if challenging him would make the whole evening worth it, or not. I felt like I was learning a lot just being there, watching him pontificate.

"I ain't gonna tell no one if you want some, ya know. I won't tell Tom, but you gotta know that Tom used to smoke with me, too. I wouldn't tell him, but even if I did, what difference does it make? It's not like you did it first."

"Tom smoked dope with you?" I asked, not believing it, thinking it was a way to coerce me into doing it so he wouldn't feel alone.

"Yeah, all the time, after work. He was like you, scared of it, worried about what people would say, but he saw, he got it, then, he was cool and chicks started liking him and he saw it was a good thing. Makes sex better, too."

"What makes you think I'm scared of it? Or, that I'm worried about what other people would say? I'm in Kansas, all by myself. What makes you think I'm afraid of anything?"

"So, you want some, then?" he asked, cheering up; thinking he had successfully manipulated me with the concept of being afraid.

"No, I want to know why it's so important to you that I do

it. What difference does it make to you? You think I'm making this decision, now? That I'm looking at you and thinking that I want to be like you and the way to do that is to start smoking dope? Is that it? Like I don't know who I am and you're gonna show me, reveal the inner me by smoking dope?"

I looked away, knowing that I should stay away from other people. Even though I knew what I was getting into, I still came out and sat down with him, because I wasn't afraid of what he would say, how he would try and coerce me, I knew who I was and that wasn't it.

"What I'm saying is, you don't know who you are," he said, setting the pipe down and digging in his pocket for something else, another plastic bag. "What I'm saying is you're just looking at the superficial you, not the inner you, not the you at the molecular level, the nuclear level. This here," he held up the plastic bag, "will let you see that."

"You're selling your goods to the wrong guy."

"I'm not selling anything; you can have some."

"Yes, you are, you're selling me some vision of myself, some vision of reality, when in fact, reality is all around us. Your reality is illusion. How do you square that?"

Roger sat staring at me and I thought he was going to get up and make a run at me, so I brought my body into position to deflect his charge and put him on the ground.

"All reality is illusion, dude," he said, grinning, swaying backward, looking up at the ceiling with bloodshot eyes. "Don't you get it? You see what the television shows you, you believe what the television tells you and it's all designed to keep the military industrial complex running, man, keep it chugging along, feeding it our young people. They wrap it in the flag and it's your reality, but there's a lot more going on out there than looking through the narrow scope of the television screen, there's life going on out there."

"I know about life. What the hell do you think I'm doing here? In Kansas? I'm sleeping in my car, living in shithole motels, eating once a day for a long time and not on weekends. You don't think I know anything about life? That I need to get it second-hand from you, through drugs?"

"That's not what I'm sayin' man, you're complicating things, blowing them out of proportion."

I sat there looking at him, his suave, hip demeanor slipping a little bit when he didn't have a wide-eyed, gullible punk to lay his rap on. I didn't consider myself "cool" or hip. I was a hick, but that didn't mean I was stupid. I liked being alone and being alone helped me to think things through, things I'd heard before and I had heard his song and dance before a couple of times.

The first one was an older cowboy, a guy named Josh, who swung between the hippies and cowboys trying to fit in somewhere. He talked me into going with him to Masonville, before I got my license and laid it all out, except he was angling toward dope as a means to something else, to some sort of sexual freedom. It all sounded reasonable and cool, but I sensed some undercurrent that I didn't understand. Then, drunk and on the way back, he started in again, wanting me to smoke dope, telling me how it would open my mind and reduce my inhibitions, let me see a different reality. He told me how he was like me once, too, but that I would be able to experience things in a clearer way, see things others couldn't see. The sexual freedom part, I liked and sounded all right, but there were no girls with us, so I didn't know why he kept bringing that part into it. I didn't see why I had to smoke dope to get to that, I had never been against sexual freedom. It was the girls that needed to loosen up, not me.

"You're killin' my high, man. Let's listen to some tunes for a while. This," he said, pulling out an album from a cardboard box he brought with him, "is some great shit."

Roger pulled the black disc out of the jacket and started the turntable. He set the record on the turntable and raised the stylus, setting it gently down. There was a buzzing noise from the speakers until the room filled with music. Drums beating, then a piano came in rhythmic-like and it was not what I expected. I thought it was going to be loud guitars and screaming voices, but it wasn't bad, not my style, but everything good didn't have to be my style. I could appreciate it for what it was.

"Meat Loaf!" Roger yelled over the music and started hopping on his bottom, pretending to be playing different instruments.

I listened to the A-side of the album and from a person who was not into rock, who preferred a simple song written by someone who lived life, real life and sung by someone who had felt the sting of betrayal and suffered long days of work for a few precious moments in a bar, having a cold one, it didn't do much for me. It was fantastic and out of control and everything that seemed farfetched and plastic. Roger couldn't see it, because he was hearing the music, each individual instrument played at a masterful level and felt connected to it in a way that I didn't. So, when he started to doze, my entertainment was over for the night and I went back to my little room off the kitchen and went to bed.

I woke in the morning to sounds I had not heard at Kevin's before, stomping of feet, voices and the slamming of cabinets in the kitchen. I listened to see if I could discern the cause of the disturbance, but it wasn't clear. Opening the door, I looked out and saw Kevin in the kitchen eating a bowl of cereal.

"Were you a part of all that?"

"All what?"

"Smoking dope in the house."

"He said you and him used to do it all the time."

"That don't give you guys the right to do it without asking me."

"Whoa there, I didn't do any of it. When he first started, I asked if he thought you would approve and he said you guys used to do it all the time. That's as far as I go with this, I have no right to tell your guest what to do or not to do in your house."

"You're my roommate, you have a right to tell people not to smoke dope in the house. You pay rent," he said, hurt and I saw it as being hurt, I had betrayed him in his mind, as if expecting me to lay down the law in his absence. I wasn't going to let him get away with the double standard. Besides, he hadn't bothered to tell me the house rules.

"I rent a bedroom," I said. "The rest of the house is yours, not mine. You invited a guest into your whole house. Had he wanted to smoke dope in my little bedroom, I would have stopped it, but you didn't bother to ask me if it was okay to let him stay here anyway, so you must not think of me as a real roommate unless something goes wrong. Besides, you never once said what you thought about dope. How was I supposed to know?"

Kevin munched on the cereal and chased some floating marshmallows around the bowl with his spoon, scooping two or three up at a time. He was thinking about what I had just said.

"Okay, I get it, my fault," he said and I went back into the room. I didn't see Roger after that.

We went back to our normal life for several weeks until disaster struck for me. I got in my car at the gas station and tried to start it, but it just cranked and cranked with no fire. Jim came out to have a look and quickly identified the problem as a broken timing chain.

"Five hundred," he said, taking my freedom. "The best I can do, with as much help as I can give, the parts and time are nearly that."

I looked at him through the window.

"I can't afford that," I said.

"I'm sorry. Maybe you could call your folks, or something."

I nodded, but knew I would never do it. If I couldn't get out of the jam I was in, I couldn't have the car, simple as that. I would have to walk for a while. By then, it was December and there was snow on the ground. I hadn't even packed a coat when I left, but Kevin let me have one of his old ones.

I got out of the car, locked it and started walking up the hill toward town thinking about what I would do. I couldn't leave the car there for very long, they would make me move it.

I was going to have to sell it. It seemed colder in Kansas than it was in Colorado, the humidity probably and the idea of walking to and from work every day was not appealing, especially in the cold. I didn't know how much I could get out of the car; broken the way it was. I assumed I would take a loss on it.

The car was everything to me, it was life itself, or so it seemed until it was broken beyond my ability to repair it. Then, it became a thing, a hassle, a problem to be solved. Not having a car didn't mean that I couldn't go anywhere, I could get a bus ticket, if there was somewhere I wanted to go. But, it was protection, shelter at times. I had to realign my life without the car and I was having trouble with that.

When I got back to the house, I kicked the snow off my boots and left them at the door. I went to my bedroom and flopped down on the bed. I was afoot in Kansas. I kept driving that fact into my brain, forcing acceptance of it. The whole world seemed to change, but it hadn't. What was I really doing with the car anyway? I drove it back and forth to work, sometimes down to buy a burger at the place on the corner of Main and Highway 69. It wasn't like I bought six sacks of groceries, if I had two sacks it was unusual, so I didn't need it for that. I could get along; I would have to get along. I went out to talk to Kevin when he got home.

"How much do you think I can get for that car?"

"Not much, it don't even run."

"A couple hundred bucks?"

"No way, maybe a hundred if you find the right guy. The junkyard will give ya fifty."

I didn't want to think of the car in a junkyard, it hardly had a scratch on it. I didn't want its life to stop, just because it was broken. I wanted to think that I could sell it to someone who would put the money into it to get it fixed. It felt like an old friend, but it wasn't, it was just metal. I had to come to terms with that.

"I'm going to have to sell it," I said and went to my room.

The next day at work, I told Jim what I had in mind.

"I need to sell it, I guess. I want to sell it to someone who's going to fix it, though. I don't want it to go to the junkyard."

Jim wore his businessman face when we discussed it, the one that had to tell old ladies that their repairs were going to cost three hundred dollars instead of twenty, the firm face, the reality face.

"What did you pay for the car?"

"I bought it from my dad, so he let me have it cheap," I said, not wanting to tell him three hundred dollars, making the junkyard the most feasible.

"You didn't pay over five for it, I know that, not with those miles on it."

"Three."

"Okay, three. The parts, the gaskets, the timing chain, assuming the sprocket isn't damaged, but it probably is, so replace that and the water pump and it comes to two hundred. Then, there's time and the whole front end of the engine has to come off. Who knows how rusted some of those bolts are? There's space in the garage that even if we knock a bunch off for labor, which is hard to do, we have to account for the bay and the income it represents, it's not just whether we are doing a favor, or not. I'm responsible for making these bays pay off the way the company expects them to."

"So, basically, you're saying I might as well call the junkyard."

"Not so fast," he said, a gleam in his eye. "What if we take it to my shop? What if I let you work on it there? It'll be warm. I won't help, though; I can't let my side jobs go, they need to pay off, too. But, I would be around for advice, to get you started and answer questions, like that."

"I don't know where I'll get the two hundred," I said, thinking about it. I did have some money saved and had been putting a little away every payday, but everything I had was for an emergency, like if I had to catch a bus.

"Think it over and let me know. This offer isn't good for very long, you need to get that car out of the parking lot."

"I know," I said and thought about it all day. I knew he expected an answer before the end of the day, but there was a lot to think about. I would have to call home and ask for at least one hundred dollars if I said yes. I could send them twenty dollars a month until it was repaid. I could do that. That didn't violate my principles and I would get to keep the car.

"Let's do it," I said.

Jim grinned. I think he really wanted to teach me something, show me how to do the job right. I heard how he dealt with the guys at the shop, even Kevin. He was a good teacher. He had the job under control and spoke in smooth, easy, tones when he explained something. Then, when they got completely stuck on what to do, he would walk over there, grab a tool and pop, it was done.

Jim was the sort of teacher I would be able to learn from, a leader I could follow. We towed the car to his shop that night. The roads were dry, but there was still snow everywhere else from the last storm. We pushed it back into his shop and pulled the big, overhead door closed, went in and had supper.

CHAPTER TWENTY-TWO

Working with Jim after work was fun. He had all the tools I needed and I looked forward to working at his shop. It was nice and warm, heated by an oil burning furnace. He got to keep the used oil from oil changes at the station to use in his furnace. It was a brilliant use of resources to me, but just common sense to him.

He didn't actually help me with the job, but he would get a break from what he was working on in the next bay, an oil change, a carburetor repair, a starter replacement, nothing that took very long, but made him some extra spending money, which, from what I heard, went to his children and step-children for expenses they incurred.

While we waited for the money to arrive from my parents, which was a bigger deal than I thought it would have been, I got started tearing the engine down to get to the timing chain.

They wanted to know when I was coming home and I didn't have an answer, because I didn't know.

"Well," my mom said, when I talked to her, "why don't we send you the money it will take to fix the car and you come home when it's done. What's wrong with that?"

"Because, I have a job here and I don't need you to pay for it, I need you to lend me the money to buy the parts. I can pay it back. Besides, I'm learning how to do a timing chain, that's important to know."

"Your father can teach you that."

"Yeah, but my car isn't broke there, it's broke here, in

Kansas."

She would not give up on the idea of using the car as a reason for me to come home. She didn't understand that if I did come home, it would have to be when it was my decision, not one made by bad times, or lack of funds or unemployment. The only way I would be able to come home and be satisfied that all of the sacrifices I made were not in vain, was to do it when times were good, when given a set of facts, it was a logical choice for me, because I wanted to be there.

In the end, she agreed to send me a check for one hundred dollars to cover the parts I couldn't afford. I didn't talk to dad about it, but I thought that he would agree with me, anyway. What could be wrong with what I was doing? He didn't have the emotion involved in it like she did.

That first night in the shop, Jim walked by the car and looked into the engine bay.

"You need to strip it down. Pull the shroud off, the fan, drain the radiator, remove it, the power steering pump, the alternator and if you get that far, come and get me," he said and went about his business. That's how it was going to go and it was more than I had hoped for.

Most of the time, he ran me back to Kevin's when the work was done, but I walked once when he had gone in early and I saw through the window that he had taken his shoes off and was relaxing. Usually, we finished working at the same time. There was only a couple of hours we could work at a time anyway. It took a total of four nights to complete the job and get it back together.

I was putting the finishing touches on the car when he leaned up against it.

"You're a good mechanic. Too bad I don't need one. If I did and you were eighteen, I'd hire you," he said.

"I'll take that as a compliment," I replied. "But, I don't know if I want to be a mechanic. I know I can do it, but do I want to?"

Jim shrugged. "Works for me."

"That's what all of this is about for me, finding out what I want to do in life. My dad works in the oil field and that's probably what I'll do, but I don't want that to be the only thing I know, the only thing I can do."

"You're a good worker, so whatever you wind up doing, you'll do a good job," he said, slapping me on the back and turning me toward the car. "The only question is: will it start?"

"Find out," I said, got into the car, inserted the key, took a deep breath and turned it. It cranked for a second or two and fired up.

Jim walked over with a flashlight and looked at all the places where it might be leaking. He checked the radiator where the automatic transmission lines fastened, he checked the gaskets around the water pump, the hoses, he checked the fan belts then he slammed the hood down and pulled down on the chain. The door started rising up, the cool air poured in and, with greasy hands, I pulled the gear shifter into drive. I waved as I went by. I pulled the car out of the shop and up the driveway to the street.

"Yeeeeeha!" I screamed and beat on the dash. I was free.

It was only a week later that I saw something that changed my life. I was driving back from the gas station to Kevin's and passed another station where an old man was pumping gas with a rag hanging out of his back pocket, the same way I kept a rag in my back pocket for checking oil and wiping off the squeegee when I cleaned windshields. He didn't look like me in any other way, but I could see myself in him. I could see my future. He was me for all intents and purposes, but much older, doing what I knew how to do, which was pump gas.

It occurred to me that continuing along the path I had set out, that's all I would ever be qualified to do, pump gas. In the back of my mind, I knew that was a lie, that I had other abilities and might be hired by Jim Crandall if I stayed long enough and a spot opened up, but then what would I be? A mechanic, making what a mechanic made, doing what a mechanic did, that's all. If that was the future I chose, I could have done that anywhere; I didn't have to be in Kansas.

Thoughts came at me in a torrent after that, putting things together, linking things. If I chose a different path, what would it be, where would I have to go to pursue it? Some of it might have come from rescuing my car, from knowing the feeling of being stuck and becoming unstuck. I went through imagined interviews like the one I had at the Co-op. I put different words in the boss' mouth and pretended he asked me different things.

"So, you dropped out of high school?"

"Yes."

"Why did you do that?"

"I wanted freedom."

"What happens when you want freedom again? Will you quit?"

"Yes."

"Thank you for your time."

The truth I came to face was that without an education every job interview would be the same. Of course, I knew that my future was the oil field, but what if that didn't work out? That was one reason I went to Kansas. What if the oil field doesn't work out? What if I put all of my efforts to working there and they discover some other form of fuel that doesn't require a drilling rig? Then what? I could be forty years old when it happened, what skills would I have that would help me get a different job? I had heard dad say it more than once: "a job in the oil field makes you uniquely qualified to work in the oil field," but not much else. In the oil field there were opportunities to learn welding, plumbing, electrical work and mechanics, but it did not make one a welder, a plumber, an electrician, or a mechanic.

I decided on the way to my room that day to go back home and go to school. It was my choice, not forced on me by circumstance, but by logic, by reasoning. I had to look for a good day to go, when the weather would not be an issue. It was a long way back home and Interstate 70 was treacherous at times;

a regular snow could shut down whole sections of the interstate within a few hours and if the wind kicked up, it could stay closed. I had to look for a window, when the weather would be good for several days.

I wouldn't be able to give any notice at work, because it was winter and the weather was unpredictable. What would happen if I gave a date and when it came, I was out of my room and out of a job and a big storm came in over the mountains in Colorado and swept northeasterly, as they usually did, and blanketed Southern Kansas? I would be stuck and with no place to stay, spending money I didn't have to spend, eating away at reserves I would need for gas.

Perhaps, I thought everything out too well. I manufactured issues were there were none. What if I did all of that and got stuck in Fort Scott and they understood and let me stay with Kevin until the weather cleared? I didn't know and once I mentioned it, it was a done deal. They might fire me right there and kick me out of the house. I had no lease; I hadn't signed an agreement. I was a guest by all logical definition.

I felt a little guilty, or ashamed for that. None of the Crandall's or Zimmers had ever done anything to make me think they would react that way. Except maybe Kathy for the past that we shared, but it was unlikely she would have a say in it. I went back and forth on how to proceed. Rent was coming due soon, but I would need that money to get back home. Then there was the hundred dollars I still owed my parents. It was complicated and the minute I found a reason to tell them, I found several reasons for not telling them.

When the day came, I left as much money as I could afford to leave on the dresser with a note to use it against rent or bills and my thanks. Whatever wages I had coming they could keep, if they could figure out how to get it. I signed the note so they would have a signature they could copy on the check. I packed my suitcase and left. The roads were dry and the sky was clear when I started out for Wichita in the early evening after work. I could drive all night and be in Colorado in the morning.

I felt bad about the way I left, but knew that it was the best thing. I didn't care for saying goodbyes anyway and I knew they would try and talk me into staying, or I thought they would and I didn't want to have to argue with them, because most of my arguments came down to the fact that Fort Scott was a nowhere town with little, if anything going for it and I didn't want to insult them.

Despite the downside of congestion, I felt a lot more comfortable around the economic engine that was Loveland. It was growing by leaps and bounds; people were starting up businesses right and left. Some of the businesses I knew of that started only a few years before were moving into bigger buildings and hiring more and more people. But, I was going home to go back to school, to delay my thirst for commerce a year or so while I got the education I was going to need to go much further than a gas pump.

I had been gone for six months, but it felt like a year. I went away as a boy who had hardly ever been out of the county and was coming back having lived on my own for six months in a different state, through all manner of poverty and privation and come out stronger, more capable, but mostly, I had proved my point that I did not need to be taught or shepherded through life; that I knew how to make it work and proof of that was the conclusion that I needed to finish my education.

Driving through the dark night, I made my way back through the small towns and toward the bright lights of the Wichita skyline, then up to Salina on the interstate passing the periodic truck stops, their lights reflecting off some low hanging clouds, making them look enormous. It was cold and I had to keep the heater running high enough to hear the fan spinning under the dash to keep the windows clear. I tossed off the International Harvester cap I had worn most of the time I lived in Kansas and reached into the back to pluck the straw cowboy hat off the seat and tossed it on my head. As I neared Salina, I started to feel myself come back into my skin and only then realized how much I had sublimated in order to assimilate to Kansas.

I hadn't changed myself consciously, it was more the fact that working in the restaurant, I couldn't wear a hat of any kind and working in the kitchen, I had to wear tennis shoes as a safety requirement. I hated them, they were some cheap pair purchased at the department store in desperation and only wore them during work. I changed the minute I got off. When I started working for Jim, I wore my cap again and continued to wear my boots, but there was still something missing in my manner, a subservience I did not feel on the ranches and farms I worked.

Then, feeling the draw of Colorado and comfortable surroundings I felt myself return, like I had opinions and beliefs that I was willing to share. Perhaps, it was more that in Colorado I felt like I had something that needed to be defended and preserved about my heritage and culture. In Kansas, I felt none of the historical connection that I did in Colorado, where my people lived and worked and marked the changes over time.

I felt a sense of accomplishment, too. I know people doubted that I would last on my own, that I was too young, too inexperienced to survive it without calling back for assistance, but I proved them wrong, or myself right and that felt good. Even the hundred dollars I had borrowed I had squirreled away, ready to be repaid when I got home.

I made the interchange and got onto Interstate 70 headed west. I went through Russell and Hays, but on the other side of Hays, it started to snow, lightly and first and picking up as I traveled west. It got harder and harder to see and the wind picked up. There was nothing in the forecast for snow. It might have been a freak snowstorm or the weatherman didn't care enough to get it right, but it was snowing and the wind was blowing.

I had driven in snow most of my life, not on the interstate that often, but the winter before, I had taken a group of kids to the National Western Stock Show and a blizzard blew in while we were there. I drove them all from Denver to Loveland in a serious snowstorm that piled up rapidly. By the time we got onto Highway 60, the snow was a foot deep and the big LTD ploughed on through with no trouble at all. The only time I had a worry was when I had to turn around in Zach Pritchard's driveway and nearly got stuck. So, I had no worries about the snow, or the wind, but they closed the interstate at Goodland and I had to stop.

I pulled into the parking lot of a small café that was still open due to the road closure. It was packed and I walked in, looking for a seat of any kind.

"Hope you're eatin' we don't have room for idlers," the heavy woman in a flowered dress said when I came in and brushed the snow off my jacket.

"If I can find a seat."

The woman looked the dining room over and picked out a booth.

"Sit with those girls, we all gotta share."

I looked to where she was pointing and was surprised and pleased to see that the girls were nice looking. I walked over and looked at the open seat on the other side of the booth.

"I'm supposed to sit here," I said, pointing at the bench seat, hoping to convey the fact that it wasn't my idea. "They say I can't stay unless I eat."

The girls, both blonde, looked up at me, jumped as if startled and one of them extended a hand as an invitation. I took my cowboy hat off and set it on the seat next to me.

"My name is Chrissy and this," she said, presenting her friend with an extended open palm, "is Alice."

"Lane, nice to meet you," I said, nodding at each.

It was only then that I realized how I must appear to them. I still had on my clothes from work that day and they were dirty, some oil stains on my pants and grease marks on my shirt. The jacket Kevin gave me was good for work, but not much else and normally that wouldn't have bothered me but the girls across the table were dressed in fine clothes, the sort of clothes rich girls wore.

Chrissy was the better looking of the two with blue eyes and a smooth complexion with a thin, tidy nose. Alice was a little less smooth, a little less attractive with a bit of acne at her jawbone. It didn't matter, but I could have been matched up with much, much worse, that was apparent from looking about at the interior and seeing crowds of truck drivers and families with crying children.

I tried to ignore them and let them have their privacy as much as possible while I waited for the waitress to take my order. I looked down a lot and out at the others gathered there. I looked up at the walls covered with pictures of landscapes and cattle. There were trophies of deer heads punctuating the art.

"Cowboy, huh?" Chrissy asked, while I was studying my hands in my lap.

"Yeah, sort of, I guess."

"Sort of?"

"I haven't been working as one for a while," I admitted, unsure if I still deserved the title. I had been a dishwasher and a grease monkey lately, the hat only a part of my attire for last six or seven hours.

"We're going to be teachers," Chrissy announced.

I nodded, looking at each in the eyes for signs of dementia.

"What are you doing driving around in this mess?" I asked, curious, thinking them brave.

"We came in with the bus," Alice said.

"Oh." I said, recalling a bus in the parking lot.

"We're headed back to Manhattan, where we go to college," Chrissy said.

It was clear that I had nothing in common with the girls and waited to give my order. I looked over my shoulder. Did they know I was there? Deep down, I hoped they would forget me, or think I had already eaten. I didn't want to buy anything.

"Do you go to college?" Chrissy asked and I recognized it as a shot, asking to be polite, but in a mean, demeaning way. She knew better.

"Nope, I'm seventeen, all I do is work."

"You're not in school?" Alice asked, shocked or appalled, I couldn't tell which.

"No."

There was a whole conversation I did not want to get into concerning school and teachers and freedom that would make sitting there unbearable.

"Why not?" Chrissy asked, innocently, but putting me on the spot at the same time.

I shrugged. I didn't want to get into it and was willing to let myself look like a fool to avoid it. I stood up and looked for the waitress, there were three of them, all taking orders. I sat back down.

Chrissy was staring at me while Alice played with her sleeve. I looked down at my hands, then over at my hat.

"Why not?" Chrissy asked again.

"I don't get much out of it," I said. I let them think I was stupid and couldn't read like Miss Tanner. I didn't care. I was there because the road was closed and the seat I was sitting in was one of the few available in the little cafe, perhaps the whole snowbound town.

"Why not?"

I told myself that I had tried to be nice, to be polite, that I was even willing to let myself look like an idiot to keep from answering her questions, but Chrissy was trying to get to something she could solve. She had the same tone as Miss Tanner, convinced that with her superior teaching skills she would be able to cure me of stupidity, so I let her have it.

"Because, I don't like teachers and I don't like the curriculum and any time I try to fix the curriculum so that it might actually teach something, to offer something of value to a student, I get labeled a troublemaker and sent to the office; so I argue with the principal for a while about the lunacy that is the public school system and I get detention or another study hall," I said, nodding to let Chrissy know that it was her turn.

"When we're teachers you would like us," Alice said, with imbecilic assuredness.

"I doubt it."

"What'll you have?" the waitress asked.

"Ham and cheese omelet with coffee and toast."

I didn't want to look at them. What I said had insulted them, I knew it. I had ridiculed their chosen profession, at least demeaned it to some degree. When I did look up at Chrissy, she was staring at me, the wheels turning furiously behind her eyes, her mouth seemed poised to fly into action held still only by determination.

"Sometimes," she began, struggling to retain control over what she wanted to say, "students who struggle with school have bigger issues in their lives that they're trying to cope with and it isn't school at all, but their condition that makes it difficult for them."

I chuckled and her jaw tightened.

"You think school is difficult for me? That's why I'd rather work, because it's difficult? The only thing hard about school is listening to the social messages being introduced and reinforced time and time again, like repeating a lie often enough that it becomes the truth. You don't think I've picked up on that, that I don't recognize it for what it is? The school work is so incredibly simple, I was on the honor roll and didn't even know it, didn't even try. That's when I lost all respect for it and started looking for something difficult just to keep my interest, but all I found, even in high school, was this constant drum of social issues repeated over and over. So, yeah, I'd rather go somewhere and work, learn something that I can use to raise my wages, advance my position and leave with the sense that I did something, that I fixed someone's car, or baled someone's hay, instead of supplied the school system with another lab rat they can affix their banners to and lead around."

"Well, school isn't for everyone," Alice said, as a fallback position taught in Manhattan, Kansas.

"No, it isn't" I said, happy to agree with them on something.

It was some time that we spent in uneasy silence before the waitress showed up.

"Here, you go," the waitress said, placing the plate down before me and a cup of coffee.

"Thank you," I said, grateful, hoping that they might feel obligated to let me eat in peace.

I realized, as I ate, that what came out of my mouth had been distilled by hours of thinking about the school system and why I could not get along with most of the classes. It wasn't thought out or rehearsed, but I was capable of articulating what was boiling in my soul at any given moment. I was disappointed in the school system, more so than I had ever acknowledged until I finally had my say on the matter. I wanted a class that was difficult, that I saw value in and would have to work hard to master, but I got A's with ease and that was their fault, because they stopped trying to make it hard.

CHAPTER TWENTY-THREE

It was ten in the morning when they opened the interstate. Most of the night and some of the morning in the café was spent dozing off or having civilized conversations with Chrissy and Alice, who had come to the conclusion that I wasn't as stupid as they first thought and they weren't going to make me love teachers, not even them.

I walked out into the morning sunshine bright enough to force my hand up to shield my eyes as it reflected off of the new snow on the ground. There were gusts of wind, but not the steady, driving winds of the night before. The snow was not as deep as I had thought it would be, but then the winds had probably driven most of the snow further on.

The car was cold and the vinyl panels of the interior seemed brittle. My breath came out like a cloud of steam and hung between me and the windshield as I turned the key and heard the slow efforts of the battery to spin the starter in the cold, but the engine kicked over, a cloud of frozen air pulsed out of the tail pipe, filling the rear-view mirror. I got out of the car, cleaned off the windows and went back into the café to watch the car warm up.

The bus had been warming up for some time. As I stepped through the doorway, I saw there was a line of people ready to leave the café and go out to the bus. Chrissy and Alice were in the last third of the line. I didn't know if I wanted to leave before they got to the door to avoid any awkwardness, or if I wanted to say goodbye. I just didn't know.

It took so long for them to decide to load the bus that I left before Chrissy and Alice got to me. I was pulling out of the parking lot when they came out and I waved, to be nice. I didn't know if they saw me or not. It was not like we hated each other, but it was a relationship that existed only for a duration of time and beyond that, it had no context. It was something held in the café for as long as we were there, but carried no further. It could not survive in Loveland or Manhattan, because it had no roots. It lived its whole life in the small café.

The roads were plowed, but they were still slick, at least through town. Once I got up on the interstate, they were wet and icy in spots, but the asphalt was visible thirty percent of the time. They had been working on the road all night and it was apparent by the huge piles of snow by the side of the road.

The Ford had a good heater and without the wind blowing fifty miles per hour, I had to keep the fan on low to keep from melting my feet. There was a brilliant blue sky overhead, with wispy white clouds streaking it here and there, almost like contrails, but shorter and curved.

It was no time before I passed the "Welcome to Colorful Colorado" sign, which I think they thought, back then, Colorado was Spanish for colorful, but in fact it means "the color red" or just "red". Every time I passed that sign, it came to mind, usually going back and forth from Cheyenne. But, maybe they said what they meant regardless of the Spanish meaning of the word, I didn't know, but it seemed like something stupid of which only a government could conceive: Welcome to the color red Colorado!

I was nearing Burlington and rolling the dial on the radio looking for my favorite country stations, but they weren't in range, yet. I pushed in the eight-track tape of Ronnie Milsap and let him escort me back into the state as he had escorted me out.

When I did pull into Loveland, a few hundred miles and a tank of gas later, it was largely under a nice blanket of snow that looked like whipped cream lying smooth over the open fields, the roofs and lawns of the houses and up to the wet roads.

I didn't expect anything when I got home. I hadn't been off on a vacation or coming back home on leave from the service. I had told them that I didn't need them and left. Not exactly a reason to celebrate the return. I got what I expected.

I pulled into the yard, swung my car around to the general area where I usually parked and someone, probably Scott, had plowed the area out earlier that day as would be expected. I got out of the car, noting what little changes had taken place over the past six months: the haystack was a lot smaller than it was when I left; the corrals had gotten a coat of paint. We did the barn a few years before and it still looked good. I took my suitcase out of the back seat and went up to the house. Mom was still at work, so was Dad. Scott was in school and Jon was working on a rig somewhere. I was all alone and I took my boots off at the door and carried my suitcase up to my old room.

There were things in the house that were different, but nothing had changed. I sat in my room and looked out the window that faced the yard, corrals and barn. I thought I should go down and see what needed to be done outside. I set the cowboy hat on the dresser and would get my International Harvester cap out of the car. It was in the mid twenty degrees and comfortable to work in, but I was happy to find my Carhart coat hanging up by the door. I had counted on the thick-lined, canvas coat that had kept me warm in cold temperatures through the winters. I was happy to drop Kevin's hand-me-down into the trash.

I had just gotten to the barn when I heard dad's company pickup turn into the drive. He pulled up to the place where he usually parked and came over to see me.

"When'd you get back?"

"A few minutes ago. They had the road closed at Goodland," I said in explanation.

"Don't have no phones in Kansas, I guess."

I started to chuckle, that was my dad. He had an incredible way of letting someone know when they had screwed up simply by pointing out the logical thing that should have been done. My mom would have been upset and scolded me on not making a phone call. My dad, however pretended to assume that Kansas had no phones, because if they had, a good person, a decent person would have made a phone call so that the people waiting for his arrival would not worry all night about what might have happened, especially during a snowstorm.

I looked down, blushing for my thoughtlessness.

"Put a timin' chain in that thing, huh?"

"Yeah."

I reached into my wallet and pulled out the hundred dollars I still owed for the parts. I tried to hand it to him.

"That ain't my money," he said, pushing it back at me. "That was your mom."

I took this to mean that he would not have given me the money and that there was some disagreement about how that had been handled. My parents were oddly separate in such things, each ruling a different part of their children's lives and the household.

Then, it was as if something occurred to him that had not before.

"Hey, you might be able to do something for me," he said, pulling back from me as if to get a better look, so he could evaluate some aspect of me in a different light. "How would you like to make some money?"

"Hell, yeah," I said, "doin' what?"

"We just come up short-handed; got Ricky workin' over right now, but it just occurred to me that you ain't in school and could fill in for a couple of weeks out at the rig. Would save us havin' to hire a new hand and keep the spot open in case Dipshit comes back."

I didn't know who Dipshit was, but it didn't matter, the thought of working on the rig pleased me, but there was the obvious hang up: I still wasn't old enough, even at seventeen.

"But…"

"Yeah, I know," he said, "we'll work that out. Get your clothes together and get out there, I'll draw you a map."

Dad was well-known for his directions, even with a map.

They were right on the money every time, but they looked awful doubtful and sounded sketchy when described.

I had to locate my steel-toed boots, hard hat and winter clothes. The last time I filled-in for someone it was summer. And, gloves, I didn't have any.

I went out to the barn, where the clothes were kept. They weren't allowed in the house, because the smell of dope, grease and oil would fill the house. They could not be washed in the machine or dried in the dryer for the same reason. We had to take them to a laundromat when they needed washing, which was frequent. I found the burlap sack and went through it. I needed some winter coveralls, too. The steel-toed boots were curled up from being packed away and did not look comfortable, but I'd put them under the heater of the car and they would be pliable by the time I got to wherever the rig was at the time, but it was sure to be somewhere around Greeley, Fort Lupton or Brighton, which was their usual area of operation.

The company dad and Jon worked for was different from a lot of companies; they didn't move their rigs around very much believing that if people could be home more and travel less, they would make for permanent employees, which would lead to better safety records and less turnover, so the hands could put down roots and be better citizens. These were all things they felt would make for a more profitable operation. They were right.

I came walking up to the car with the burlap sack as my dad came out of the house carrying a piece of paper he had been drawing on.

"I need a pair of winter coveralls, some gloves and probably a pair of wool socks," I said, opening the trunk and putting the sack inside. I held the boots in one hand, destined for the floor of the car.

"Tell you what," he said, pointing a finger at me, "you take that hundred dollars you got for your mom and go buy those things. You'll make plenty enough to pay her back over the next few weeks. I'll call the rig and let 'em know you're comin'. Here's where it is," he pointed at the piece of paper.

I took the piece of paper and looked at it while I closed the trunk.

"What's this here?" I asked, pointing at a circle with lines drawn in four directions from the circle.

"Water tower," he said, like I should have known that.

I nodded.

"If you think you went past the lease road, you probably did, turn around and go back."

Having followed his directions as much as I had, I trusted that when I got there, I would see what he meant.

I remembered when I was a kid, my mom was taking us out to the rig and trying to follow his directions. We were bringing him his lunch or something. The directions he left her relied on us turning at a corner where there was a hawk on a power pole. All the way out she kept complaining about it.

"How am I supposed to know where to turn? What if the hawk flies away? What if it's somewhere else, eating, or hunting? You can't give directions like this. I'm out here in the dark, with three kids and I'm supposed to rely on a hawk being on a power pole?"

But, when we got to an intersection, there was a hawk on a power pole, we turned there and wound up at the rig. He used other markers that seemed unreliable, until it was encountered.

"There'll be a herd of cattle all jammed up at the corner, go one mile past that and turn left." "After you pass the barking dog, go another two miles." "If you think you've gone too far, it's just a little further on."

I looked at the directions, got in the car and left. They would have the clothes I needed at the farm supply store. I drove out of town that way and stopped there, got my things and drove on to the rig, it was near a town called Firestone in Weld County. I had been with dad when they were drilling wells out that way before, so I had no anxiety about being able to find it.

I showed up at the rig about four in the afternoon, the snow had been plowed off the road by someone, probably a local farmer dad hired to do the job. He tried to use farmers for as much as he could, when he could.

I pulled onto the location and saw Fred's four-wheel-drive truck. It was brand new the year before, a '78 Ford. He was a legit biker, but cheap. He belonged to one of the motorcycle clubs in Colorado, had a patch and the whole thing, but he liked to make money and did not like to spend it. He lived in a tiny trailer house down by a river in Evans. I had been there and the place he lived in did not correlate with the man I'd known since he first started working for dad. He was a meticulous individual, owned nothing that was not first class and well taken care of. His motorcycle looked like it fell off the cover of Easy Rider, but he lived in a rusty little place on a small lot. It just didn't jive.

The new Ford was a result of his miserly ways. The accountants at the office had been calling him for a few months asking him to cash some of his paychecks, because they could never get down to a reliable figure with so many checks showing as debits, but the balance was tens of thousands of dollars over what the books showed. Fred had been getting them in the mail and putting them in his top drawer. When he did cash them in, he went down and bought the new truck with it and put cash in his drawer. The paychecks would pile up again, though, because he didn't need the money.

Fred was also the welder on the rig, because he was good at it and very particular. Everything he built looked like it was manufactured, except that it was normally unpainted and left as bare metal. There was no humidity or salt in the air to destroy it like there would be on an offshore rig.

I went into the change house on the ground level. The drillers had lockers in the doghouse, which was up a flight of iron steps. Everything on the rig was made of metal. Even things that could be wood, were not, except the handles on the scrub brushes, which I knew would be in my hand most of the day, even in the winter.

I found an empty locker and claimed it, putting my "going-home" clothes in there and pulling work clothes out of the burlap sack. The new coveralls would garner some comments, it was not possible to have anything new without it. Once decked-out, I went up and into the doghouse to talk to Fred and see where he wanted me to start.

Fred was standing by the geolograph that marked the feet being drilled across a chart that marked the time so it was possible to know how fast the rig was drilling. He glanced at me when I came through the door, but looked back at the chart. He was nearly six-feet tall, with long, dark hair pulled back into a ponytail. Even his work clothes were clean and neat. The doghouse, so unlike the one up by Walden, was immaculate. I was afraid to touch anything, even though my clothes had been laundered since the last time I worked.

"Gonna stand there all day or get to work?" he asked.

"You're the boss, where do you need me?"

"You can't figure that out on your own?"

"I could," I said.

He nodded toward the door at the other end of the doghouse that led out to the working floor.

"Go grease something."

I nodded and went out to find a grease gun wondering if he didn't want me, that he felt I would be a burden. Just being the boss's kid did not and had never meant that I got any breaks, but I was usually met with a little more friendliness.

The grease gun was hung by the handle in a pipe collar that had been welded to the back of the draw-works, where it had always been, right next to a wire brush. I found a rag in a box by the doghouse and went about greasing the draw-works, which was a lot like greasing the fluffer back in Walden. The truth was, "roughnecking" was a combination of being a mechanic and a farmer or ranch hand in its daily tasks, but different from almost anything when making a connection or tripping pipe into or out of the hole.

It was getting dark when I got there and was full-on dark

by the time I got the draw-works greased and oil checked, the rotary chain and compound. The kelly was getting low, meaning we would have to put another joint in the string to drill another thirty feet pretty soon. The others came up to the floor, from whatever they had been doing on the ground, ready to make a connection.

"Hey, hey, Lanie, how ya doin'?" Eddie called to me when he saw me, knowing I hated the feminization of my name. We had been through it before.

I shook my head as if disappointed that he had not respected my preference, but I knew it would happen. I had no illusion that he would do anything other than annoy me.

"Oh, you don't like that, do ya? Well, Lanie, life's a bitch, then ya marry one."

Eddie was a stout little guy, shorter than me, but wider. He tried to grow a beard, but it was splotchy attending to either his Mexican or Native heritage, no one knew which and he didn't either. I would work with him most of the time, both of us having the same duties, except for where we worked on the floor. I was in "worm's corner" and he was a chain hand. The derrick hand came up the steps, his clothes white with bentonite powder that he mixed to keep the mud thick. He was tall and thin with long, blonde hair tied back into a ponytail, a common hairstyle that kept long hair from getting sucked into the omnipresent spinning machinery on a drilling rig. Tad was his name and the guys made fun of it at every opportunity. "That's Tad-bit stupid." "That's Tad-bit lazy." "That's Tad-bit crazy." I think my dad gave it to him, a debt that I was sure he would like to repay.

Moments later Fred came out and operated the draw-works through the connection and went back into the doghouse when the kelly was thirty foot higher in the derrick and everyone went back to what they had been doing, except, I followed Eddie to see what projects he had going on.

"Aw, we just gotta dig out this ditch," he said, pointing.

I nodded and went to get another shovel lined up neatly

by the substructure.

"Took off on your own, I heard."

"Yep," I said, sinking the shovel into the ditch, that was filled with water and the ambient heat of the engines running at high revolutions kept from freezing. Even though the engines were ten feet above us, the warm air blew down inside the enclosed substructure and kept the ground warm.

We talked and worked and made connections until the night had been used up and we were relieved by the next crew that came on. The shifts were only eight hours long, like the rig up in Walden and it seemed like I had just gotten there when the crew change happened at ten-thirty.

I cleaned up the best I could, put on the clothes I came in while I let the car warm up outside. Tad studied me while we changed.

"So, you workin' for us, now?"

"Just fillin' in for a few weeks."

"Then what?"

I shrugged. How should I know? He seemed perturbed by it, as if I wouldn't pull my weight, but I was seventeen and nearly old enough to do the job, so he shouldn't worry.

"Rig move and all?"

"I suppose."

"I got some shit I need to teach you, then."

"That's what I'm here for, to be taught."

"Well, I didn't have to teach Dipshit nothin'."

I could have gotten into it, if that's what he wanted, but I let it go. I didn't have to win every argument. I would work hard and learn fast and let that shut him up rather than argue with him about the fact that I knew he didn't know anything his first day on a rig, either.

"At least Lanie fuckin' works," Eddie said, either to stick up for me, or, more likely, to annoy Tad, because that is what Eddie did, he annoyed people for entertainment.

CHAPTER TWENTY-FOUR

I worked on the rig for two weeks and took home seven hundred dollars. I made more in one week on the rig than I made in a month in Kansas at either job. I could see how working on the rig steadily that I would be able to afford a place of my own, a new car or pickup and even a boat if I wanted one. No college degree, no technical school, nothing but hard work and surviving in the cold would present a neat future. But, I came back to go to school, just in case the rig did not always run, or they developed a better source of fuel and it shut down for good.

Mom had been talking to Mr. Schmidt at the high school to get me registered the whole time I worked on the rig. I was allowed to be listed as a junior, despite the fact that I would still have some sophomore classes to make up, health and oral communications, swimming could wait. Being a junior, though, I was allowed to attend Vocational Technologies, or VoTech in the afternoons where I would learn some sort of trade. I looked over the options and decided that appliance and refrigeration repair looked like it would supply me with some practical experience. And, it was the only class that was not filled half way through the school year.

The first class I had on my schedule was oral communications. It seemed like a challenge from Mr. Schmidt more than anything else. That first day back at school was odd. A number of the cowboys from before had quit and gone to work and there were a few new faces. Ronnie was still there, Brad, Frank and Juan. Zach quit to work for his dad in construction. Annie was still at school, but I didn't see any of them except passing in the hall, because they all had junior classes to attend and I did not. Then, we went to different classes at VoTech, too, because all of the good ones, like welding and auto repair were filled by the time I showed up.

The appliance and refrigeration instructors, there were two, were skeptical of my ability to get much out of the class, coming in half way into the course. All of the other students had focused on doing the classroom part of it during the first half of the course and were going to be out in the shop for the remainder, so they put me in their office space adjacent to the shop, where they could watch me and be on hand when I had questions, but I was expected to do all of the classroom work by myself and at an accelerated pace so that I would have some time for the shop portion before the school year ended.

I wasn't sure how I was going to complete the classroom portion by myself. I didn't know anything about what they had studied. They sat me down in their office and every day they would point to what I needed to cover, which chapter, where to find the questions at the end of it and they went out to teach the practical side to the others.

It was enlightening. The experience changed my views of a lot of things, particularly, the very structure of school. That was where I flourished. It was the way I should have been taught from the very beginning. I read and studied the chapter, turned to the questions, answered them and moved on. I went at my pace, which was fast. I sometimes did two chapters a day. The instructors were shocked by it. I didn't get a wrong answer and they spent no time at all giving me special instruction as they feared they would.

I was left with only one question: Why couldn't all of school be like that? If it had been, if I had experienced school that way, it would have changed my whole perception. I completed the classroom portion in half the time that the others had and joined them out in the shop for the final quarter of the year.

The rest of school, however, did not go as smoothly. I went to one class of oral communications, then stopped. I was pulled into the office to be informed that unless I attended oral communications every day, I would not be able to attend Vo-Tech. So, I attended oral communications every day. I would show up ten minutes before the end and sit there until the bell rang and left. That went on for a week.

"I told you," Mr. Schmidt said, pointing his finger at me, "that you needed to attend that class, every day."

"I did."

"Yes, I heard, you show up ten minutes until the end of class and wait for the bell. That's not what I meant and you know it."

"Okay," I said, "I'll try it, but it is so completely pointless that it's like Chinese water torture, it just keeps coming, drop after drop until it drives me crazy."

"I don't care. By all reports you are doing well at VoTech, but you can't flunk out here and still go there, it doesn't work that way."

"I said I'd go."

"Okay."

I went to oral communications the next day and was there before the bell rang to start the class. I looked around at the sophomores in the class. Most of them did not know what mind-numbing crap was coming their way. I was sure that they were all like me, that when they saw the sheer stupidity of it, they would rebel.

"Okay, class, get into your study groups," Mr. Guiterrez said, clapping his hands together. He was short and heavy with thick-rimmed glasses and a small mustache.

I sat there. I had no study group.

"You, get into your group."

"I don't have one," I said.

He looked around at all the different groups and picked one out.

"Over there, with them," he said, pointing.

I moved my desk over into the circle they had formed. Two others scooted their desks apart to make room for me. They were just kids, some with long hair, some with Rolling Stones T-shirts, some with button down shirts and long sleeves rolled up, but with wild patterns printed on them. They were jocks, or hoods, or nerds, none of them were cowboys and they didn't like me from the start. I was older and I did not give a damn.

I sat in the circle and watched as the guy in front of me, a nerd from all indications, held up pictures of people dressed differently, some men, some women, all seemingly with different occupations and, from what I could grasp, we were supposed to say what we thought they did for a living, or who they were in society: teacher, doctor, farmer, etc.

I was not going to play the game. I did not come all the way back from Kansas to sit in a circle and tell people what I thought some person did for a living based on a picture some nerd held up in front of me. I just was not. I watched as the nerd got responses from those before me in the circle.

"Farmer," one said.

"Gardener," another responded.

Then, it got to me. I sat there staring at the nerd wanting to physically shove the picture down his throat, because it was an insult, not just to me, but to him. Did he not see that his life was being wasted in the most ridiculous manner? Worse, did he not care that he was being used as some sort of guinea pig? Did they not understand the social messages being shoved down their throats with exercises like that? Were they oblivious to the fact that they were being manipulated into arriving at the same conclusion by force of peer pressure? That the one guy who said it was a farmer would be outnumbered and the group would decide that it was a gardener and that would be the conclusion, forcing him to recognize that either he was wrong, or that his individual perspective was irrelevant, because the group had decided for him what the person was?

"Get that fuckin' thing out of my face," I said, as calmly as

I could.

The whole group gasped and the nerd quickly shifted the picture to the next person in the circle, a girl, not particularly attractive and thin as a rail, who did not look at the picture, but stared at me as if I had just grown another head. She was put off by it, even angry or contemptuous, but stared as these emotions swept over her face each expression blossoming as the thoughts came to her.

"What was that?" Mr. Guiterrez said, walking sideways toward the group, his ear aimed at us as he came. "Did I hear profanity?"

I looked at my groupmates, which one would rat me out? Which one wanted to be the good little Soviet? Then, I ratted myself out, fearful that one of them would beat me to it.

"Damned straight," I said, standing up, ready to throw in the towel on school all together. I would miss VoTech, but nothing was worth the soul-sucking experience of being indoctrinated.

"Explain yourself," he said, sweat appearing on his forehead, his face flushed with anger.

"You don't want that," I said, knowing that had I not spent time with Chrissy and Alice in the café, that I would not have my opinions galvanized, would not have even yet consolidated the ideas that I had concerning school and teachers, that it would be some cloudy, half-formed opinions of school, rather than the teachers themselves, the curriculum and the means of delivering groupthink to the rest of us, using a form of democracy as a bludgeon that I had often recognized, but hadn't been able to distill as the reason I hated school. I thought it was just the waste of time, but I had come to recognize that I detested being forced to accept the social messaging that was being inserted into every class. It was much more pronounced in oral communications than any other class and why I could not tolerate the message much more than the insult of wasting my time. But, knowing that now, I knew that Mr. Guiterrez, for all of his education, all of his ability to speak publicly, was not prepared for a student with so well-organized ideas as I had at that moment. He was used to the average, the type who just wanted the grade and move along, who did not care what the class was or the sinister intention of it.

"Yes, I do!" he screamed at me, losing his composure in his building irritation with me, seeing me as a weak opponent to his superb reasoning. He wanted to crush me and he wanted to do it in front of the whole class, with their rapt attention to his brilliance. Okay.

"Well, junior nerd over here kept holding the picture in front of me demanding that I play this silly game of pretending we don't know what subversive messages are being shoved down our throats. This molding of all opinions to those of the majority, erasing individual thought, individuality itself. Because, that's what it's designed to do. I've seen this work its way through the school system ever since seventh grade and I finally got tired of it.

"Don't you guys see it? Don't you recognize that this class is nothing but propaganda? That its whole purpose is to streamline thought?"

"That's not true," Mr. Guiterrez objected, but it was a weak objection.

"Yes, it is!" I yelled, starting off reasonable and nice, but growing angry about it as he tried to deny it and I directed my message to those in the class.

"You all have got to feel the oppression of this place, don't you? How some things are taboo, that you can't say, even though you know it's true? That this class is bullshit, that it's borderline socialist? That it's preparing you to accept messages and thoughts that are alien to you? That are inconceivable in a capitalist society that values individuality? It quashes individuality. It makes the individual subservient to the group. That there is a subtle means of punishing individuality and praising acceptance of the group opinion? This isn't a speech class it is indoctrination, pure and simple. Look at it objectively, don't let this clown," I said, nodding at Mr. Guiterrez, "force his view onto you, look at it for yourself, evaluate it."

"You need to go to the office," Mr. Guiterrez said, abandoning the argument, determined to get rid of me and get everyone else back on track, destroy my argument in private, with no rebuttal.

"How am I wrong?" I asked him, taking a step toward him.

"In every way."

"Then, explain it."

"I don't have to explain anything to you!" he yelled.

"You're right. I'm asking you to explain to them. I'm gone. You know, I'm gone. This is my last day, but you owe an explanation to them, these others, these sheep you've been shearing. Tell them how I'm wrong, but I'd like be here to call you on your bullshit."

"You're disrupting the class. I'm going to have you removed," he said, walking toward the phone to call the office.

"I'm trying to save the class! At least one of them."

I saw him talking to someone on the phone.

"I'll go, you don't have to do that," I said. "He's going to lie to you, but you have to be smart enough to call him on it. You have to care enough to defend yourselves from his lies."

I walked out. I met Mr. Schmidt halfway to the office as he pushed his mass through the hall on stiff legs, trying to get there. He was sweating and red-faced with anger or exertion, it didn't matter which.

"What the hell did you do in there?"

"It took me all this time to figure out why I can't stand that class and others like it," I said, conversationally, as if talking to Ronnie or Zach.

"I know, you think it's a waste of your time."

"No, that's what I used to think, but I finally figured it out."

"What is it?"

"I'm a dyed-in-the-wool individualist."

Mr. Schmidt was confused, befuddled.

"So? What does that have to do with anything?"

"That class and others like it are not, they are pushing a socialist, communist message and I can't stand it. I see the machinations of it and it ticks me off."

Then, I saw something in Mr. Schmidt I hadn't seen before, a sudden recognition and respect. "Let's go have a talk," he said, guiding me to a table in the cafeteria.

Mr. Schmidt sat next to me in the cheap, plastic chairs, his hands stretching out over the faux-wood lamination on the table.

"I really should throw you out of school," he said.

I nodded.

"There aren't many classes left for you to take."

I nodded. Was he expecting me to argue with him?

"Plus, you're not completely wrong and it isn't going to get any better. The school system has been leaning left the past several years and all of the momentum is in that direction. I don't know that I need you around stirring up trouble in every class, starting some sort of rebellion, though I think it might be a good thing. I'm just trying to get to retirement here and while I might have recognized the same things, I'm trying to run a school with the least number of headaches as I can. So, I have a proposition for you. I don't even know if I can make it work, but I'm going to try."

"Okay."

"What I'm going to try to do and this is no promise, but what I am going to try to do is let you go to VoTech and that's it. You won't even have to attend classes here. They don't like that sort of thing and to talk to them, it isn't even possible. I will leave you enrolled here and that's it."

"Or, I can stay here and start a movement," I said, grinning, teasing him.

"No, if I have to, I'll ban you from school and that'll be the end of VoTech, too."

"I was just joking."

I left school that day for the last time. Whatever my

future held; it would not run through Thompson Valley High School. They were as glad to get rid of me as I was to be rid of them. I continued at VoTech and nearly went to the state competition. I didn't know they had a state competition for fixing appliances. There was a lot about school that I didn't know, but I never felt any worse for my ignorance.

CHAPTER TWENTY-FIVE

A lot of things happened the summer of 1979. Ronnie and Lisa got married after the rabbit died. Ronnie went work on the ranch full time and Lisa started building a nest for the child growing in her womb. At least, she graduated high school first, unlike a lot of us.

I had only months to go before I could legally work on the rig when I started visiting the recruiters in Fort Collins. I might not be old enough to hold a dangerous job, but I could enlist in the military and get shot. That sort of reasoning was abundant. I couldn't drink beer, even though it was a legal substance, but I could get my hands on acid any time I wanted. I could drive around with a shotgun in my car, but I couldn't shoot a duck after sunset.

After spending some time with the Army recruiter, I decided to stop in and see the Air Force recruiter, just to say I researched the options. On his desk was a folder with an F-15 Eagle on the cover, some big, twin-tailed, two-engine jet that looked like it was going a thousand miles an hour sitting still. The recruiter saw me looking at it.

"F-15," he said, "hell of a jet, brand new. Didn't come out until '76."

"It's beautiful," I said. "Better looking than a Corvette."

"Have a seat."

We talked for a long time and there were three things he said that resonated with me. One was that I could work on that jet. I wanted to fly it, but he said I had to go to college to be a pilot. The second was that the Air Force had two-man rooms while the Army required their soldiers to live in forty-man barracks. After my experience in Walden, I knew the Army would be a mistake. The third was that I would see the world, at least the United States.

So, I took the folder home to read through the information. It was all about the benefits of being in the Air Force. It didn't cover the downside. Laying there on my bed with the window open and a breeze coming through, looking at my rigging bag and going over the idea of trying to make rodeo a career, I decided to talk to dad about it. I waited outside for him to come home.

I was putting up some hay when he pulled into the yard and parked the company pickup. I walked over to him and waited for him to finish talking to the rig on the radio and to get out. He looked at me and he saw something in my face that bothered him. He looked at me again, to see if the look was still there, then he got off the radio and opened the door.

"Problem?"

"Yeah," I said, backing up to let him get out and close the door.

"Big problem?'

"Not really."

"What is it?"

"I'm thinking of joining the Air Force."

"Big decision."

"Yeah."

"I wasn't in the Air Force; I don't know anything about it."

"Yeah, but you were in the Army."

"Not by choice."

"What do you think of it?"

"Me? You can't judge by me. It was war. I didn't want to go. My experience was a long time ago. There's really nothing about it that would apply."

"Yeah, but do you think I can handle it? I can't even handle school."

He stopped and appraised me. I don't know what he saw, what he thought of me at all, to be honest. Dad recognized my talents, my ability to work hard, he noticed when I had done something wrong and what I would do about it when I got caught. But, I never got the sense that he had an overall opinion of me and if he did whether it was good or bad. I was his kid and he took the good with the bad and raised me to be honest and to have integrity, a thing he thought I took too far sometimes.

"What I do know about you, is that if you decide to do it, you won't give up. If it's someone else's idea, you'll bail the first chance you get. So, if it's your idea, if you want to do it, I think you'll be fine. If you're only doing it because your friend is and you want to do it together, you won't last very long."

I nodded. He was right on the money about that.

"I thought you wanted to work on the rig, you only have a few months to go."

"Yeah, but I feel like I need a backup plan, something I can do besides the oil field that still pays pretty good. Ranching won't do that, farming either. Workin' on jets, though, that would pay pretty well, I think." I looked at him. "I want to see something before I settle down to anything for the rest of my life. I want to go somewhere, experience a few things. You may not have wanted to go, but you got to see something, Korea, Japan, San Francisco, right? I can always come back home to this, where I belong, but with memories and knowledge of the world."

He looked down and when he looked up, I saw in his eyes that he had come back different, having seen the things he had, been the places he had, even though it wasn't under the best conditions, he had discovered something there that made the rest of his life work out.

"I might need you to sign for me, though, being seventeen."

"If you can tell me this is your idea, I'll sign."

I went back down to the recruiter's office the next day. I walked into the small office on Howe in Fort Collins, past the

Army guy with the folder in my hand and saw the look of disappointment on his face. I went into the paneled office where the Air Force recruiter, a man with short dark hair and a face that looked flushed most of the time, sat behind his desk. I sat down in the padded chair. The guy's name was Freeman, it was on his shirt.

"If I can work on that jet," I said, pointing to the one on the folder, "I'll join the Air Force."

"No problem," he said with a smile and I saw him shoot a glance at the Army recruiter looking in from the hall. "But, you have to take some tests. If you score well enough on those, I can get you a job on that jet."

They set me up with a testing session upstairs from their office in a big conference room. There was no other person there, so I figured business wasn't too good four years removed from the end of the Vietnam War. They had already made a number of concessions that allowed me to join. First, I wasn't eighteen, but there was a plan for that. Second, I was not a high school graduate, it was the first year they were allowed to recruit for the Air Force from non-graduates, but I would have to get a GED in the first year. Third, I had a juvenile record and they would have to get waivers so I could join. All I had to do was pass the entrance tests with high enough scores and I was in.

I couldn't remember the last time I took a test when I wasn't sure I would pass. I had not been nervous about tests in five years. The truth was, it was the first time I had taken a test when I cared about the outcome. So, I went at it with determination. I had two goals, to score high enough on the mechanical aptitude to be a mechanic and low enough on the administration part to be excluded from ever working in an office. When I was done, I was told I would get the results in the mail and I should contact him as soon as I did.

It was a week before I got the little card with my scores. If I remembered right, he said I had to get at least eighty percent on the mechanical aptitude to be a mechanic. I had done enough mechanic work that I thought I did well. There were some questions that were tough, though. I walked back from the mailbox with a handful of mail and held the card out in front of me as I walked.

Mechanical aptitude was eighty-seven percent; electronic aptitude was ninety-two percent; and administrative aptitude was thirty-seven percent. I tanked that one thoroughly. But, they were going to try and make me take some electronic job, but they didn't understand, that was not natural aptitude. Most of the questions on the electronic part were stuff that I had learned in appliance and refrigeration and therefore skewed.

I called the recruiter and we set up a time to talk. He didn't ask what my scores were, which I thought he would want to know. Maybe, he already knew and the mail part gave me time to digest the fact that I could not be what I wanted to be, before talking to him. He didn't think I would pass. Freeman thought I would fail and wanted me to get used to the idea. People usually expected me to fail. I don't know why.

We had to do some official things in Denver and he drove me down. The physical was a big part of the day. I didn't worry about that, either. I was in better shape than most of the others. Hard work had never let me down. Then, I met him back at the busy office he shared with two other recruiters. We hashed out my job and he had to go do some things to confirm this and that. We talked a lot about Lackland and what it would be like, how it was a shock, but that I would get used to it and fit right in. I took that with a grain of salt.

"So," he said, calling my attention to him instead of all of the other busy things going on around me, "when do you want to go?"

"Now," I said, causing Freeman and the other recruiters to snap their attention to me.

"Right now?" Freeman asked.

"Yeah," I said, I had already made the decision. We were in Denver, where we would board a plane for San Antonio.

"Don't you want some time to say goodbye to friends and family?"

"I already did that. I thought I would leave from here."

"Well, look, you ought to take some time, a month or so."

"What for?"

"To get prepared, you know, finalize some things at home."

"I don't have to. I don't have anything, except a car and they know what to do with that. I don't have rent or any obligations to anyone."

"At least a week," Freeman said and since I got the feeling that it wasn't me, but him that needed the time to get prepared, I agreed to a week.

That Friday night there was a party out at Lone Tree lake, where we often partied. It was far enough out of the way that cops didn't bother us. We would all drive our cars and pickups out there and build a bonfire. Those who were eighteen brought beer and there would be some liquor and occasionally someone would bring some weed and smoke it, but not often. That was usually an interloper, not one of the regulars. If we had wanted to smoke dope, we could have, there were few drugs that were not readily available, but it seemed to me like taking drugs was to prove something and I had nothing to prove. I didn't have to go out of my way to be a bad boy, that was natural, attested to by the legal waivers.

Annie Brewster was there, Ronnie brought Lisa, pregnant Lisa. Brad and his girlfriend, Julie, Zach, Frank, Will and Juan were there. If I had wanted a going away party, that would have been it, but I didn't tell anyone I was leaving for the Air Force that Monday. They knew I had joined and I didn't like the attention of that sort of thing. How could I maintain my solitude if they thought they had to make some big gesture about saying goodbye? I did let the thought of saying goodbye to Annie properly drift through my mind, but that was hijacked by Beth, who tagged a ride with Ronnie for some reason.

"Hi," she said, coming up to me in the dark, between Zach's pickup and my car.

"Howdy."

She was older, fifteen, but I hadn't seen her much since I came back from Kansas. With Ronnie being married in the summer and me spending the winter in school and working at our place, I hadn't gone over as often as usual. That relationship had fallen away.

"Air Force, huh?"

"Yeah."

She was prettier than when she was a little kid. She had grown into her body, but she had matured some, too. She was more serious and judgmental than I remembered. She was going to be a real beauty in a few years and whatever she had for me when she was little would disappear while I was in the Air Force. I might be married by the time I saw her again and I let my guard down, stopped protecting her from the truth of the matter, which was we were never going to be together. I didn't know how much of the old feelings she retained, but that much had to be certain.

"When are you leaving?"

"Pretty soon," I said, not wanting the truth to get around and spoil the situation as it was.

"When are you coming back?"

"I might not."

"Ever?"

"I don't know," I said, chuckling. "Forever's a long time."

"Can I write you?"

"I don't know where I'll be," I said.

"You know where I'll be," she snapped, her temper flashing. I was making it too hard for her. I was trying to.

"Yeah."

"You're such an asshole," she said and walked away.

She had to find out sometime. I couldn't keep pretending that something would happen that wouldn't. I took a drink of beer and wandered closer to the fire. Annie was talking to Zach. Where was her boyfriend? Annie was a pretty girl, she ought to have a boyfriend somewhere, didn't she? Where was Doug? I hadn't seen him for a long time.

I went up to Annie and bumped into her as if it were an accident. I knocked the beer out of her hand and she cussed me as she picked it up and slurped the foam coming out of the top.

"Fucking Air Force?" she said, angry.

How was I ever going to have a going away party when everyone was mad at me? I guess that's why I didn't want one, people would treat me different and just when I wanted to see them for the last time, just as they were, they would change and get all gooey.

"Gotta do somethin'."

"I thought you were going to work for your dad."

"I might, we'll see how this goes first. I'm not making it a career."

"Yeah, but I thought you were going to stay around here," she said, sounding like she had something planned and I was screwing it up.

"Hell, I already left. I went to Kansas, remember?"

"Oh, that was stupid, everyone knew you'd be back."

"Everyone? I didn't know I'd be back."

"Some of us know you better than you know yourself."

"But, you didn't see the Air Force coming, did ya?"

"Just shut up," she said and pulled Zach off further around the fire to get away from me.

Ronnie and Lisa were sitting on the tailgate of his pickup, surrounded by people. Ronnie was the friendly one, the admired one, the attractive one out of the two of us. I was a by-product, a leftover, an oddball in the equation and I liked that role, but I had only started to realize that I made a lot of people mad. They seemed to have more of a stake in whether I went to the Air Force than I did. Maybe they were just angry because they weren't involved in the decision, that I had consulted none of them. I decided to see how the winds were blowing with Ronnie. I knew Lisa would be happy that I wouldn't be around. At least, there was that.

I stood by the tailgate of the truck and listened to what was being said, the funny story Ronnie was telling.

"Yeah, so there we were, trying to report a crime and the cops weren't having any of it, a couple of kids, who had been drinking, underage, in the police station, reporting stolen gas, something they couldn't prove and there's Lane, just letting them have it.

"'You sonsabitches ain't gonna do a damned thing, are ya?' he said, and man, I'm just standing there looking for a way out...'"

Those gathered around laughed as Ronnie put on a face like he was ducking swooping birds or something, like he was looking for a way out of a trap and trying to sneak past some danger. It was the way Ronnie told stories, the images he created that made them funny, not the facts themselves.

"'Fuck these assholes,' he says and turns around to walk out, just like that and I'm already at the door, holding it open so he can make a break for it. I'm wavin' him in, like I'm waving him around third base and he's just as calm as hell and pissed. You know that look he gets when he's about to clobber someone? Yeah, like that..." And, they all laughed along with Zach who made a determined face. Hell, I even laughed, despite myself and took a drink of the beer. They were making fun of me, but it was funny. Ronnie could tell a story.

"So then, this big cop, the one he had been arguing with comes around the counter and starts walking toward Lane and I'm trying like hell to get him to run and he's just walking like he doesn't give a shit..."

"I didn't," I interjected.

"So, this cop claps a big hand on Lane's shoulder and Lane spins around and decks the cop, right there in the police station. I'm gone, I left, nothing for me to do, but go to jail, too. I don't know what happened after that, I was running down the sidewalk wishing I had drove."

They all laughed as Ronnie made motions with his arms like he was running for all he was worth. They were all having fun and I wanted to talk to Ronnie, but the attention was squarely on me, so I took a drink of beer and decided I would go listen to the radio in my car. Maybe later. I knew he told that story a bunch of times, it was one of the times when good-natured Ronnie was involved in one of my many adventures and he liked to tell it.

"What did happen after that?" Brad asked when I had gotten to the far end of the fire.

I looked back at all of them gathered around Ronnie's pickup, the fire lighting up their expectant, smiling faces as if I had the humor that Ronnie did, but I didn't. Nothing I could say would be as funny as Ronnie. Maybe, I didn't have the self-deprecation that he did, or the ability to pull it off. Maybe, I was too serious. I could be humorous, I had held the crowd's attention at times, but I had to be in the mood and I wasn't. Ronnie was always on.

"What did happen?" Annie asked, just as I thought my non-answer would cause them to lose interest.

"I went to jail," I said and kept walking. When I looked back, Ronnie had them engaged again. It was one of the reasons I had to have a waiver for the Air Force. The cop dropped the charges, at least down to something that didn't carry much weight, a mark on my file, underage drinking, I think, but nothing happened to me. I spent the night in jail until my dad showed up to get me out. He was livid for having to come out in the middle of the night and get his kid. I was afraid to make it worse, so I didn't say anything until we were in the pickup, when I thought I would really get it when the door closed. I pulled the door closed and looked at him, waiting for whatever he had to say, take whatever he wanted to give.

"You know, I was really angry when I came down here to get you out," he said.

I nodded, feeling bad.

"But, I talked to that cop for fifteen minutes and I wanted to kick his ass."

He put the pickup in gear and drove away with his son.

I stopped at the cooler and got another beer out of the ice and popped the top. I took a big drink and went over to my car. I reached in and turned on the radio and sat on the hood, drinking the beer. If I drank too much, I'd just sleep in the car. I'd done it before. I was seventeen and felt older than any of the others that night.

Annie came up, I saw her coming, but pretended I didn't.

"Hey," I said, pretending to be surprised.

"What did happen, Lane?"

"Nothing. I ain't as funny as Ronnie is, never have been. I can't entertain a crowd like that."

"You can," she said, having been present when I was in the mood. "But, you're surly a lot these days."

"It's not surly," I said.

"Depressed?"

"I don't get depressed, but I do think about things and when I'm thinking about things, I don't talk much."

"What are you thinking about?"

"Nothing."

"Do you know how often you say that?"

"It is nothing. Nothing to share. Inside shit, is all."

"Did someone hurt you, or something? Someone break your heart?"

I laughed out loud, where did that come from? She knew as well as I did that I had never had a serious relationship with anyone, how could I get my heart broken? It had never been involved.

"In Kansas, I mean," she said, realizing the same thing. "You're different since you came back, everyone says it."

"I feel old," I said. "Stupid, I know, I'm seventeen, but I feel old, like I know how the world works and it's mostly hard times, hard work."

I took a drink of beer and saw Beth coming out of the firelight, headed right toward us. She walked up and stood there for a moment, breathing hard.

"Can I talk to you for a minute?"

I looked at Annie. If I went with Beth, whatever might have developed between us was over. I knew it and she had a look that said the same thing. As if there was a choice being made between her and Beth. But, I could see Beth was nearly in tears and I felt responsible for it, so I took a deep breath and slid off the hood. Beth turned around and walked toward the lake where there was a big, fallen tree that was little more than a log, the branches having been cut off and used for firewood. She stopped and looked up at me. The bonfire reflected in her dark, brown eyes and I thought I had never seen anything more fitting.

"I love you!" she said, almost screaming it, standing there, shaking. "I have always loved you. And, now you're going away? For years?"

I stood there, what was I going to say?

"I know you think I'm a little girl, that I'll forget you, but you don't know shit about love, not real love."

"Beth, you're fifteen, I..."

"That doesn't matter, that, don't pull that on me. You're only seventeen. My parents are five years apart, that's more years than us. If you would just wait, just wait, that's all, but you don't even think about it. You don't think about me. I'm waiting, I've been waiting."

I felt like she needed to be held and told that it's all right, but that would just send everything out of whack, send too many mixed signals. So, we stood there in the dark, by the log, near the lake.

"Why can't you see me?"

"I can see you."

"Not the way you see Annie, not the way you see other girls. Is it sex? If we had sex you would see me?"

"No, don't say that shit," I said, looking over my shoulder.

"Then, what?"

"What am I supposed to do? I'm too old for you, have always been too old for you. You've always been too good for me. You are now and you will be in ten years. But, I'm supposed to hang around like some dog? You think Ronnie wants to see me chasing after his pretty little sister? How do you think that would go down? Really? You're asking too much of me."

"It's asking too much for you love me back?"

"Beth, I've never loved anybody; I don't know what that is. I can't figure it out. Love? Do you know that I have never talked to a woman for more than a few minutes that it didn't end with them being pissed off or me being absolutely confused to the point of insanity? I have no clue how you go from that to love. I don't even know how you get there."

"You get there by admitting that you at least like someone. Do you like me?"

"I've always liked you," I said, honestly. She was funny and clever, positive and brave. I admired her more than liked her. She was emotionally fearless.

"Prove it, sit down on this log with me and let's just talk and see where it goes."

I looked over my shoulder at the fire. It would look weird, like I was trying to put the moves on her, or something.

"Don't worry about them, they all know. Everyone knows. They all think you're an asshole, because you won't do the slightest little thing to acknowledge me," she said, losing control, sobbing, tears running down her cheeks. "Sit down with me, Lane Daniels, right now," she said, gulping, putting it all on the line, "or break my heart."

I left for the Air Force on Monday. I sat in the window seat of the plane. As it flew south, I looked out at my beloved mountains, tiny white spots of snow capping the massive purple peaks that filled half of the horizon. Beth would be sixteen before I came back in almost a year. What would I do, then? She carried with her the fiercest love I had ever known and whoever got to be her true love would be loved like no other. And, though we talked the rest of the night and I had my arm wrapped around her, her snuggling close to me, almost purring, I didn't know what was going to happen, who I would meet, what sort of things I would do, places I would go.

In the back of my mind there was some guy out there, much better looking than I was, kinder, sweeter, more attentive, the sort of man she deserved. I could see him in my mind, humble and gentle someone who would get all giddy when she looked at him. He would stumble and say stupid stuff and they would laugh, because he was so madly in love with her. Every time I thought of him, the man she deserved, I saw someone else.

I looked at the piece of paper with her address on it and put it in my shirt pocket.

ABOUT THE AUTHOR

T. L. Davis

T.L. Davis held a number of dangerous jobs while maintaining a writing career as a novelist, screenwriter and playwright. His first two novels Shadow Soldier and Home to Texas are highly rated for their complex and deep character portrayals.

BOOKS BY THIS AUTHOR

Shadow Soldier

After the Civil War ends, J.D. Wilkes is seventeen and has worked for his father as courier between himself and Jefferson Davis, is sent into the west to start a new life. He struggles with morality and survival as he encounters outlaws and unscrupulous lawmen, but he survives only to find out that his father has betrayed those who served him in the war to gain favor with the occupying forces of the Union.

Home To Texas

J.D. returns to Texas to build a ranch, but the other ranchers and the Union Army that occupies Texas for several years after the end of the Civil War are not hospitable to the young man's aspirations.

Made in the USA
Coppell, TX
02 June 2023